Presented by
B.O.N.E.S. Entertainment
(Based On Never Ending Success)

I Am Abaddon, The Nefarious Son:
An Erotic Thriller

K. "BONES" LOVELACE

I0550339

I Am Abaddon, The Nefarious Son: An Erotic Thriller
Copyright © 2020 K. "Bones" Lovelace

Books may be purchased in quantity and/or special sales by contacting the publisher, K. "Bones" Lovelace, by email at Lovelacek35@gmail.com.

Editing and Formatting: Tanisha Stewart
www.tanishastewartauthor.com
tanishastewart.author@gmail.com

Cover Design: Thaiala Gardner
Major Ink Publications
Thaialag16@gmail.com

First Edition

Published in the United States
by K. "Bones" Lovelace

K. "BONES" LOVELACE

Table of Contents

I Am Abaddon, The Nefarious Son:
An Erotic Thriller

K. "BONES" LOVELACE

I Am Abaddon, The Nefarious Son

Prologue

Letter from a Serial Killer

Dear Reader,

May this letter find you cluelessly awaiting my arrival. I recently viewed a documentary titled, The Creation of a Serial Killer. On which several psychologists offered their theories as to what makes a killer, a killer.

Some believe it to be the nature of circumstances that impels an individual's murderous instincts to surface. As if some imaginary kill-or-be-killed switch clicks on in the brain. In turn, the killer proceeds in driving on to believe it to be their duty to rid the Earth of lower beings as a form of survival.

Other ideology consists of it being in the killer's DNA. Basically, deeming some children to be Natural Born Killers, conceived with an inbred taste for death.

In my expert opinion... and I did say expert opinion, I do believe, being in the midst of a killing spree, in which I have claimed twenty-three lives and counting at the moment of this letter, should qualify me as somewhat of an expert.

So in my expert opinion, I say bullshit! What makes a killer kill is society! And since they'll never admit it... Fuck them! Fuck you and fuck me!

Since they got so many fucking answers... Tell them to answer this: Which one am I?

Sincerely,
On My Way

May 12, 1988
Fort Hood Texas
Marine Corp Base
Family Housing A - 23

Tick-Tick-Tick!

Michael sat listening to the second hand of the old wall clock in his bedroom. It read 8:30 p.m. And he knew it would begin soon again. Sitting quietly with his hands in his lap, Michael fidgeted and played with his fingers while he prayed.

"Please, God, no…" he silently begged a god who seemed to enjoy his torment. There it was. That music coming to life from Mother's room. She loved that song.

"I promise, Father God…" The first tear rolled down his young handsome cheek as he began to stiffen. "I'll never do anything bad again... I'll attend church without being…"

Michael paused his prayers as the familiar creak of the bedroom door sent chills up his spine. Blood curling chills. Her footsteps made his heart race as her feathered slippers slid across the industrial tiles of their base housing floors. Mother loved those slippers. Closing his eyes, Michael continued his pleas for mercy from God, but still his bedroom door slammed open while he sat. His back was toward Mother and the door, but he knew. He felt her nakedness behind him.

"Please, God, I'll never touch it again... Please don't make me…" he silently begged God, in a rush.

"Boy!" Mother sternly whispered, standing just behind him.

Michael slowly stood from the twin bed. Mother had made it perfectly clear to never be dressed when she came for him. So hard he had prayed for his father's return from Iraq. Then Mother would have no reason to come to him and his Glory for pleasure. "Glory," that's what Mother had named it.

"Boy, are you spilling your seeds on that floor again? If I told your father what you've been doing with the gift he gave you…" She whispered the threat lustfully.

"Please, Mother... don't!" he begged as he slowly rose. The tears rushed down his handsome young face as he willed himself to rise. "Mother…" He paused so her eyes could take in the sight of Glory filling with blood. "I'm ready for you," he said as he held it in his hands.

"Good boy," Mother said and smiled from just inside his small bedroom door. Her nakedness boldly stating her intentions. "Because Mother really need you to work it tonight. I need you to kill it!" Then she smiled through the crimson red lipstick.

Mother was what most men would call a full-figured woman. Some would even enjoy her thickness. The long curly reddish weave she wore down her back, the large breasts with thick beige nipples like jelly beans, the large round hips and full ass cheeks. Even the thick bushy lips of her flower.

"Come on, Boy!" She demanded, holding her hands out. "I want it now, and you better remember how I taught you to work it, Boy. Make Mother scream out in pleasure, Boy," she softly cooed.

Mother led him into her bedroom again.

"That song," he thought as his eyes instantly went to her nightstand. "It's Father's favorite song." He thought to himself as a tear escaped his young eyes. He knew that his father made love to his mother while that song played at night. He knew the song word-for-word.

"Do it, you filthy boy!" Mother giggled as her fingers found her lips. As usual, she spread her thick thighs wide. "Let Mother see you explode again," she moaned. This was her routine as she helped him masturbate at the foot of the bed while she masturbated on the bed.

They both exploded together.

"Don't you stop!" She screamed as he kept himself hard for her. "Mmm…" She moaned. "Mother's ready, Boy."

Slowly she held out her glistening fingers for him to taste. Closing his eyes, Michael climbed onto the bed with his mother. She had raised her legs to his shoulders so he could fully enter her body.

Chapter One

Hello Brotherly Love
May 2012

THE DEAFENING SILENCE of the night became soothing to his existence. He sat there in awe of his Glory. That's what Mother always called it: his Glory. She claimed he was a curse from Satan for their nights of lustful fornication. The nights he spent with the Angel of Light. Mother confessed that his father was Lucifer himself and that that alone accounted for his Glory, which Mother used at an alarming rate from the day he reached twelve years old. Now he sat in total darkness, in front of the looking glass. He watched the pure evil image of his demon stare back at him, loathsome.

He often rubbed and stroked his Glory, just to watch it erupt its seed to the floor; its 'molten seeds of pleasure', as his mother would say. He knew his actions displeased Mother and she would scream obscenities and make him perform until she shook in total ecstasy upon her queen-sized bed. Her words of encouraging threats, which made him strive harder, made him slam into her Devil's Flower with such violent force, trying to end her torment, and her life. With every stroke, with every deep thrust... hoping... no, praying that somehow he could do as she coached him to do. Every night, she'd scream as he entered her the same words of encouragement: "Kill it, you son of Satan!"

Yes, and it was those same words that kept him inside of her Devil's Flower until he just couldn't hold it any longer. That's when his seeds of lustful pleasure would mix with hers and death would take a little more of his sanity.

"Kill it, you son of Satan!" Her voice continued tonight as always; and as usual, here he sat in awe of his Glory, watching it as it began to rise for Mother once again.

"Kill it, you son of Satan!" was her scream.

He stood from the vanity high-back chair in the suburban home's bedroom.

"I'll kill it this time, Mother. I promise." Then he began to cry, slowly unzipping the bag. She watched him from the bed and he realized that she'd wished that she had run away. He saw it in her eyes; she wanted to be away from this Giant. But that was impossible now. She was in Union with her dead husband. He had bound their legs together at the ankles, their torsos at the waist, their arms at the wrist, and their necks at the throat. This was the Union, the making as one.

Slowly he pulled the dark red wig from the large arm duffle bag; a wig long and curly like Mother's hair. Smiling, he pulled it onto her thick natural black Afro. Her lips needed more color.

"Redder," he said softly and smiled as always. He then dug out the crimson red lipstick once more.

Fuller, he thought.

"No, please... please... don't... please... God," she cried softly now, too afraid to anger the Giant again. He had snapped Matthew's neck, her husband, for yelling too loudly. He had told both of them not to scream or resist.

Matthew did both and he had died horribly.

"I won't, Mother. I'll do it much longer this time," he whispered delicately, applying the lipstick. His body shook as he shot his load onto her breasts from the excitement. He stabbed the thin wire post of the large hoop earrings through the meaty flesh of her earlobe, causing her to squeal in pain. He shot another jet of sperm onto her breasts.

"Look what you've done, Boy. Your father would laugh at your weakness!" Mother's voice scolded him as she lustfully giggled. "He would have never given up his seeds to be wasted in the Earth. You better stay ready for your Mother or..." she continued to torment him.

"I will, Mother..." he stuttered. "I will, Mother."

The woman looked up in horror as both voices seemed to merge and come from his mouth together. Her name was Carol McDermott and she realized at that moment that she was going to die.

"Please don't," she begged.

"Oh, Mother, where is the beaded rosary you love so much?" He continued to mumble to Carol who was now transformed into his mother. "We must please God."

"In that ugly shirt pocket. To be the son of Lucifer, you sure are dumb as shit. Now hurry up and kill it, you son of Satan. Kill it with your beautiful large Glory," his mother said from his lips.

"Oh wait, Mother," he said, smiling. "I almost forgot." He climbed from the bed once more. He pressed Play on the Bose Airwave system CD player.

Mother screamed and clapped her hands in disgust. "Look at it, Boy. It's going limp! Just like you, a limp wimp! All those weights can't help you none! You're still going soft on Mother." She laughed as the music began to play.

The song was Mother's favorite and she began to sing it as she always did. That was enough to cause him to get erect once again. The tune was an old Isley Brother's song, "Livin' In The Life", and Mother sang it beautifully.

"Somebody said…"

Suddenly, Mother stopped singing and giggled, showing her pleasure at the sight of his Glory growing once again. "Do it now, Boy. Kill it, you son of Satan. Don't you dare stop, Boy, until you've killed it." She continued as he flipped the couple over so that Carol was on top. If her husband was still alive, he would probably have suffocated from the pressure of his wife's body. The Giant mounted Carol McDermott for the first of many times that night. Parting her legs with his strong oversized legs. He rubbed his Glory into her vagina and found it moist from nothing else but fear. "I'm ready to take it, Boy! Now kill it!"

Slowly the Giant slid deeply inside of her body as the blade sliced her neck, clean through the muscle behind her windpipe.

His sperm filled her stomach cavity.

Bleep-bleep-bleep-bleep-bleep!

"Shit!" Joanna growled, reaching for the New Wave Escape Tron alarm clock. It swiftly rolled from her hand as it was designed to do with its rubber wheels.

Bleep-bleep-bleep-bleep-bleep!

"I heard you, you son of a bitch!" Joanna slammed the down filled pillow over her head. She cursed the gift her former part-time lover, Al, had given her for Christmas last year. She had this nagging feeling that he was really getting rid of it more than giving her a present. "Shut the fuck up, dammit!"

Bleep-bleep-bleep-bleep-bleep!

"That's it, motherfucker!" Joanna shouted, jumping from the bed totally naked. The Escape Tron crashed into her oak armoire and reverse pivoted toward the wall. "Come here, you noisy bitch!" She then grabbed the high tech alarm clock by its rubber wheels. It instantly activated its voice alarm.

"Good morning, Joanna!" It beeped twice and shut off.

Joanna read the large red numbers. "It's six thirty-six pm," she whispered.

The sun was still high in the sky and she knew she still had at least three hours before her shift started. That was just enough time to do her usual evening workout. She needed her daily forty-minute sprint to the park and back. It was a ritual.

She smiled, knowing there were three things she always started her day with. First, she'd brush her teeth and wash her face. Second, she'd come back into her Chestnut Hill bedroom and stand naked in her full-length mirror in front of the open window on the second floor of her apartment so that Tommy could masturbate for five minutes. She'd pretend to be either examining her body or exercising. Every now and then she would bend, giving him a full view of her flower. She was his dream girl, he claimed, over and over again. Third was her daily run. And that's just what it was, a run. She didn't jog or trot as most. She straight out ran three miles, full speed. This was the secret to her beauty and figure.

"All right, Tommy. Where are you, cutie?" Joanna said to herself as she searched the mirror for the big teenager. "Oh there you go, cutie. Good evening, big guy." She smiled and pretended not to notice his stare as always.

Seductively, she swung her shapely hips as she headed for the bathroom to pee.

"I'm such a perv," she giggled. "Bitch, he's only seventeen and that makes you a pedophile."

But Joanna loved to tease Tommy. Had been doing so since he was sixteen.

Entering her bedroom, Joanna stood with her back toward the window and slightly parted her thick, muscular legs. She began her daily stretches with straight leg bends, followed by breast bounces, which were really jumping jacks. She loved the heaviness of her 38D cups.

The looks and frowns on Tommy's face said it all.

Joanna rolled her thick deep brown nipples between her fingers and lifted the roundness of her breast to her mouth.

"Let it go, Baby," she whispered and smiled as Tommy came on his room's window, unnoticed by everyone except her, this being between the two of them.

Slowly and deliberately Joanna dressed in a pair of skin-tight biker shorts and a sports bra without any undergarments. She felt his eyes on her every move. She giggled, knowing he'd be on the patio waiting by the time she made it outside. Looking out of the peephole, she spotted him as always.

"What, Boy," Joanna said as she opened the door. Brushing by him she felt his semi-erection brush her stomach. She paused and looked down as it came to life between them. Tommy said nothing.

"No, let me guess," she said, then giggled. "You love me, right? Wow!" Then she stole another glance at his obvious erection. "Mmmm, shit!"

She backed away, then said, "No, you love me and can make love to me better than that big guy, am I right?" Looking down again, she said, "Wow, Boy."

"Ummm... Right on both accounts," Tommy said. "I wanted to tell you there's a white dude in that Chevy Tahoe over there who's been watching your front door for hours."

Tommy smiled as her eyes rose from his erection and focused on his.

"Where?" Joanna whispered.

This news put her on alert, especially with this case.

"Behind you."

"He's still watching me?" she asked, standing defensively.

"Nope! He's coming this way now," Tommy told her as he stepped around her.

Then she noticed that Tommy held an aluminum bat.

"Hold up, big guy," said the detective, holding up a gold badge. "Detective Robinson Paison."

"You the captain's man, right?" Joanna said, then smiled as she rubbed Tommy's arm to let him know it was safe.

6

"That's me," Detective Paison said. "And you must be his niece, but I won't hold that against you if you don't hold it against me. There's been another one last night."

Joanna quickly held up her hand to halt him from saying any more in front of Tommy, her protector. "See you tomorrow, Baby. Both of you."

Joanna looked down and then back up into Tommy's eyes.

Tommy blushed.

The detective didn't notice the sexual intent.

"I gotta get my run in, then we can-"

Detective Paison cut her off. "Sorry, Detective Staley, there is no time," he informed her. "The brass wants you now… no really, more like two and a half hours ago. I lied and said you weren't home. Please… let's go."

"That bad, huh?" Joanna said, then frowned.

"They are threatening job status and pensions," he whispered. "Let's go, please."

The blue latex gloves snapped around her wrist. She pulled the cloth shoe slippers over her Gotex hiking boots.

"That's four in four days," Joanna whispered, checking her surroundings as always. "He's picking up steam."

"Correction; that's seven in the same amount of days," Detective Paison said, leading the way to the crime scene in the small, quiet urban neighborhood. "The connection wasn't made until recently."

"Dammit to hell!" Captain Jackson yelled as he looked at one of his technicians. "Move the hell out of the way!" he barked. "Jo Jo, come this way, please." Then he held out a hand and looked the tech up and down.

"Is it our boy?" he wanted to know.

"Wait! What are you doing out in the field?" Joanna asked.

The captain looked in her eyes. All she saw was anger in his.

"The big wigs got their noses up my ass," her uncle, the captain, whispered. "Listen, they want answers, and frankly, so do I. Not to mention the city's in fear. Some heads are about to roll, Jo. Most likely mine and the Sex Crimes Unit's. This bastard gotta be downed."

"Everybody out," Joanna said with authority. As they filed out, she looked at the coroner and said, "Finished, Tim?"

"Yes. Same cause of death on the women. Severed aorta. The husband had his neck broken by someone strong. And, Joanna, he's big," the coroner, Timothy Rankins informed her and her uncle.

They both nodded in grim understanding.

Rankins held up his hand to indicate length and said, "Very deep penetration."

"Then it wasn't you," Joanna joked.

Her uncle looked disgusted.

"It could have been, sugar," Rankins said, then laughed and cleared his equipment from the bed and the floor.

"Joanna," Captain Jackson said. He only used her full name when he was about to get bossy or needed a favor. "When you've done your creepy..." he stopped and waved his hand to indicate her thing. "Transformation... I need you to meet who you'll be working with. She's out of the 21st precinct. It's the scene of the first two."

"No," Joanna barked. "Fuck that... sorry, Unk."

"This ain't no damn request, and don't try to piss further than me. Mine is larger," the captain said. "Besides, it's the commissioner's orders!" He then turned on a uniformed officer. "Didn't she say, 'get the fuck out'? Are you special? Do I gotta hold your hand? Get the fuck out! All of you!"

Captain Jackson said, "Joanna," then frowned.

"Yes, Boss?" she said and rolled her eyes as he kissed her forehead. "See you for dinner Sunday."

"Thanks, Jo Jo."

And just like that she was that little eight-year-old again whose parents were just murdered in their sleep.

Sitting in the high back Victorian chair, Joanna looked down at the semen on the floor, then the semen stains on the edge of the floral cushion. Lifting her eyes slowly, she stared at her reflection and imagined the erection as she masturbated. She was him. She was completely naked again in her mind. This was his ritual and she had to become him. The killer! She knew him. In her mind, she was him.

Standing, she turned toward the bed. Joanna headed for the bodies tied together back to back in some kind of ritualistic killing. Her eyes fell on the CD player. It sat where most of the others sat, on the night stand. The button said Play and she pressed it. Just as she expected, the song came to life, that song again.

"Somebody said… I was living the life."

Joanna smiled as she climbed on the bed. She stared down into the cold black stare of the dead Mrs. McDermott, who wore the long dark red curly wig and lipstick.

"Why the wigs? The music? Why the lipstick? What did she do to you?" She asked herself, whispering as she caressed her face.

Slowly, Joanna pulled open Mrs. McDermott's mouth. It was there as always. "Why?" she whispered while pulling the plastic beaded rosary from her mouth. "What does God have to do with such an ungodly act?"

"I have those same questions," the tall white woman said from the door.

Joanna quickly sized her up. The long auburn hair pulled back into a pony tail. The long swimmer's body with the slightly bowed legs and designer clothes.

"Can you please wait out there with the other reporters and press," Joanna barked rudely.

"Is the rosary there?" Detective Veronica Rawls asked. "I got the feeling the rosary is the key."

"Who the fuck are you and what do you want on my crime scene?"

9

"Don't you mean, our crime scene? I'm Detective Veronica Rawls. I'm from the 21st precinct. Your captain had to see the commissioner and the mayor, and yes I've heard about your special gift. The ability to transform into the sick minded souls we're trying to catch."

Joanna relaxed. "Yeah," she began, "well it's my curse. I've had it ever since one killed my folks for a few bucks, just to get high."

Veronica took it all in, looking over the scene.

Joanna climbed off the bed, her hospital scrubs covered in blood. "It's his mother," she stated flatly.

"Who's mother?" Veronica asked as she stepped further into the room.

"The perp's," Joanna let her know. "It's his mother he's dressing up to kill." She stopped the CD player. "Somehow it's turned sexual to him or it started out sexual." Then she pulled the rosary from Carol McDermott's mouth, and it went into a plastic bag.

"What turned sexual?" Veronica had to ask. "You're losing me."

"The perp hates his mommy for reasons unknown. And it's either turned into a sexual thing or started out that way. But over and over, he is killing her and raping her. The question is why?"

"I don't give a shit!" Veronica exclaimed, showing her excitement. "We need to catch this freak and kill him before he kills a child." She whispered as she made note of everything in the room as she had always done at a crime scene.

"That won't happen," Joanna said, looking under the bed. "He desires them 35 to 40 years old, black, middle class, working and slightly chunky. Children and teenagers are not his priority. So, I'm finished and now I'm hungry. So, where do I go?"

Both detectives stood quietly for a moment.

Veronica said, "There's an all-night Wendy's not far from here. Let's send an officer down to…"

Joanna cut her off, her mind still on the perp. "No need. He's a product of either an overbearing mother or a very abusive repressive mother. Either way she'd turn him against fast food joints or any other large public audiences. He'll seek home-cooked meals or a private, small restaurant. The perp is a "creature of habit.""

They studied the room together, quietly.

Deloris smiled while watching the white 1996 Caprice Classic pull into the small private lot again. She knew that checking the wall clock would be useless. It was exactly 7:00am as always.

"Hey, Mack. Start the two number fours." Deloris quickly checked the silverware on the table. Six in the rear by the window, two spoons, one fork, no knife.

When he walked in, she studied the muscle the size of Ronnie Coleman's in his left arm. "Yep, Mack. You was right. It's bigger today." There was no way she could fully grip it. "Go sit down, sexy, before I forget I'm 58 and jump your bones."

"She'll do it too, Michael," Mack said. "And I can't stop her." He spoke from the grill top. "She's a sexy starved woman."

Michael Angel's erection began to grow as he rushed to seat himself facing the door.

Deloris poured his hot water into a 16-ounce rock glass instead of a tea cup. One by one, Michael dunked the three tea bags ten times only to leave them floating while he stared at Deloris' wide hips. His fantasy was interrupted by his only friend.

"Hey, big guy," the small Spanish man spoke as he came through the door of the mom and pop kitchen.

"Jesus Manuel, you're late," Michael blushed as he pushed his erection down under the table.

"Puta," Jesus chuckled childishly.

"Hey, guys!" Deloris barked, turning like a mother whose sons just cursed. Her look was scolding.

11

"Sorry, Deloris," Michael said, more excited than before. He fought hard to control his erection. "You know, breakfast is on you, Mr. Savior." He mugged his friend.

"It's not pronounced like God's son. It's Jesus, like my uncle from Mexico City. It's not my fault that my bus was late." Jesus sat down and admired his friend's physique. "Damn if that chest of yours ain't grown another two inches over the weekend, Muscle Butt. Shit, look at that shirt. It's gonna rip any minute, Amigo."

Both men looked up as the bell over the door rang violently when it flew open harder than necessary.

"Oh damn!" Jesus said as he shook his head. "They're early this morning." He quickly shifted his eyes.

Jesus noticed the changes in Michael's demeanor as his voice became dark.

"So what if they're early," Michael said as he watched the two white men and one black man sit down, talking loudly.

"Hey, sexy," the large white man yelled, slapping Deloris on her ass.

"Do it again and lose a hand, pervert!" she screamed.

"Oh come on, Momma, You ain't that old to have forgotten what sex is," he said, blowing kisses.

"I ain't playing with you guys! Don't try it again! You understand me, Tony, Joe?" Deloris yelled.

"I hate those guys. Did you hear what they did to the last new guy? They held him over the edge of the framing machine by his feet," Jesus whispered. "One day somebody is gonna teach them a lesson." He giggled, using his hand to cover his mouth, then made a gun with his fingers and fired off three imaginary shots at make-believe targets.

"Hey!" Deloris screamed.

Michael noticed Tony had wrapped his arms around her waist and pulled her into his lap. She struggled to get up and he roughly held her down.

"I want your pussy, old-ass woman," Tony growled. He grinded into her large ass while his best friend, Fat Joe laughed.

Vinny shook his head. He didn't like the two white guys he ate with. Mack came from behind the counter holding the unloaded .38 Smith and Wesson. "Let her go, Tony!" he postured as if ready to fire.

Fat Joe moved like a cat. He quickly grabbed Mack's hand and twisted his arm behind his back until he dropped the gun from his 62-year-old grip.

"What's the gun for, Mack?" Fat Joe wanted to know.

"Let him go!" Michael stood from the table.

"Whoa, whoa, whoa, big guy. I can't fight," Jesus whispered, but Michael paid him no mind.

Michael crossed the room. "I said, let her go. And get out. I haven't had breakfast yet and you're slowing it down."

"Oh shit, the retard speaks," Tony yelled, pushing Deloris to the floor. "Move, bitch. I think the retard has a crush on you."

"I'm calling the police," Mack said, pulling his cell phone from his apron.

Fat Joe slapped the phone away.

"Now!" Tony smiled. "You got something to say, retard? How about you, wetback?"

No one said anything.

Tony stood up to show his full 6'4", 246 pound frame, staring at Jesus.

"Come on, fellas. The engine will be here in another hour. They don't want no trouble, Tony." Vinny tried to calm the situation down. "Let's have a quiet day for once, Tony."

"Vinny, you sound like the retard there," Tony said as he crossed the room, followed by Fat Joe. "Maybe you should leave, unless you want to help your soul brother here. 'Just leave, Tony'," he mocked in a feminine voice. "Get away from my table… Boy," he told a smiling Vinny because he knew what the outcome would be.

13

"It's your hospital bill. I warned you," Vinny said, then began to laugh as he exited with his coffee. "Michael," he nodded, before he went outside.

"Now what was that, retard?" Tony said as he turned his attention back to Michael, who was within a foot of both men. His sheer size dwarfed them both. Now Tony had to stand his ground. "Huh, retard?" He used his hand to cup his ear as if Michael was hard of hearing.

No one saw it coming until the snap of the ribs filled the silence in the diner. The bone in his jaw crumbled from the next powerful blow. Tony hit the floor, unconscious, and the size 15 steel-toed boot fractured his skull on the tile floor.

Fat Joe ran for the door and Jesus chased him as far as the first table, acting like he was in the fight, helping his friend Michael, who needed no help.

"What happened here?" Detective Williams asked the patrolman. The ambulance lights flared as it pulled away.

"Fella in the ambulance assaulted the owners of this here establishment. He and his buddy took a legal gun from the owner… Um, Mister Jefferson there," the officer pointed. "Another customer and his coworker didn't take too kindly to the assault and opened a can of whoop ass on the attackers."

"More than one attacker?" Williams asked.

"Yup. The second one is in my back seat. He'll be booked for assault and attempted robbery," the officer said and then smiled. "You gotta see this freakishly big mothafucka."

"Where?" the detective asked, and the officer pointed. "Damn, be Jesus Christ! What's his name?"

Chapter Two

They Must Know My Name

"SHHHHH," HE WHISPERED calmly, rocking the infant in his large rock-hard arms. "It's time for nighty-night. Yes, that's a good boy," the Giant cooed at the baby while she watched in horror. He was pure evil, but so gentle with her child.

"Please, don't," Vivian Phelps cried quietly. "Oh God, is my husband dying?" She could hear his gasps. She knew he was dying.

Holding the baby at arms' length, the Giant whispered, "See, Mother, he's sleeping." He smiled so genuinely, so gently.

"Please… Oh God, please untie me so I can help Jonathan. Don't let him die." Vivian's voice rose slightly. The Giant looked at her sternly while the baby slept peacefully in his large hands. "Sorry… sorry… I'll be quiet," she moaned. "Please don't hurt my baby," she begged.

Without a word, the Giant walked out of the room. He returned empty-handed.

"My baby… please," she cried. "Where's my baby?" Her eyes searched the door in panic as if the baby would appear.

"He's sleeping, Mother. Be quiet! He needs his rest to grow strong like me." The Giant growled while standing by the Lay-Z-Boy chair in the corner of the bedroom. Slowly he began to undress while staring at his own image in the mirror. Mother began to speak to him as always; he expected it.

"Don't you start that touching and rubbing, Boy."

"Yes, Mother," he smiled defiantly. A tear rolled down his face. He didn't want to do this again, but he could not stop it.

"Let me see your Glory, you son of Satan. I want it to stand in awe of my Devil's Flower, Boy!" Mother demanded.

"It will, Mother. I promise it will." He rubbed the length.

Vivian screamed, "Oh my God, my baby!"

The Giant paid no attention to her outcries now. He was no longer there.

"When your father Lucifer entered my Flower I screamed out for God, Boy. But your Father made me love it and that made God angry," Mother said and then giggled. "Your father spilled his seed in my small Flower with pain and ecstasy. So God cursed me. He sent you, Boy."

"Yes, Mother." He rubbed quicker and he sat. Vivian heard the Giant moan out as he masturbated. "Ummm."

"Stop it, you son of Satan, before it-" Mother screamed as he erupted his long jets of semen to the carpet. "Now look what you done! Your Father would laugh at how easy you released your seed. Boy, you can't hold onto your own pleasure seeds. Boy, you better be able…"

"I will, Mother. You'll see. I will, Mother," he cried. He began to masturbate faster this time.

"Stop it, Boy!" Mother screamed. "Shut your mouth and kill it, you son of Satan. Kill it for Mother, Boy!"

"I will… I will… I will… I…" he exploded again onto the carpet with a large volume of semen.

"Stop that!" Mother screamed.

"Why, Mother?" he smiled. The Giant stood from the chair. He crossed the room and pressed the Play button on the Bose Airwave system. The sound was crystal clear as the Isley Brothers came to life.

"Somebody said…" Mother sang as the Giant slid deeply inside of her Flower. The carotid split easily as he sliced her throat. The Giant exploded once again and Mother continued to sing.

"Did you see that circus show? The Mayor's news conference was a joke. What a bunch of bullshit," Detective Veronica Rawls mumbled. She looked around the upper office of the Sex Crimes Unit in the police administration building. "What was that shit?" she complained.

Demonstrating with her small hands, Joanna made choking sounds. "Stupid bastard! How could he promise the city that they're safe?" She reached for the tea on the desk. "He sounds so sure that-"

She was stopped mid-sentence.

"Let's go, ladies. We got another one. Fairmount Park, Creston Hill Drive," the Captain said, standing in his doorway.

"Wait! Outside job?" Veronica asked and shook her head. "Not our boy, sir." She was certain of it.

"She's right, boss!" Joanna said, clipping the Glock to her belt, following them both.

"The M.O. fits. Let's go," Captain Jackson said.

"It's not him, Unk!" Joanna said again.

"This is Gloria Velendez, Fox 29 News. We're in Fairmount Park in the Creston Hill Drive section of the park where the gruesome discovery of a naked woman's body has been found by a young teenage boy and his dog. It's not known if it's the work of the Midnight Creeper who's been terrorizing the Tri-state middle class families in mostly black neighborhoods for weeks now. But earlier reports have stated that it bears the same earmarks of the Creeper's work. The red wig, the red lipstick, and throat slashing…"

The beautiful Spanish reporter continued reporting as the Giant sat on the edge of the blood-soaked bed rubbing the hardness of his penis.

The reporter continued: "The discovery was made around 8:45pm tonight by the teen out walking his family dog and it wasn't a pretty sight. The child's name and face are being withheld due to his age. Now to Jim Connelli. Jim," she said, and the TV screen filled with the face of a male reporter.

"Thank you, Gloria, and as you've said, it was a very gruesome and horrifying sight. With me we have the teenage boy's uncle and father whom the teen ran and got after he discovered the dead naked body. They themselves are shaken from the sight…"

The Giant sat erect, listening to them speaking of things he knew nothing about. "First of all, Mother would never let me take her outside in the open," he softly mumbled, stroking himself once again.

The reporter continued: "She was raped repeatedly, then sodomized before she was stabbed in the neck and facial area…"

"No!" the Giant cried out loud. His cry seemed to shake the room.

"That's filthy, Boy," his Mother whispered. "We can't let them get away with these lies. God knew this day would come. That's why He never allowed you to use your new name. It's God given," Mother said. "Now the world must learn to fear it."

"They will, Mother." He stroked harder and faster.

"Quiet, you son of Satan. You're the seed of your Father's. Now finish what you started with me. Kill it, Boy!" Mother moaned in pure ecstasy as he shot a load on the floor.

"I will, Mother," he cried softly, mounting the dead body of Vivian, who stared blankly into his eyes. "I will, Mother. Ummph… ummph… I wil… uumph," He slammed into Vivian's

Flower again and again as his Mother screamed his God given name in his ears.

"Fox News 29 hotline. If it's news, we're on our way," the young female intern answered cheerfully.

"Gloria Velendez… please," the low, raspy voice grunted, sending chills down her spine. "Ssss... uumph…uumph."

"Ummm, who's calling and what does it pertain to, Sir?" She pressed the RECORD button on the desk. "I'm sorry; we don't take personal calls…" she tried to say as his rage broke through the line.

"I am Abaddon! Put that cunt on the phone! Now! Uumph. Uumph," he continued to grunt.

The desk intern froze with fear as she heard an older woman's voice take over and scream into her ear.

"If she doesn't listen to you, Boy, take another one tonight!"

"I will, Mother… uumph! Uumph!" he grunted as if he was her boyfriend on those long nights when he'd make love to her like an animal and was about to cum.

The intern pressed the alert for the news program's director who instantly picked up.

"Hello… who's calling?" the program director answered after seeing the fear in the intern's face.

"Mmmm…" he paused for release. "Abaddon!" he moaned in pleasure. "The story Gloria Velendez reported two hours ago was a lie, and Mother hates lies."

"Listen, pal, we don't have time to play games around-" the program director pressed and was cut short.

"1954 Ashley Street. The door is open," Abaddon whispered. "Mother is waiting." And the line went dead.

The desk intern and the program director's eyes locked on each other's. She was visibly shaken. So was he. "Oh shit!" she whispered. "Was that for real?"

"Let's find out," the program director said and realized his mouth had gone dry. He dialed Gloria Velendez while she was still out, roaming.

She answered on the second ring.

The white van sat just outside of Temple University's Shriners Hospital. Gloria Velendez ate the soft-shelled taco filled with roasted pork and veggies as the phone rang twice on the dashboard cup-holder.

"Gloria," she answered, and then listened.

"No shit? Abaddon? Like from Revelation? The King of the Abyss?" she questioned.

Jimmy, her cameraman and driver, watched while shoving more fries into his mouth.

"Yeah, got it," Gloria scribbled the address down. "1954 Ashley Street, two blocks off of Cheltenham. Got it, boss." She shook her head in disbelief. "Abaddon? Let's go, Jimmy. Ashley Street."

"I know just where that is," Jimmy said, then smiled. "I live about six blocks from there. Who is Abaddon?" he asked.

"That's it right there," Jimmy said, pulling into an empty parking spot. A few people sat on steps up the street, watching in amazement.

Gloria Velendez checked her makeup before climbing from the van. By then, the neighbors began to gather.

"Hey, y'all going into Vivian's house? What's happening?" the next-door neighbor asked as Gloria pushed the heavy steel security door wide. The neighbor came up behind them. "Her name is Vivian."

"Vivian... hello..." Gloria yelled out twice.

"Jonathan, baby," the neighbor yelled over Gloria's shoulder. "That's her husband. Jonathan! It's me, Ms. Hamms."

The baby cried out from upstairs.

20

All three froze and listened for movement. Jimmy raised his camera and turned the bright light on. He shrugged his shoulders. "After you, Miss Reporter," he smirked.

"I'm calling the police," Ms. Hamms said, rushing from the house.

"Dammit, we gotta hurry, Jimmy," Gloria said, climbing the stairs.

"Vivian, Jonathan… y'all here?" she yelled as they hit the top stair. The baby cried from the darkness of the back bedroom. They found him unharmed in his crib, wet, scared, and hungry.

All along, Jimmy filmed.

Gloria Velendez picked the child up into her arms. "That's a big boy," she cooed to him softly. With him pressed to her chest she headed toward the master bedroom. The door was closed, adding to her anxiety. "Vivian… Jonathan…"

"Gloria, you sure about this?" Jimmy asked from behind the camera. She could see he wasn't.

Holding the mic in one hand and the infant in her other hand, she whispered, "We got to…" Slowly, she eased the door open to her horror.

The scream escaped her throat before she knew where the sound came from. The baby screamed seconds later and so did Jimmy. He closed his eyes in terror. The camera kept filming the horrible scene inside the bedroom.

"Freeze!" the two officers yelled as the flashlights found them standing in horrid stillness. "Don't move! Not one damn muscle," the second officer said as he approached the terrified news crew. He froze also as he read the writing on the wall in the victim's blood.

I am Abaddon.

"This isn't our boy," Detective Rawls whispered, using her hands to shield her mouth from onlookers.

"I know," Joanna said and still surveying the scene. "She's been stabbed repeatedly. Our boy slices. And look around. What's missing?"

Veronica scanned the area for twenty yards in all directions. "The music for one, and the chair."

"What else?" Joanna asked.

"The mirrors."

"And?" Joanna pointed to the grass.

"Son of a bitch! No sperm. We got us a copycat," Veronica almost screamed before catching herself.

"Yeah, someone is trying to disguise their own shit by blaming our boy. Let's see if it's there!" Joanna said.

They gathered four officers to hold up a makeshift screen around the body made from sheets from the Crime Scene van. The officers formed a circle around them and the coroner. The coroner pulled the dead woman's mouth open as the three examined her mouth cavity.

"It's empty except for the traces of semen in her throat," the coroner whispered.

"Where's God?" Joanna laughed and Veronica joined her in the private joke.

"Detectives," an officer called from outside the new made tent. "They're radioing for you two. There's another one up on Ashley Street. They believe it's your boy for sure."

"Shit!" whispered Veronica.

"What the fuck is an Abaddon? And why has he all of a sudden changed his M.O.? Why now?" Veronica Rawls asked out loud as she spoke to herself, staring at the writing on the wall. "I am Abaddon," she whispered and shook her head.

Joanna sat on the foldable card table chair by the dresser in front of the dresser's mirror. Her feet were parted around the semen. Slowly, she surveyed the small bedroom inch by inch with her eyes. It was neat with everything in place. The closet was open, small and over-crowded. The flat screen hung on the wall at the foot of the bed and the cheap entertainment center sat beneath it. She knew exactly who slept where by the belongings in the nightstands. The watch, the ring, the oversized chain and pendant made of gold. The Airwave Bose Sound System CD player on the dresser.

"Dammit!" she barked. It was like someone had slapped her in the face with it. "Son of a bitch, Veronica." She groaned, like she felt pain from the discovery.

"What?" Veronica turned her attention to Joanna.

"I'm semi-retarded."

"What are you talking about?" Veronica laughed, crossing the room.

"What's the thing at all the crime scenes that no one's paid attention to? Think Ronnie."

This was the first time Joanna called her by her nickname. She didn't realize she knew it. "What didn't we check? There was no need to."

Veronica studied the room again. There was the sperm, the rosary beads, and the CD player. She froze as it dawned on her what Joanna was talking about. Quickly she pulled the small notepads from her leather carryall. She fanned through one pad, then two more. "You're a goddamn genius, Jo. I was so busy concentrating on that damn song I never gave the system another thought. I just assumed it belonged there." She fanned through another pad. There it was.

"A Bose Airways 1000 Sound System. It was in all of the scenes. On the night stands," she said, looking at the one on the stand now. "Son of a bitch!"

"Ronnie, I need a moment to do my thing," Joanna said from the chair.

Veronica knew it was time for her partner to transform. She needed to become the perp, to re-enact the crime scene in her mind and Veronica needed to question the two news crew members.

"Do your thing. I'll be with this, ummm…" she checked her pad. "Yeah, a Ms. Gloria Velendez and James Carter Jr." Closing the door behind her, she heard Joanna mumble something about momma or mother. She shook her head and headed downstairs. No sooner had she hit the living room than Gloria Velendez spoke. "Detective, we must get back to our station to-"

"No, what you have to do is answer my questions first. Then you'll have to turn over that baby to its relatives," Veronica said. She took note of the protective way Gloria Velendez held the sleeping baby boy. "Now what the hell were you two doing here?"

Instantly the tears rolled down Gloria's face and Veronica realized she was truly beautiful.

"It was an assignment," the cameraman said.

"Oh God! This poor baby!" Gloria cried.

Chapter Three

THE SUN ROSE two hours ago.

She was beat and her stomach growled like it was a living creature of its own. But all she wanted to do was soak in a tub of hot water and get some sleep. She knew breakfast would be the normal coffee, two pieces of buttered toast, and a banana.

"Good morning, detective," Mrs. Flint said from her porch as Veronica climbed the steps of her row home. It was located in the middle class section of Overbrook.

"Good morning, Mrs. Flint. How's Mr. Flint this morning?" She forced a smile. It wasn't that she didn't feel friendly, she was just tired. The husband and wife were really quite lovable and friendly. Mrs. Flint was a little nosey, but loveable nonetheless.

"I'm great, beautiful. How you doing?" Mr. Flint yelled from the hidden vestibule that sat opposite her front door.

Whispering, Mrs. Flint said, "He's in his Billy Dee Williams mood this morning, child. Thinks he's a player."

This made both women laugh.

"Billy Dee Williams was an amateur. Shucks, he used to call me for advice when I was younger. You know, Ethel, you remember don't you?" he giggled. "That's how I got you, woman."

"Oh yeah, sexy, I almost forgot how fine you are." Mrs. Flint smiled and winked at Veronica, who laughed some more. "Honey," Mrs. Flint said, touching her arm. "Last night we had some boys smoking that stuff and cussing behind our houses. Playing that foul language music and spitting on the walks. I called the police, but they got away."

"I'll have a car patrol tonight, Mrs. Flint," Veronica promised and made her way inside. She felt like she was being watched for some reason.

The steam rose up around her as she closed her eyes to enjoy the muscle-soothing bath. The vanilla scented bubbles crowded around her full, thick breasts. Veronica opened her eyes to watch the droplets fall to her toes from the tub's tap. For some reason the Airwave System on the hamper frightened her, forcing her to turn away. She smiled as the music played softly. She recognized the tune, but she couldn't place it, the name of it. It was something her dad used to dance to when she was a child. She closed her eyes once more and began to hum along with the man's falsetto as he sang: "Somebody said..."

The room seemed to grow darker, no... that wasn't it. It grew more dense and dingy. And for reasons she couldn't fathom, it aroused her to a point that she needed release.

Softly, Veronica pinched the thickness of her swollen pinkish-brown nipple with her left hand while the bubbles played tickle with the other nipple. "Mmmm," she heard herself moan through the ridiculous crimson red lipstick she now wore. But why? She had no idea and it frightened her even more, but her lust was stronger now. Her hand slid down her stomach and under the water. She felt the bubbles popping against her soft skin. The music still played.

"I tried talking about it…"

Her body now shuddered from the caressing of her large breasts and nipples. Her other hand was softly parting the lips of her labia and it happened again, the shuddering, then the moan from her crimson red lips. Her strokes were magical and deliberate. She wanted release and she knew she was close. It became painful as she frantically rubbed in search of a name she felt would send her over the edge of pleasure.

"Say my name," the heavy voice moaned from behind the bathroom door. "I release you," he growled hideously.

"Ssss! God, what is your name?!" Veronica moaned, only a few rubs away from ecstasy. "Please tell… Oh God, yes!" Her red crimson lips moaned loudly. "Tell me so I can…" Her fingers worked feverishly. "I'm gonna cum… I want to say your name… Mmmm, shit, tell Mother your-"

The bathroom door slammed open. In the doorway a Giant of a man stood there blocking her exit as she came. Her climax shook the room violently as he whispered, "I am Abaddon!"

Veronica heard the scream but didn't realize it came from her throat, until she noticed the bubbles on the floor where she lay gripping the Glock .40, frantically searching for the Giant named Abaddon. The Killer! Unconsciously, she wiped her lips, trying to remove the crimson red lipstick.

He knew she was there, and he would be there until she had finished.

Every morning it was the same routine. She sat back away from the bedroom window just out of sight. If someone like his father happened to enter his room, they wouldn't spot her before she was able to escape. But this morning, she wanted… no, she needed to cum.

"Yes, cutie, ssss… mmmm… yes, cutie," Joanna was saying this as she rubbed in circular motions with two fingers on her right hand while pinching her plump dark brown nipples with her left. "Oh yes… here… I'm… almost…" she moaned as she lifted her breast into her mouth to engage her thick tongue. "I'm… cummmm!" She squealed softly with a deep intake of breath. Then Joanna slid into her king-sized bed, naked as usual and very satisfied.

Looking at the clock on his dashboard, Kenneth began to worry.

"Fucking supervisor," he barked, turning on to 29th and York Street. Scanning the streets from his beige and navy conversion van, he could not find her. She had to be just right. Five-three or four, no more than a hundred fifty-five or sixty-five pounds and chocolate brown skin.

"Dammit!" he almost screamed.

He thought about the racist supervisor who always picked on him. Always picking him to work the extra overtime. Sure he needed the money, but why not let him come in early to stock the shelves? Why cause him to miss his chance to meet his hero? It was true he didn't know the Creeper yet, but he was his hero nevertheless. Single-handedly, he had the city in the grips of fear.

"I'm gonna be like you," he whispered unconsciously. "But first, the city must recognize me too. I'm not trying to take your glory…" He paused as she walked out of the corner store. Her hair was tied under a blue scarf that was filthy. Her jeans looked old and dirty. Under her arm she carried a forty-ounce of beer inside of a brown paper bag. The way she searched passing cars with an inviting smile was his cue. This was his victim. Quickly he circled the block with hopes that none of the old white men had picked her up by the time he made it back to the corner. "There she is," he said to himself, pulling out the taser from the bag. Reaching into his pocket, he pulled out two more sixteenths of crack that he got from his brother's stash in the closet.

The conversion van pulled past her and the horn sounded as he pulled over in front of the abandoned houses.

She quickly ran to the passenger door and climbed inside. "You want a date, handsome? I bet you got a big, fat dick. I'll suck it for ten dollars. We can fuck for twenty, baby," She reached for his zipper.

"How about this?" Kenneth said, smiling and holding out his hand.

Her eyes opened wide at the sight of all that crack. She knew she would have to suck more dicks than a few for that much, and she was willing. "What I gotta do, baby?" she cooed, pulling him free. He was small but that didn't matter. Her pleasure came from the crack, not the sex. She could take or leave that. She went down as he drove off, his penis in her mouth. Two blocks later, he exploded in her mouth. She was very good at her job.

"Here!" he moaned as he laid back in his seat. Then he said, "Climb in the back and get undressed in the bed. When we get to the park, I'll join you back there." He handed her one of the sixteenths.

She smiled.

"Is the pussy any good?" he asked.

Startled from her sleep, Joanna looked immediately at the Escape Tron.

It was silently still and read 3:20 p.m. "But what…" she thought as the banging started again. "Fuck!" she growled. Slowly, she rolled from the bed. Not stopping to cover her nakedness, she headed to the front door. "Wait, dammit!" she barked as the banging started more aggressively now. "Who the fuck is banging on my door?"

Joanna snatched the door open only after peeping out the peephole.

"Grumpy, aren't we?" Veronica smirked. "Wow!" she said and looked Joanna up and down. "Now I'm jealous."

"What?" Joanna said, letting her inside.

"That body, bitch! How you stay so… wow!" Veronica smiled, tapping her on the booty.

"Watch it, pervert," Joanna laughed. "Now like I said, what brings you here so early?" She flopped down on the sofa. Her legs sat open, wide and inviting.

"We got us another one," Veronica whispered.

"Abaddon?" she asked.

"Nope! The copy cat. This time up in Manayunk," Veronica said, her eyes staying glued on Joanna's naked body.

"Dammit that's twice I missed my run." She headed to her bedroom to dress.

Veronica followed behind her, watching her booty bounce.

Once in the bedroom, Veronica saw that she was not the only one who enjoyed naked black beauty. "Hey, you little freak!" She yelled at the peeping Tom across from Joanna's bedroom. "Damn Peeping Tom!"

Joanna just smirked.

"You should do something about that," Veronica said as she pulled the blinds shut.

"Why? He's my boyfriend. Well, sort of," Joanna said, then laughing as Veronica stared in disbelief. "What, you never seen a young boy with a hard on?" She giggled. "Take a peek."

"Not that big," Veronica said and then giggled as she eased the blinds up.

The brown skinned woman lay in a pool of blood, naked.

Beside her laid a forty-ounce bottle of Olde English 800, inside a brown bag.

"She's been stabbed numerous times with what looks to be a large kitchen knife," the coroner said, pointing at the wounds around the neck area. "My first guess is that she was unconscious before the murder. No defensive wounds. Also, there's no clothing again." Tim Rankins stood over the body. "This guy either wants to be sure we know he's a copycat, or he's stupid. I'll bank on the first being true."

30

"How deep is the penetration, Tim?" Joanna asked.

"Not as deep as mine. You remember?" He laughed at his own joke. "But nowhere close to the Creep…"

"Abaddon," Joanna corrected. "He wants to be called Abaddon."

"What?" Tim frowned and shook his head. "Crazies. Anyway… Abaddon is very, very well endowed. This guy is not even average. And one more thing. His sperm count is not normal. The little fellas don't swim no more. But the Cree… I mean, Abaddon's is twice the volume of a normal man's. I also found traces of steroids. The legal kind. I'm sending you a list by fax as soon as I get back. My guess is a professional body builder."

Tim walked out to his coroner's van, mumbling under his breath. "Abaddon my ass. Crazy mutha is more like it."

The women stayed behind him, at the crime scene.

"Want to pass it on?" Veronica asked.

"Naw, it's ours," Joanna said. "It's connected."

"I knew you'd say that," Veronica said, stepping away to search the grid. She instantly pulled out her notepad.

"Who are you?" Joanna said, sitting beside the body. "Why like this?"

Joanna's eyes found the only other thing besides the body on the grass. It was the beer bottle inside of the brown paper bag. With the latex gloves she pulled the half-full bottle of Olde English from the bag. It looked normal, then she looked into the bag and froze. "Ronnie!" she yelled. "Check this shit out!"

"Hey big guy," Jesus said as he jumped on Michael Angel's back.

"I heard they arrested Tony in the hospital bed and Fat Joe agreed to testify. No more of those bullies! Man, teach me how to fight."

"You too small... Jesus," Michael grunted, pulling Jesus over his shoulder. "Buy a gun, little guy." He laughed, holding him like a small, struggling baby.

"Yeah, yeah, yeah! Put me down," Jesus said, smiling. "Did you hear?"

"What? That you can't fight?" Michael said, then giggled.

"No, everyone knows that already," Jesus joked. "I'm talking about Abaddon and Apollyon."

"Apollyon?" Michael whispered, and Jesus had to step back. His voice didn't sound the same. If he was asked, he could have sworn Michael was an old lady. But he thought he was mistaken because his voice was back to normal when he spoke again. "Who's Apollyon?"

"The guy killing girls in the park. At first they thought it was the one they call The Creeper," until he named himself Abaddon, and made it clear he wasn't the same killer that plagued the park. Now this guy left his name and said he was called Apollyon. Did that mix you up? It did me, big guy."

"What the hell are you talking about? Who is Apollyon? Not that copycat. Where did you hear all that stuff. I..." Michael stopped mid-sentence to regroup. "Abaddon only announced his name last night."

"Man, y'all need a radio up here. It's been on 1060 AM all day. I'm glad he don't like Puerto Ricans amigo. I worry about my mama."

"Yeah, she sure is fine," Michael said, only to catch Jesus mid-air flying at him.

"Take it back!" he yelled.

Both men laughed as Michael put Jesus down.

"Face it, Jesus..." Michael said as he took two steps back. "I may be your step-daddy one day." He turned and ran as the alarm sounded to end the day of fun.

The conversion van held its speed as he cruised down Grand Avenue.

And Kenneth smiled as he watched the women walking up and down the streets. So badly he wished he could stop and pick one of them up and maybe have some fun. Just to prove to the city he was Abaddon's equal. That bitch on the news this afternoon had the nerve to call him a wannabe.

"What does she mean, wannabe?" Kenneth screamed to himself. He looked at the clock on the dashboard. It read 9:30 p.m. And he had an hour and a half to make it to work which was only thirty minutes away. "Look at you, bitch!" he mumbled as the brown chubby who was obviously on drugs stumbled across the street in front of his van as he was idling at the red light, looking up and smiling. She even licked her ashy, crusty lips and winked at him. "I should take you to forever."

He smiled back as he unconsciously massaged his penis. He said, "I'll see you again."

The beige and blue van pulled into the park and headed west toward City Line Avenue.

Kenneth noticed the police presence everywhere and he knew he was now being noticed, along with his hero. "Say hello to Apollyon," he mumbled as he drove past the patrol car.

Chapter Four

THE JAHEIM CD played loudly as Kareena Saleem pulled away from the gym.

She felt good about the workout tonight and had planned on a hot bath, a small snack and David Letterman. Tomorrow was the beginning of her weekend, which meant bill paying and relaxation. Maybe some sex.

"Just in case, I don't make it home tonight," she sang along with the song loudly as she pulled onto Cheltenham Avenue, only to travel the few blocks before making a left onto Wadsworth and a right onto the eight-hundred block of Rugby Street.

Kareena snatched up the few bags from the back seat of her ATS Cadillac, and climbed the few steps to her home. She closed the front door and threw the bags onto the sofa. Then she flicked on the dining room light as she made her way to the kitchen. Pulling open the refrigerator door, she grabbed the bowl of fruit salad and spring water.

"A hundred and fifty-two pounds," she said and then smiled. "That's eight pounds, bitch," she whispered to herself.

Her plan was to get down to one thirty-five by her birthday, which was only two months away. "I can do this."

Kareena danced a little and sat the salad on the table. Sitting down, she kicked the cross trainers off and plucked a grape from the bowl. She ate her late supper and climbed the stairs to her bedroom.

Entering her bedroom, Kareena smiled to herself. There it laid, unashamed and proud. She shook her head as she lifted up the eight-inch dildo from the nightstand where it had laid since last night.

"Hey LL," she said, then giggled. LL Cool J was the name she gave her dildo because he was who she fantasized about while masturbating at night.

Kareena stood and slid her sweatpants to the floor, followed by the rest of her clothing. Slowly, she inspected her chunky body in the mirror. "Thick my ass! I'm fat!" She frowned, lifting her full breasts with both hands. She spun to look at her hips, ass and back in the full length mirrors on the walls and ceiling. It was her ex boyfriend's idea to have them installed. "Fuck you, Abdullah! Fuck you, Tazera!"

She giggled as she reached for LL Cool J. "I got another friend now. Too fat, my ass, punk. Wait until you see me again."

Kareena walked naked into the small bathroom to start the hot water bubble bath. Scanning the shelf, she selected Peach Cream by Victoria's Secret Bath and Body. She froze and looked up, thinking she heard a moan, but brushed it off. "Bitch, you trippin'."

"Stop it, Boy," Mother whispered as he peeked at her from the walk-in closet.

"It's going to get everywhere, Boy," Mother warned. The explosion shook his body as she leaned over the tub. "See, she heard you! Be ready, you son of Satan!" Mother scolded in his ears.

Instantly, Kareena stood straight up.

Her eyes went straight to where she heard the old lady's voice whispering. The closet. "Was that a moan?" she thought as their eyes met.

The scream escaped her throat as she ran for the door. It was too late. The Giant stood in front of the bedroom door. She noticed he was naked and extremely large. She screamed again, only to feel the Giant's hands, one on her throat and the other covered her mouth. She felt something hot and wet running down her back as he pressed their bodies together.

"I am Abaddon," he moaned.

"Wow!" Kenneth moaned, listening to the news in his conversion van.

His right hand masturbated feverishly as the reporter told of the call received by the police this morning, informing them of victim eleven. "It's too… mmph… too soon… I can't…" He shot his load onto the floor of the van.

Then he started the van and pulled from Pathmark parking lot, heading toward Cobbs Creek Park. He needed a new hunting ground for a while. The police had Creston Hill covered. The clock read 4:15 a.m.

"Come on, Darlene," the dark skinned woman said nervously as she shifted from foot to foot inside of the vestibule of the old home on 58th and Springfield Street. "These boys trippin," she said to her girlfriend who had her body being used by two teenage boys at the same time.

"Get out, bitch!" the tall boy laughed, slamming into Darlene as hard as he could.

"Cheap bastards," she frowned, watching her best friend being tag-teamed by the two boys for twenty dollars of crack. The short stocky one was cumming. Melvina could tell by the way Darlene began to choke. "Bitch, I'm gonna… fuck it!"

She turned and left.

Two blocks away, Melvina still mumbled about the situation she had just left behind. Her mind was so preoccupied that she hadn't noticed the van cruising beside her til he spoke.

"Hey baby, what's up?" he said and smiled.

"Get the fuck outta my face!" she snapped. Melvina felt pissed that the bitch would double cross her for such a small amount of crack. They could have made them nut ass tricks pay at least two twenties apiece.

"Look what I got for you, momma." He held out a handful of dimes from his brother's stash.

That did it. She smiled and straightened out her dirty skirt. She wore no panties already. "What you want to do, sexy?"

"Fuck and suck, girl. Climb in," he said, smiling and looking to see if anyone had eyes on them. No one did.

Moments later, she had him cumming in her mouth. "Here." He handed her two dimes. "Get undressed and in my bed. It's alright to smoke until I find a spot to chill in Cobb's Creek Park. I want some of that pussy." He smiled innocently.

"Park near Pine Woods Crossing. Nobody hangs over there," Melvina said as she spread her legs, exposing her hairy vagina. "And I'm clean," she whispered, spreading her thick lips with her fingers.

"Pine Wood Crossing," he said, then smiled.

"Mmph! Mmph! Mmph!"

Michael grunted as he threw the four sixty-five into the air for the tenth rep in his third set of benches. "Mmph! Ahhh!" He screamed loudly in the basement of his two bedroom home on Lambert Street. He stood up in front of the full wall mirror to look at his chest. "Too small," he snapped, slamming another plate to both sides before climbing back under the safety catch bar of his bench, which kept the weight from crushing him if it slipped. He drank the protein mix drink straight down and looked at the wall clock. "5:15 a.m.," he mumbled, sliding under the five fifty-five. "I need ten reps. Ahhh!" He broke the weight from the rack with no spotter.

Veronica Rawls yawned and rubbed her temples.

She closed her eyes a second to think. Suddenly, she whispered, "This guy is huge." She lifted the fax from the desk and read, "Methadrostenol, oxymethobol, drostanozol... what the hell is Boldenodrol or Cyclostanozol? Muscle hardeners, steroids, and listen to this one, sperm volumizer."

"The company's name is Hardcore Anabolics Legal Steroids. It's a mail-order service. How much you want to bet it has a clientele list longer than Broad Street?" Joanna said, sitting back in the hard wooden chair.

"You know our boys most likely struck again last night and this morning. Going home would be a waste of time. They'll just wake us anyway, "Rawls whispered with a yawn.

Joanna's desk phone rang and she debated whether to answer it at all, but finally did after the third ring.

The voice on the other end was horrifying.

"Mother, please don't do this," he begged as the sweat dripped from his naked body. His muscles ached so wonderfully, but Mother dialed the number she wasted the thirty minutes getting. Michael should have known Mother was up to something strange when she purchased the pre-paid from Walmart last week.

"Shut up, Boy. I just want to talk to the bitch who thinks she's gonna stop my Boy. Don't you start that rubbing, you son of Satan," Mother barked as Detective Staley answered the phone.

"Detective Staley."

"Is this the little bitch who thinks she can call my boy The Creeper?" Mother yelled then moaned.

"Excuse me, Ma'am, but I have no..."

"Shut up, bitch! Do you know who you are speaking to? I'm his mother! Mmmmm, yeah Boy."

Detective Joanna Staley sat up straight and snapped her fingers at her partner to listen in. "The Creeper? Like, as in that freak Abaddon or Apollyon?"

"Mmmm, yes… I'm almost…" Abaddon's deep harsh voice moaned out over the line, into their ears before Mother took over again.

"Stop that, you son of Satan! You better not shoot your… dammit, Abaddon! Look at my floor! You're so weak, Boy!" Mother scolded as the two detectives listened in horror. "Hey, bitch… you still there?"

"Yes, Ma'am. I…"

"Call me Mother. He's Abaddon, the son of my lover, Lucifer. Well, anyway, my Boy left you something inside of the Devil's Flower this time." Mother let loose a disturbing laugh.

"Where is the Devil's Flower, Mother? How am I supposed to find it," Joanna whispered. They both knew she meant another murder, another rape, another dead body.

"No, Mother. Don't," Abaddon grunted.

"Mmmm… God, that feels too good, Boy. But you're messy. Look at my floor, Boy." Mother moaned. "8032 Rugby Street." Mother laughed, then Abaddon's laugh took over.

"Detective, one more thing," he whispered. "I'll find Apollyon before you and he'll be placed in the abyss." He continued to laugh as the phone went dead.

Shaken, both women stared at each other for what seemed like hours, but was only seconds. Detective Rawls had a page full of notes she wrote during the call and it was now a fact. They obviously had a crazy man on their hands, but she had to ask the question: "Was that for real? I mean… shit! Did you hear him masturbating?"

"He's both… Mother and Abaddon," Joanna said as if uttering a revelation. "Let's go. He still may be there."

"Shit!" Detective Rawls yelled. "Captain, we got us another one. 8032 Rugby. The bastard just called it in himself."

"I'll have the patrols there in seconds," the Captain yelled back as the women detectives ran past his office. "Wait… he's calling who?" The Captain was at the door with his phone. "Send everything you got free to 8032 Rugby," he said into the phone.

"We got four out back and we've been out here all along. No one has come out or gone in," the patrolman said to Joanna and Veronica as they dressed in evidence protective clothes.

After pulling on the blue latex gloves, Veronica chambered a shocker flat head high velocity round into her ACP .40 Glock. They watched as the SWAT team entered the house ahead of them.

"Clear!" the sergeant yelled from the front door. Both detectives climbed the stairs. "It's your boy for sure. He left you a message on the wall upstairs. Only me and my second read it."

Mike shook his head and said, "He's got a hard on for you."

"Thanks, Mike," Veronica winked. "No one in until we finish."

"How about him?" Mike pointed as the captain pulled up in his black LTD Mercury sedan.

"Nobody but brass," Veronica said, smiled and followed Joanna inside. At the top of the stairs, they both paused, standing in the puddle of water from the tub that still ran.

"Shit!" the Captain whispered from behind them. "This is some…" He stopped as he read the writing on the wall, written in crimson red lipstick:

Detective First Class Joanna Staley. So sexy and chocolate you are. I've watched you run by in Valley Green. What an ass. But Mother thinks you're skinny.

And Detective Veronica Rawls, I wonder if white pussy feels like black pussy. Who knows? Mother might allow me to let you feel my Glory. Maybe that pretty old black woman next door who called the police on me the other night can be Mother.

Apollyon can never be me. I am Holy.

At the bottom was an arrow that pointed toward the master bedroom. Water could be heard running somewhere inside the room behind the closed door. The hardwood floor was soaked as the water ran under the door. Their eyes all followed the red arrow to the door.

"Shit!" Veronica said, disgusted as they all stood staring at the message in the hallway. "He's just a crazy sick son of a bitch. We can't let him…" She froze, quiet as she slung open the bedroom door. Written in hundreds of lines covering up every wall in crimson red lipstick sentences, it read, I am Abaddon!

"Detectives," Tim said, visibly disturbed.

"Can I do my thing, Tim?" Joanna asked the coroner as his team exited the room.

Shaking his head, he sat on the edge of the bed. "Do you know the Bible? He does." Tim handed the captain the plastic evidence bag which held moist strips of a Bible page. "That's Genesis six, verses one through four. It has sperm samples on it, so handle with care."

"Ain't his name from Genesis also?" Captain Jackson said, then frowned, holding up the bag.

"No! Abaddon and Apollyon are from the Bible also, but it's from Revelation nine, verse eleven," Tim said. "Your boy may be sick, but he knows his Bible. Call me when you're finished. We'll take the body." He walked away, mumbling as always. This time something about Giants and Nephilim, whatever that was.

"What's up, Joanna? Where you been?" Tommy smiled, sitting on his balcony looking down. "You going to bed?" He stood and tossed her the club sandwich wrapped in plastic wrap. "Made it myself for you this morning."

"Thanks, Tommy. Baby, do you have a Bible?" she asked as she unwrapped the sandwich and paused.

"Ain't no mayo or mustard, don't worry." He smiled down at her. "See, I pay attention, and of course, we own a few. Why?"

"Who's Nephilim?" Joanna asked as she bit into the sandwich.

"It's what. They were a mixture of angels and the daughters of men. The Bible says they were Giants and heroes of the old days. Wait a minute," Tommy said as he went inside. Moments later, the front door to his father's house opened. "See, right here in the book of Genesis." He opened the book as Joanna finished off the club sandwich.

Tommy read from chapter six of Genesis: "When men began to increase in number on the Earth and daughters were born to them, the sons of God saw that the daughters of men were beautiful, and they married any of them they chose. Then the Lord said, 'My spirit will not contend with man forever, for he is mortal; his days will be a hundred and twenty years. The Nephilim were on the Earth in these days, and also afterwards, when the Sons of God went to the daughters of men and had children by them. They were the heroes of old, men of renown."

Tommy paused and smiled then continued. "That is why a woman should sleep with a man on his request, no matter his age."

"It says that?" she said, and then leaned into the book to read it for herself.

"Of course, it does!" Tommy pulled away just enough for her to touch him. "Make love to me, Joanna. Please?" The warmth he felt from her touch caused him to grow excited.

"If I did, you'd fall hopelessly in love with me," Joanna said and then laughed, snatching the Bible. "I gotta go take me a long cold shower now." She softly brushed his erection with her hip. "But first I better exercise." She shot him a sly smile.

The Escape Tron read 12:02 p.m. As Joanna undressed in her bedroom, she had to smile as Tommy stood in his room and watched naked. With every stroke, he performed and for the first time, their eyes locked until they came together.

"Nigga, twist up!" the teenager yelled, opening the forty ounce beer.

After taking a deep swallow of the beer and then replacing the cap, he said, "Here! I got to piss."

"Piss over there, muthafucka! I don't want to smell that AIDS infested shit." His friend dumped the cigar tobacco into the dirt.

"I got it from Bernise," he joked back, referring to his friend's mother. "I knew not to eat that fat ass of hers."

Calvin Dykes walked twenty feet into the wooded area and that walk would change his life forever. He saw it. He saw her. Slowly, he backed up, but he never stopped peeing, even as he fell backwards over the fallen tree limb his best friend sat upon.

"Man, watch that shit!" Isaiah yelled as pee sprayed everywhere. "What the fuck wrong with…" He started laughing as Calvin jumped up and ran down the hill. Two minutes later, Isaiah caught it and passed his best friend on the way home. He had seen her cold, dead eyes.

"Her name is Melvina Williams. Last seen by her best friend Darlene Goodjones after a night of sex, drugs, and alcohol," the officer said. "She was found by two teenagers out to smoke a little weed away from the crowds. One of them had to pee and did so on her face, on his best friend, and himself."

"Bet he won't smoke no more," the detective said with a smirk.

"Or piss," the officer laughed.

Veronica Rawls held the ACP 15 Glock .40 at her side as she checked the back door again. She titled the aluminum six foot ladder against the door. "If you open this bitch, I'll hear that ass." She smirked. The hair on her neck stood up and she turned and looked at the closet at the back of the basement. It sat cracked open. She had no idea if she had left it that way or not. "Shit!"

"If you're in there, Abaddon, life's over." The door swung open to the emptiness of the closet. "Fuck this!" She giggled nervously. She climbed the stairs to her bedroom. "Not this time." She laughed and wrapped the .40 in a plastic sandwich bag. She turned on the tub water very hot, no bubble bath this time. She bathed, quickly soaking. "Just stop it! We can't let him get in our heads," she whispered. She sat on the edge of the king sized mattress. "Besides, I'm white. He prefers black women."

It was Saturday afternoon and she had two days off. There was no way she would let this freak ruin her weekend off. Veronica laid across the bed to sleep. She looked at the clock. It read 1:30 p.m. When her eyes popped open again, the clock read 2:30 p.m., but why did she awaken? Under the silk sheet, her hand slid to the Glock without thinking. "What is it?" she asked herself. Something had driven her out of her sleep, but what? Quickly she ran over a checklist in her mind, starting from when she drove to her home.

I locked the car. I walked around to check the back door. I came back around the front, checked my basement and locked the screen door... Veronica sat up frantically.

She leapt from the bed and ran toward her front door, clutching the ACP Glock.

"God no!" she screamed, heading for the front door. One lock, two locks, the security chain. She knew she had to get in there. They may need her help.

But her legs wouldn't move.

"No," she whispered.

Veronica had originally read it and brushed it off as an attempt to frighten them and so did Joanna. Oh my God, Veronica, she thought. Do something.

Slowly, Veronica climbed the three steps and entered the vestibules of the Flint's home. Her heart sank as she looked at the family portraits over the mantelpiece. She had become so color blind that she had forgotten Mr. and Mrs. Flint were black. He had said it. His words ran through her mind once again: Maybe that pretty old black woman next door who called the cops on me.

Veronica screamed and rushed up the stairs ready to kill. She charged into the bedroom and they were tied to the bed, but still alive.

All across the walls was written: I AM ABADDON.

Veronica rushed to untie the Flints. She pulled the duct tape from Mrs. Flint's mouth first.

"Oh God, Veronica. He's still here!" She got the words out right before she fainted.

"Detective..." Veronica heard far off in the distance. Was she dreaming?

Why am I in Mrs. Flint's house? Who called me? She wondered. There it goes again.

"Detective Rawls... Veronica Rawls... Can you hear me?" the voice was heard again.

Oh God! I have to save the Flints! "It's Abaddon," she said, and struggled to move as she stood in the Flint's bedroom.

"I'll save you, Mrs. Flint I promise..." That was the last thing she had heard before everything went black again...

Veronica came to again, with hands holding her firmly as she began to panic.

"Detective Rawls, you're safe. We have you! You're safe..."

"It's us!" the paramedic said as Veronica fought him and his partner.

"Ronnie!" Joanna yelled. "Stop fighting, Ronnie!"

Joanna wrapped her arms around Veronica and pushed the paramedics away. "Calm down. It's me."

Veronica struggled a second longer before she became more aware of her surroundings.

"He was here, Jo. Because of me, he was here!"

"It's over," Detective Staley whispered, rocking her partner. "It's over."

"No, Joanna. He's just starting!" Veronica cried.

Chapter Five

BE QUIET NIGGA! Kevin thought as he crept into his oldest brother's room.

The keys were where he left them - on the dresser. So many times he watched Kenneth sneak into his closet and steal crack and not once did he complain. So, if Kenneth wakes up and catches him, fuck it. Fair play ain't no robbery. "I'm only going to be an hour. To the mall and back," he thought as he lifted the keys. Ten minutes later, he was driving up 69th Street with his homies and a trick crackhead named Darlene Goodjones.

"Damn, Kev! Mmmm, shit!" Jamal moaned as he laid back in the bed inside the conversion van. "This head is the bomb!"

"Nigga, I ain't trying to hear about it. Hurry the fuck up!" Flip barked, playing with his dick as he watched Darlene deep throat his man.

"What, you some kind of ball gazer, nigga? Turn around!" Kevin laughed, turning onto Market Street.

"Fuck that, nigga!" Flip laughed. "This shit like a porno."

"Shit, boy!" Darlene moaned. "You gotta cum soon, my jaw hurts." She licked around his helmet before putting him back into her mouth.

"Fuck that!" Flip yelled, climbing into the back and onto the bed. He slid his jeans down to his ankles and pulled Darlene's dirty biker shorts to her knees. Slowly he sank into her and she moaned out as he reached into her stomach.

"Uhhhh shit... Sssshit, stop," she moaned as Jamal came instantly from her moans.

"Damn nigga! What's that?" Jamal laughed, as Flip changed Darlene's position and began pulling her legs further apart.

"Hell no, boy. That shit too... awwww!" she moaned as he slid back into her with her leg over his shoulder. Five minutes later he exploded into her as Kevin pulled into the parking garage.

"Darlene, smoke this," Kevin said, then smiled. "We'll be back in a few minutes. I want some head, too." He laughed as she held her stomach and rolled her eyes at Flip.

"Here bitch, chill out," Flip said and tossed her a twenty.

"Pussy," Darlene whispered as she pulled her glass straight shooter from the plastic imitation Louis Vuitton purse. "All that dick and can't use it unless he hurt a bitch." She continued to complain. "Shit," she cursed when she realized her lighter was empty. She looked frantically around for a lighter or some matches. Her eyes spotted a green lighter that she knew was Flip's. She had watched him light his blunt with it earlier.

"Mine now, fat dick," she said, then giggled, climbing from the bed, naked now that big dick Flip had stripped her. "I'm gonna teach that young boy how to use that shit when he gets back. I'm on top this time." She giggled again, reaching for the lighter. "Ooops!" she whispered when she noticed the pearl earring on the floor.

Darlene picked it up and spotted the Reebok sneaker under the front seat. She instantly knew whose it was. Panic set in as she rushed to dress herself.

"Oh God! Oh God!" she cried, pulling the cheap, dirty flats onto her feet. "Please, Lord, protect me," Darlene prayed as she jumped from the van and ran toward the L train, still holding her crack and straight shooter.

"Sit up, Mother. The news, it's coming on. You promised to watch it with me," Abaddon whispered, pulling the crying heavy-set woman up into a sitting position. The red wig had shifted slightly and he straightened it.

"Is my son alive?" Pamela Sample whispered, too afraid to move. The Giant who called himself Abaddon had easily strangled her husband to death. She hadn't heard a thing as she put their son to bed.

"Of course, Mother. I'm not a monster; I would never hurt a child."

"Please; he's only three and… I'll do anything… I won't try nothing, I promise."

"Shhhh! It's on!" Abaddon said as Gloria Velendez began to speak.

"This is the scene outside of one of the lead detective's homes in the serial rape and murder case that's held the city hostage with fear for weeks now. It's the scene of an assault believed to serve as a warning to the Philadelphia Police Department to back off," Gloria said with a grim look on her face.

"Sources say that in the house to my left lives Detective Rawls, who has had the job of questioning me and my cameraman Jimmy only three days ago when he received a tip from Abaddon of the gruesome rape and murder of a husband and wife in the nineteen hundred block of Ashley Street. Early this afternoon, it is said that Abaddon somehow attacked an elderly couple next door to the detective, to serve as a warning. The detective was injured in a struggle with Abaddon when she entered the couple's residence to investigate. It is not known at this time if the detective got a look at the suspect or not. We do know, however, that the elderly couple was taken to Hannamens for observation and will not be returning to this home tonight, maybe never. Now to Jim Connelli with a follow-up on today's discovery. Jim."

The scene switched to a darkened wooded area with Jim Connelli standing by the yellow tape the police use to keep out intruders. "Thank you, Gloria. As reported earlier, this is the scene of another copy-cat murder. Police believe it's the same sick individual who named himself Apollyon. As you may know, it is the Greek name for the Hebrew name Abaddon. The young lady was found by two boys out to have a good time. They are teens, so their identities are protected. Police say the wig and lipstick prove it's the copy-cat..." he continued.

"Sick?!" Kenneth screamed, throwing his boot at the television. "Mutherfucka, I'll show you sick!" he screamed again.

Kenneth stormed out of his room and out into his van. It was his day off and he had all night to himself. He smiled, knowing that Abaddon was out somewhere making magic once again. Too bad he had to wait until daylight to send his own message.

"Sick, huh? A sick copy-cat, huh? You son of a bitch, I'll show all of you. You'll fear Apollyon as you do Abaddon. Even more muthafucka!"

He pulled off, squealing the tires.

"See, Boy!" Mother said, then giggled. "Now they respect you."

"I see, Mother," Abaddon said as he rolled the tape around their necks to make the Union. "But..."

"Quiet!" Mother yelled loudly.

He whispered, pleading. "Mother, please… the baby…"

"Oh God, please…" Pamela Sample cried as she watched the two voices come from his mouth almost simultaneously. "His name is Michael Sample, and he's only three years old," She began to sob.

"Don't listen to her, Boy," Mother hissed as Abaddon paused hearing the child's name. "The baby's safe… as long as you kill it for Mother. Remember…"

"Noooo!" Pamela screamed. "Help! Help! Help!"

"Shut…" The blow was swift and very hard. "Up!" Pamela Sample made no more sounds.

"Mother, you killed her," Abaddon whispered. "Her neck is broken. Look what you've done."

He began to cry.

"Cut the Union, Boy. It's over tonight," Mother said in disgust. "See what happens when you defy Mother? It's your fault, Boy." Mother smiled. "You know what we can do with this one, don't you?"

Abaddon smiled.

"Fox News," the intern answered.

"I am Abaddon," he growled. "Apollyon, beware, for the son of Satan will find you. I will lock you in the abyss forever."

"Oh God, wait…" She pressed the alert for the director again. He instantly answered.

"Abaddon?"

Abaddon smiled and so did Mother. "Let this serve as a warning to Apollyon… you copycat… you abomination of my father. You are like wormwood; bitter to taste, and Abaddon will serve you up to the darkness of the abyss. You will dwell with my father, the Father of lies." Abaddon laughed. "Detective Joanna Staley knows where she awaits as warning."

"Who?" the director whispered.

The phone line went dead.

The big breasted, red-headed, white woman opened the door and there stood the muscular black man. He watched excitedly as his hand massaged up and down.

"Ma'am, I heard your plumbing needs unclogging and your husband's tools can't run deep enough to do the job."

"My pipes are deeper than he can reach," the redhead cooed sexily. "Do you have the right size pipe wrench?"

Unzipping his pants, the muscular black man pulled his larger-than-life penis free of his pants.

"Oh goodness, that's more than enough," the redhead exclaimed with a look of pure delight on her face. She reached out and grabbed the 15 inches in her small hand, then pulled the black guy into her bedroom.

"Oh, Johnny Piper, unclog me," she moaned, dropping to her knees. Her mouth barely engulfed his helmet.

Kenneth's hand stroked faster. "Bitch!" he growled.

"Detective Staley," Joanna answered on the first ring.

"Detective, this is Bob Thortonson, the program director for Fox 29 News. I'm the one who sent Gloria Velendez to that home on Ashley Street last week."

"Oh yeah, I remember that," Joanna said with sarcasm. "Bad move, Bob."

"Well. We all have our jobs," he said unapologetically. "I'm calling to inform you that he's called again." Bob paused for effect. "And he's requested we relay a message."

"Shit!" Joanna sat up at her desk. She knew this meant another rape/murder.

"Please listen to this," the program director pressed Play. As the voice came through the phone, Joanna closed her eyes and listened to Abaddon declare war on Apollyon. "Detective Joanna Staley knows where she awaits as a warning," he growled.

Instantly, Joanna knew somewhere in Valley Green Park there was a murdered woman.

"Detective, we've done the right thing by informing you of this. Now can we be there when you go get the warning?" Bob Thortonson asked.

"Bob, is it? Well, Bob, I think we can help each other. Send that Gloria Velendez to the entrance of Valley Green Park, east entrance," Joanna said, then smiled.

"Oh God, Johnny Piper. Yes, go deeper!" she cried out as almost fifteen inches disappeared into her clean-shaven vagina. "Ohhh, God, open my pipes."

As Johnny Piper pumped into the small, large-breasted redhead, a man watched from the closet, masturbated and thought to himself, Yes, fuck my wife with that Giant cock, Johnny Piper. Fuck her harder… deeper.

Kenneth Taylor exploded into the condom.

"Can I sit here?" she whispered in the dark movie house on 23rd and Market.

Kenneth looked up.

The Valley Green Park exploded with flood lights in the early morning hours. Joanna looked at her wristwatch. It read 3:22 a.m. In less than two-and-a-half hours, the park was set to open to the public. Most of the yuppies in the upper-middle class neighborhood liked to jog the trails early morning.

Joanna had an idea which trail she would be found on or around. The message was clear. Just as it was to Veronica Rawls, her partner. He knew them but they had no idea who he was. All they knew was that he was Abaddon.

"Jo," Detective Rawls called, slamming the door to her Chevy Impala.

"What the hell, Ronnie?" Joanna said, then smiled.

"Can't let him win that easy. Did I tell you I caught a glimpse of the bastard? Big motherfucker! I mean HUGE!"

"Yeah, that's what Mr. and Mrs. Flint said. They kept referring to the guy in the Green Mile," Joanna said, leading her partner toward the trail she used daily. It was mid-terrain steep.

"Bigger!" Detective Rawls whispered. "Bigger!" she clambered a round into the 16 gauge. "Much, much, much bigger." She shook her head.

Stopping at the edge of the command center, which was just the SWAT truck, Joanna and Veronica addressed the team of cops.

"This bastard is very, very big… and he kills. Stay in groups of three. I believe we'll find the victim on the mid-range terrain. It's where I run every day and this bastard has a thing for me and my partner."

From somewhere in the distance, Veronica could hear her name being called.

"Joanna Staley!"

"Someone has a question for me and…" Joanna started to ask.

"Shhhhh!" Veronica said as the voice yelled again from somewhere in the distance.

"Joanna Staley… Veronica Rawls. Up here!" The voice was barely audible.

"Goddamn!" the SWAT leader said, "There! Up on the cliffs!" he said and pointed behind Joanna and Veronica.

They all turned.

There he stood with something high over his head. "I am Abaddon!" he screamed, and tossed whatever it was he held over his head off the cliff and into the deep pond below. "Soon I'll be gone, but not before I end Apollyon's terror!" Abaddon yelled again.

With that, he disappeared over the cliff. Joanna knew there was no point in trying to follow him. His car had to be there on Henry Avenue, ten feet from where he stood. Seconds later, they all heard…

"I AM ABADDON! KING OF THE ABYSS!"

"It's a body, a woman… she's dead," an officer yelled as he and two others pulled the body from Devil's Pond.

"How did you know?" Gloria Velendez asked as they sat in the back of the news broadcast truck. The monitors were full of different scenes from the day's crime scene events at the park. Monitor one showed SWAT team members preparing to enter the trails. Monitor two was of Detective Staley and Rawls looking over maps of the park. Three and four were the monitors everyone was watching.

"Lord God, Jesus Christ! He's a Giant!" the Captain said in awe.

"He's smart. Look," Veronica said, pointing toward the mask and gloves he wore. "You think he knew?"

"Nope, he's just cautious," Joanna said. "Wait! What's that?"

The news tech stopped the film and reversed it a few frames.

"There!" Joanna said. "Can you zoom in on this?" she asked as she pointed to the corner of the screen.

"It's a goddamn car front end. White," the tech said, zooming in on the bumper.

"Bingo!" Veronica said and smiled. "His first slip-up."

"You didn't have to stop because of me," the white girl said, then smiled over at Kenneth who had his limp penis with the condom full of sperm under his hat.

"What you want? I heard about you faggots cruising the Triple X spots. Beat it, I'm straight," Kenneth barked angrily. He needed to masturbate one more time before going on the hunt. Now this pretty white faggot boy was trying some gay shit. "Get the fuck lost, I said!"

"Do I sound like a man or something? I ain't that bad am I? A man?" she said. "Man, that's fucked up. I guess I sold too much pussy. It's fucking up my looks, huh?" She smiled, pulling up her skirt to reveal the dark bush on her vagina. She parted her legs and rubbed her slit to prove her point.

"Sorry," Kenneth said and then licked his lips. "I thought…"

"Don't apologize, handsome. I understand, but my husband Billy wouldn't let no punks in here to hustle like the Max does. Me and my sisters work these old dudes in here. We don't get many young black guys in here." She sat back a second, quietly watching the movie. "Watch this," she said as her hand slid under his hat. He was erect again. "Damn, you thick," she whispered as Johnny Piper exploded in the big-breasted redhead's face. "I'm better; want to see?"

"Yes, mmmm, yes, please," Kenneth moaned as she rubbed up and down on his cock. "How much?"

"Twenty-five for head. Twenty more for the best pussy in Philly. If you want I'll just beat you off for ten dollars." She quickened the pace of her hand.

"Can I take this off for some head?" he moaned and shook as he came in her hand. "Mmm, shit!"

"That's ten bucks, sweetie," she smiled, pulling the condom free. She dropped it to the floor.

"Alright, alright! Please suck me. I'll pay!" Kenneth cried as her hands wiped him clean. Slowly she slid her mouth down on the length of his still erect dick. "That's it, suck it, bitch," he whispered as the screen filled with the Giant cock slamming into the redhead's anal cavity as she screamed for mercy. Two minutes later, he exploded in the whore's mouth as he watched the knife stab into her throat.

She was still forever.

Kenneth rushed from the Triple X movie theater with an erection.

"Where are you?" he mumbled, driving up Snider Avenue as the sun rose. The city would soon be awake and moving. He needed to make a statement.

South Philly was notorious for its crackheads, and there was no way he wouldn't find what he wanted.

"I should have went uptown..." he paused. There she was. "Perfect," he laughed, pulling up on the chubby smoker standing on 18th Street. "What's up, sexy," Kenneth smiled.

"You looking for company?" she said, then smiled as she stepped into the van. "You got a smoke?"

"Don't smoke, but I want company."

"You a cop ain't you? Let me see your dick," she ordered.

"Bitch, I ain't no cop! Besides, look what I got," he said, then laughed, holding out the handful of crack. "And I got a bed in here." His eyes searched for witnesses.

"All that for me?" She looked suspicious. "For what? What a bitch gotta do? I don't take it in the butt."

"No, I just want some head and pussy. That's it!"

"And you'll pay me for all that?"

"Hello," Abaddon growled. "Do you know who I am?"

The intern whispered, "Yes," and instantly the director cut in.

"Abaddon?" he asked, afraid of the answer.

"Yes, it's Abaddon," he paused and the director heard an old woman speaking to Abaddon. "I need your help and I'll give you the location of the body."

"Whose body?" the news program director whispered, too afraid to speak loudly.

"The copy-cat's... after I kill him."

"Listen... can we interview you?" The director licked his lips. This could be career making. "We'll keep it safe for you, no one will know we're meeting."

"Gloria Velendez... alone..." Mother's voice interrupted. "And one cameraman."

"Yes, yes we can do all that... wait! You'll have to promise their safety also."

"I am Abaddon!" he roared. "82011 Park Side Drive, 703A. Death is mine to hold under chains. She has nice yellow carpeting. Her panties are in the third drawer down and the picture of her mother and father sits next to this..." The hum of the vibrator came through the phone, "abomination."

"Oh God!" the program director cried out, snapping his finger at the intern who was already dialing the police to give Gloria's address.

"Don't bother! She's in Maryland for the weekend and I'll be gone. I'll call with the time and place. Remember..." Mother's voice took over again. "I'm always listening."

Before the line disconnected he heard her singing an old Isley Brothers tune: "Somebody said... I was..."

Chapter Six

"HEY PAL, YOU CAN'T park this monster here. It'll be towed," field reporter Jim Connelli said with disgust.

"What's wrong with some of these assholes?" he said loud enough for Kenneth Taylor to hear his arrogance.

Kenneth smiled as Jim Connelli entered the Fox News studio in Roxborough, Philadelphia. Slowly, he slid from his van down to Wilson and Henry Avenue and killed the engine.

"You know, I'll be asleep in two more weeks and three days, Boy," Mother whispered as they drove down City Line Avenue.

I wish you would sleep forever, woman! Abaddon thought, then he realized his mistake.

"I heard you, Boy! How could you say that to me? We only get to enjoy each other's company once a year, Michael. Why do you want to hurt me like that?" Mother cried out inside the car.

"Mother... I'm... sorry." Michael began to cry along with Mother. "I was only-"

"No, you weren't. You meant to hurt me, Michael."

"I'll make it up to you, Mother. I promise."

"Tonight?"

"Yes, Mother… please forgive me…" he cried.

"I want to be happy, Michael. Is she beautiful?" Mother whispered.

"Yes, she is, Mother."

"What's her name?"

"Katherine, and she's married."

"How old is she, Boy? Where does she live?"

"Trust me, Mother. Trust your son, Abaddon." He massaged his erection at the red light as the children giggled from the Astro van. As the light changed, the little boy in the window yelled and laughed, "Crazy man!"

"Son of a bitch!" Jim Connelli yelled, standing there looking at the words scratched into the paint of the hood of his Gold SL 5000 Mercedes Benz. Jim looked around as if he would spot the vandal. "Fucking kids!" he screamed. "Little bastards." He climbed into his car, whispering the words written in scratches in his paint job.

I am coming soon. Hold onto what you have, so that no one will take your crown. I will write on him the name of my God and the name of the city of my God… Jim Connelli paused to re-read it. "What's that supposed to mean, you little bastards? What happened to throwing eggs?!" He pulled away, more upset at himself than at the vandals. Two blocks away, he stopped, and the beige and blue conversion van pulled up behind him.

Jim Connelli paid it no mind.

"Where are you, cutie?" Joanna whispered, searching the mirror. "Ain't this a…" she thought, a little disappointed he wasn't there. In two years, that never happened. Slowly, she walked into the bathroom. It was Saturday and she had the day off. She would cook a complete meal. Chicken, stuffing and broccoli, maybe some dinner rolls and a beer. She came from the bathroom of her bedroom and froze solid. Her eyes darted to her nightstand, where the .40 Glock sat.

Ting ting! There it was again, the sound of pans and utensils.

Slowly, she realized what it was, or should she say, who it was. Veronica, her partner. She claimed they needed to stick together until Abaddon was either dead or in jail, for their own safety.

Joanna knew she was afraid to go back home alone. She told her it didn't make sense because if he wanted them dead, it was over weeks ago. But Veronica didn't feel safe alone; besides, Joanna had an extra bedroom.

Walking into the living room, Joanna smelled the pies baking in the oven, and on the table sat a roasted chicken, rice, greens, and what looked like cornbread. "Damn!"

"Oh, my God, Jo! Close your eyes, boy!" Veronica yelled as Joanna stood there in the nude.

Turning, Joanna realized Tommy sat on the sofa by the window, smiling and ogling her body, which he had seen hundreds of times, just never up close.

"I told you, she's my woman!" Tommy laughed.

"I said, close your eyes, or go home!" Veronica ordered. And Joanna blushed, heading back to her room to get dressed. Ten minutes later, she returned fully dressed in her running outfit.

"We eat in an hour, with or without you," Veronica said as Tommy stood to follow Joanna outside. "Where you going?"

"I just need to speak to Joanna a moment," Tommy said.

"Well, hurry up. I want to test my sweet potato pie," Veronica said, storming back into the kitchen. "Shit!"

Joanna smiled as they made their way outside.

"How long she staying?" Tommy wanted to know, looking at the door. "I mean, she's like my mom used to be before she left."

"She is sort of like a mother hen," Joanna giggled.

"So…" Tommy whispered.

"She'll be gone soon. It's just this case."

"Abaddon and the copycat, right? I watch the news. Damn, he's bigger than my dad. But I was talking about us and this morning."

"I was wondering where my Tommy was. That was a mistake," Joanna lied to cover her lustfulness.

"No, it wasn't," he said, and turned to re-enter the apartment. Suddenly, he stopped and said, "You should teach me now so I'll satisfy you later on."

"Boy!" Joanna said and then giggled and took off running to avoid the situation. She didn't want to admit that she was turned on by the seventeen-year-old boy.

"Excuse me, sir. Can you point me toward..." Kenneth said as Jim Connelli stepped from his car, still pissed over the scratches. The blade entered below the rib cage into his heart. "Son of a bitch! Copycat, huh? A goddamn sick individual, right?"

Kenneth laughed as he twisted the blade deeper. He let Jim's body drop in the parking lot of Saks Fifth Avenue. Slowly, he ripped the back of his Calvin Klein shirt open, and with a switch blade he began to write his message to Abaddon.

Here I am! I stand at the door and knock. If anyone hears my voice and opens the door, I will come in and sup with him and he with me. I, too, am Apollyon.

Skillfully, Joanna maneuvered the rough terrain of the steep course in full sprint. Not once did her mind conceive that he might be out there, waiting, lurking, and, if given a chance, ready to pounce. She leapt the log, barely missing the large rock sticking out of the dirt. She didn't slow down once.

The bend led to a deep decline and only a skilled mountain trail runner could take it at full speed. The reason was that it came from a blind in the bend and if you didn't know it was there, you would drop thirty yards before you eventually hit the first of many trees. She took the bend at full speed, so she never had a chance as the large hands wrapped around her neck, and began to squeeze.

Someone had her.

Self-defense classes, she thought as her elbow found what felt like a brick wall. She kicked back with force as the darkness came over her. She heard him whisper in her ear, "I am Abaddon."

Twenty minutes later, Joanna awoke, totally naked, spread eagle on an empty patch of grass thirty yards off the trail. Beside her lay a note. Her clothes were nowhere to be found, and she was sore.

The taste of your nectar fills my palate. The smell of your skin lingers on my touch. The silky softness I'll always cherish. Tonight she'll suffer the cruelness of Abaddon in your stead.

After reading the note, Veronica said, "Dammit! That bastard is getting bolder."

Joanna sat in the tub. "But he still didn't kill me," she mumbled. "But I think he tasted me." She giggled nervously, feeling sore inside.

"Shit, if he wasn't so crazy, he could taste me," Veronica said and then laughed. They both were afraid now, but for different reasons.

Why didn't he kill us? The women thought in the quiet between them. Why?

Joanna thought she knew why.

"Katherine, honey, can you bring me that slice of cheesecake now?" Anthony yelled downstairs from his bedroom. "Honey?" he called out again, then hit the button on the remote.

Katherine stood with her back against the Giant's stomach. His hand across her mouth. She could feel his breath on the top of her head, his erection pressed into her back. So badly she wanted to scream. But he said he would kill them both, and he could. She knew it. He told her he was the plague of the city, then he whispered his name in her ear. "I am Abaddon."

So badly she wanted to scream, but would she? If his hand wasn't covering her mouth, would she call out to Anthony for help? Or would she tell him to run from this Giant who killed with ease. Yes, she would! He was Abaddon and that meant death. Why should they both die?

"Dammit, Katherine!" Anthony cursed, coming into the kitchen. "All you had to do was say-" He froze as the Giant dropped his wife to the floor. His speed was incredible. Anthony had no chance as he began to try to fight back. Two punches was all it took, one for Anthony and one for Katherine who put up the best fight out of fear.

"This is ABC New Center Command with shocking news involving Fox 29 news correspondent, Jim Connelli and the copycat killer, Apollyon. Jim Connelli's body was discovered earlier this afternoon in the back of his vintage SL Mercedes Benz outside of the parking garage of Saks Fifth Avenue department store. He had been one of two Fox investigators covering the terrifying serial murders plaguing the City of Brotherly Love. It is not known how he died, but it is known that the murder was carried out by the serial killer who's been copying the murder rituals of another terrifying rapist and murderer named Abaddon. As we all know, it's become sort of a love/hate relationship between the two and it is yet known their personal connections…" the pretty, young white news anchor continued.

Abaddon switched stations.

"It saddens us to bid farewell to one of our greatest and beloved family members…" the anchorwoman on Fox News 29 paused as her co-host anchorman placed an arm around her shoulder for comfort. It was easy for the public audience to see they were both crying over the loss. The camera cut to an older man sitting by himself.

"As you can see, this is very hard on us. Jim Connelli was like family, and we're going to miss him dearly…" The camera zoomed in on the older man. "Most of America doesn't know me, and wouldn't recognize me on the street. I'm the man behind the scenes of the broadcast every day. My name is Bob Thortonson and I'm the program director here at Fox 29 News,"

He paused to wipe away a tear.

"To my very big friend out there… I'll say no names. He has disgraced you and crossed the line. The call we had will be honored and all information leading to this… this… we'll call him what he is, a copycat, a son of a (beep) will be given to whoever listens.

I am now authorizing ten thousand dollars to anyone who can lead us to the fake Apollyon and another ten thousand if he is caught. The hotline number is 555-3355 and will be manned twenty-four hours a day, seven days a week. You will be given a four digit number to collect the reward. No names are necessary or wanted. Thank you. This is Fox 29 News. See you in heaven, Jim."

The television rolled clips of Jim Connelli on different assignments over the years. At the end it displayed his dates of birth and death. Jim Connelli was smiling.

"See, Boy, they'll help us now," Mother whispered. "You must find him. He embarrassed me, son."

Katherine looked up, horrified. She was duct taped to her now dead husband. The Giant's voice had changed to someone other than a male's voice. It was an old lady's voice she now heard coming from Abaddon as his semen splashed on the floor.

"Please God, save me," she prayed silently as the Giant positioned himself to enter her body. "No, please!" she screamed as the large blade severed the carotid and he slid completely inside her.

"That's right, kill it, Boy," Mother moaned.

Chapter Seven

THE SMALL OFFICE in the basement held two desks with phones connected to Celco recorders, no windows and a small television monitor that showed the daily broadcast of the news, three times a day. The morning shift had just come in: a college student from Temple's Journalism School and a student from a local high school with intentions of going into broadcasting one day.

"Do you think this is what it'll be like when you finally graduate and get a bachelor's in Journalism?" Sharon asked him. She stared at the phone on the small motel desk.

"Shhhh," David said and pointed at the television, where the early morning weather report was being given by an old college buddy of his who graduated two years prior. "He's good."

David smiled and Sharon wondered if maybe he had some sugar in his bowl of flakes.

"I used to watch William practice in the mirror for hours in college."

"No mystery there," Sharon mumbled, reaching for the novel she brought to work this morning. She had learned yesterday, this job was boring as well as lonely and David spent way too much time listening to his own voice as he faked live broadcasts there in the basement.

One hundred calls yesterday and ninety eight were lunatics, one was lonely and another plain scary. He kept insisting he needed all the caller's names and numbers or he would visit her when she turned thirty-five. Sharon had the feeling he was masturbating when they spoke.

She looked up at the monitor and the time and weather sat in the bottom left hand corner of the screen. "6:23 a.m. and a cool 68 degrees," she mumbled, imitating David's posture and clear pronunciation.

"That's good!" he said with excitement. "No, that was REALLY good! Did you go to speech class? Wow!"

"Really?" Sharon said, then giggled. What a dork, she thought as the phone rang on David's desk.

"Hello, Fox News hotline," he said, smiling. "Yes, ma'am, this is for the reward for tips on the copycat. But first, we need you to explain why you believe you can help us."

"This is Thortonson, David. Spit it out," the program director said with irritation. Even the high school intern didn't call him with every worthless crazy who claimed to know Apollyon.

"Bob, I think we got it," David whispered as if he held the secret to eternity.

"Mr. Thortonson… David," the program director corrected, irritated with the intern's liberty. "Why?"

"Sorry, sir… she claims to be her best friend and the last to see her alive."

"David! David… David… stop and listen to me," Bob Thortonson said, rubbing his temples. "Who are we talking about, son?"

"Caller 6326-"

"David! Listen, who did the caller say was her best friend?" The program director knew David would never make it in big city media. At least not in Philadelphia. He was too self-absorbed.

"Sorry, Bob... I mean Mr. Thortonson. Melvina S. Williams, sir. She claims to have been the last to see her alive." David paused. "She slipped and gave me her name, sir."

"What is it, David?" Thortonson mumbled, opening the stolen police report on his desk.

"Darlene, sir."

Bob Thortonson froze. There it was on the first page of witnesses. Darlene Goodjones. Questioned by homicide on the day of the murder. Melvina's murder.

"David, put her through... and David..."

"Sir?"

"Forget her name, and destroy anything incriminating, understand?"

"Yes, sir." David smiled, shoving the paper into his pocket.

"Hello? Who dis?" Darlene's voice immediately came through on Bob Thortonson's line. "Dis who I got to talk to, to get my money?"

"Yes, this is Bob Thortonson, the program director. Can we meet for lunch, say around 11:30? My treat, of course."

"Lunch?" Darlene sounded distrustful.

"I promise, Miss... I'll be alone and I'll have a small ummmm how can I put this? Payment... nothing to do with the reward amount I assure you. Just like a trust payment of sorts, to prove I can be trusted." Bob whispered those last words, his headache surprisingly gone.

"Fourteen women and ten men. All married except the single women, four to be exact," Mayor Nutter barked. "Now we got this kook Thortonson from Fox 29 pressing the public in my city for info on this copycat who, by the way, has his own body count of... of... what is it now, William?" he asked his assistant.

"Seven, sir."

"God damn, seven murders! That's thirty-one dead on the streets of my city, Commissioner!" the mayor said as he sat back in his big leather chair in his City Hall office.

"Look, Michael-" the police commissioner started.

"Mayor, goddamit!"

"Alright… Mayor, goddamit," the commissioner said, then laughed.

"Don't start with me, Uncle Frank. This is not time for the BS. The city is afraid. My own wife left for south Florida last night…" the mayor continued as Uncle Frank thought to himself, Lucky man! Abaddon wouldn't fuck that tooth pick anyway.

"…and I got a call from the governor this morning. He wants one of them caught now!" Mayor Nutter finished.

"All right, listen. First of all, there is nothing we can do about Fox. They have the freedom of press thing. Second of all, we're getting close. William, can you show Captain Jackson in, please?" the commissioner asked. "Listen Michael, Captain Jackson has his top detective on this. She's some kind of clairvoyant. She's the one who ran down the Strangler two years ago."

"Yeah… I remember that. Jaqui… Josephina… something like that, right?"

"Her name is Joanna Staley. She's my niece and you're right. She did run down the Strangler after she broke his routine. No one could figure out how he was selecting his victims until my niece became him in her mind," Captain Jackson said, entering the office.

"Captain Jackson, Mayor Nutter," William, the assistant, made the introductions.

"Sit, sit, captain," the mayor said. "That's right, he was some kind of stockbroker, right?"

"No, he was a city planner and she figured out he was selecting his victims from city files."

"So how is she doing with this?" William, the assistant, seemed to almost demand.

Captain Jackson gave him a look of disdain and never answered.

William took notice of the fact.

"Yes, tell me. Captain, is she closing in on him? Either one of them?" the mayor asked.

"We're making way. The guy is a ghost. No DNA in the NCIC system. No prints. We sent his voice to Washington and still no match. But Jo... I mean, Detective Staley and Detective Rawls seem to have made some kind of connection with him."

"What do you mean... connection?" William, the assistant, asked again, as if it was his right.

"Can he leave, Mayor? He's irritating the shit out of me," Captain Jackson growled.

"I'm the mayor's personal assistant. Show some respect," William smirked.

"William, shut up and get out, will you?" Mayor Nutter whispered.

"But Michael, you may-"

"Yeah, get the fuck out!" the commissioner said, then laughed.

"What a sissy! Anyway..." Captain Jackson continued, giving William no more attention, "we have a film of him throwing a Ms. Pamela Sample from a cliff into..."

The dark maroon Toyota Corolla pulled into the Adam's Mark Hotel only fifty feet from Bob Thortonson's Audi A6. David Thomas killed his engine and smiled.

"He's going into T.G.I.F.," he whispered, checking the mirror for blemishes in his makeup, then his very white teeth.

"I don't know about this, David. We can lose our internship for this if we get caught," Sharon explained with the heavy 34 quick-focus field camera in her lap. "Besides, I can't even work this thing. It's heavy."

Pushing the sun visor back over the steering wheel, David spun in his seat, looking a little irritated.

"See that trigger thing with the red marking? That operates the filming. The square piece is what you look through to see what you're filming." David reached for the round disk on the lens. "And see this? All you do is twist this left or right to focus. Now wait here while I go see our target. She has to be in there with Bob." His smile was defiant.

"I really don't think we should be doing this, David."

"Look, it's the nature of the job!" he snapped. "Either toughen up or choose another profession. It's journalism, girlie!"

"So she got mad at me and left. She had on a denim skirt, yellow tube top and those ugly Reeboks. I hated them sneakers. She got them from Benny for some head," Darlene whispered. She quickly downed the 22 ounces of Budweiser beer. "Can I?" she looked at the empty glass.

"Sure. It's all on me," Bob Thortonson said, flagging down the waitress to the table. "Two more Buds."

"So I stayed with Maniac and Fats, and they found her later on, dead in the park." Darlene stopped to pick up the burger.

"So why do you think it's this Kevin guy?"

"I told you," she said, then swallowed a large bite. "I found her sneaker in his van. The police said she was found naked, right? And besides, why would she leave only one of her sneakers? She only had one pair. Those ugly black and white things. I'm telling you..." Darlene paused again to shove the three-alarm fries into her mouth. "These guys are tricks and they probably did it together."

"Who is they? Wait... are you telling me there may be more than one?"

"Okay, wait. I forgot to tell you that part. This is how I found the sneaker. I get high, right? And crack is expensive, so a bitch do what she does."

71

"Like with Maniac and Fats, right?" Bob smirked.

"Of course, but this time I was with Flip, Jamal, and Kevin. Kevin was driving. So when I was getting my swerve on with them, they drove up Sixty-Ninth and Market so they could shop. They told me to stay in the car while I got high and my lighter ran out, so I needed to use the one Flip left in the thing up front-"

"The dashboard?"

"Yeah, I guess that's it. The dashboard. So I dropped it to the floor and there it was under the mat. Her ugly ass sneaker... and this pearl earring..."

"Wait, did you say pearl earring?" Bob flipped through his file. There it was. Karen Mets was found with only one pearl earring, dead in Creston Hall.

"Is that important? Can I get the reward?" Darlene asked, smiling, hearing his excitement.

Sliding the white envelope across the table, beside her plate, he tapped it. "This is two hundred and if the van is where you said and the address checks out, I'll get you your money. Will you show me the home and van?"

"Yup!" she smiled. "These are good." She shoved the last handful of fries into her mouth.

"The woman you are watching behind me is the witness to who Apollyon's identity really is. She called Fox 29's tip hotline this morning and personally gave me the identity of the freak copycat killer, Apollyon," David said as Sharon kept focus on the woman with Bob Thortonson. "We do know her name is Darlene, and that's it."

"David, they're getting into his car," Sharon whispered.

"Shit! Out!" David yelled, starting his car to follow.

"Oh, yeah, Daddy... fuck me... fuck me... shit yeah," she moaned out to push his orgasm along. "Aaaaagggghh!" she screamed as the cloth came up in his right hand and covered her mouth. She felt him cumming inside her as she blacked out.

"I'll see you again in the Fur Buer," he said, then laughed, holding the rag tightly to her mouth and nose.

Chapter Eight

THE VOYAGER MINIVAN pulled to the parking area just after eleven am. It was loaded with the last year's softball champions, the Cougars, a forty-and-older women's league team. Dorothy, the captain, who also ran the carpool and organized the fundraising, unlocked the hatch in the read so that the team could gather the equipment and coolers before the rest of the Lady Cougars arrived at the ball field.

"Carla, I made the finger sandwiches you love so much," Dorothy said, climbing from the driver's seat.

"Girl, please!" Carla said, and then laughed, sliding the side door open.

"We had the shits for days from that old ass meat you called yourself saving thirty-five cents a pound on. I'd rather eat grass," Mona Lou said and then smiled as she grabbed the bag of bits. Besides-" she froze as the bag hit the ground at the edge of the field. Her eyes remained locked on the naked figure lying in the middle of the basketball diamond.

"What you say, Miss Thang? Old ass-" Dorothy stopped speaking as her eyes found the still, naked body of what seemed to be a young black woman. "Oh, no! Somebody call 911!" she screamed as her medical experience kicked in. She darted to see if she could aid the poor girl. But her instincts told her that whoever she was, she was already dead.

Three more Lady Cougars stood beside Mona Lou as they watched Dorothy run to forty-five feet, only to stop and turn away in horror. It was only Dorothy's scream that brought the women out of their shock.

Mona Lou finally made the call.

"Hello," Joanna whimpered as her eyes found the Escape-Tron alarm clock.

It was her last day off and her body still felt the soreness. Deep inside her vagina, her stomach ached from his brutal assault. So bad she wanted to tell someone he had had her while she lay unconscious and defenseless. But Joanna couldn't bring herself to admit she was a victim. Especially his - Abaddon's.

"Good afternoon, sexy," he laughed. "Or should I say, 'lover'? So tight and so fresh... mmm."

"Bastard!" Joanna whimpered as she sat up. Her eyes found the bedroom door. She wondered if the phone had woken Ronnie or was she already up.

"Hush, you whore!" Mother's voice raged through the line. "My boy spared you again," she said. "Why he loves you, I don't know."

"Mother, don't!" Abaddon barked. His roar was so strong, Joanna jumped unintentionally. Her body cringed as the pain shot through her once again. She hadn't noticed the tears streaming down her soft, beautiful face as Mother cut back in.

"Boy!" she screamed. "Don't you ever speak to me in that manner of tone again! Do you hear, Mother?"

"Mother, I'm sorry... please..." Abaddon could be heard crying.

"Now, now Boy." Mother cooed like she was comforting a small child. "I forgive you, Boy. You're my Giant Baby Boy. Now tell me."

"I love you, Mother," Abaddon cried.

"Then why did you spare this whore? Tell her, Boy."

"I... I..." he struggled for words.

"Boy," Mother whispered.

"I love her, Mother. She's mine. I won't let you hurt her."

"And why is that, Boy? Tell her."

"She reminds me of..." Abaddon said, then paused. "She reminds me of you, Mother. Now please don't."

"See, bitch? There is a God," Mother squawked.

"Why me?" Joanna cried softly. "Why?"

"6224 Norwood Street. She's waiting," Mother said, then her laughter was cut short as they hung up the phone.

"Jo," Ronnie whispered over the buzz of the empty line.

"Ronnie, don't..." Joanna said and began to cry loudly.

Moments later, she sat in Ronnie's arms, letting it all go.

Through the window, Tommy watched.

"Is that Kevin right there??" Bob Thortonson asked.

"Nope!" Darlene frowned. "But that's the van. And look," she pointed toward the small two-bedroom house as the man climbed the steps onto the front porch. "That's where Kevin lives."

Bob Thortonson wrote the address down along with the license plate, make, and model of the van. He even wrote the color down.

We'll know by evening who owns the van and home, he thought.

"How about the reward?" Darlene said, then smiled.

"Yeah, I think you'll-" Bob paused as the front door opened and out walked two men. "Shit! Who's that?" he asked as they headed up the block toward them.

"Oh shit!" Darlene whimpered, now afraid. "Pull it out." She reached for Bob's zipper.

"Stop!" he complained, pushing her hands away.

"They carry guns… Shit, they see us!" Darlene quickly pulled Bob free and dropped her mouth into his lap.

"Oh God… ummm shit…" Bob murmured as she engulfed him completely.

"What the fuck is this nasty bitch doing?" Flip laughed as her head bobbed up and down slowly.

"Sucking a dick, nigga, what you think?" Kevin said and then smiled.

"Darlene…" Flip tapped twice on the passenger window. "Bitch, you hear me… Darlene." He tapped again.

Slowly she lifted her mouth away from Bob's penis and smiled out the window.

"Wait your turn, boy! Can't you see I'm busy?" She wiped her mouth on the back of her right hand while masturbating Bob with her left.

"Bitch, take that shit somewhere else," Flip said, then laughed, watching the older white man with a look of fear in his eyes, getting his dick jacked off, turn pale white.

"If you stop looking, it will be over by-" Darlene stopped talking as she felt the hot liquid sliding down her fingers and hand. "See!" she said and smiled.

"Damn cracker, you look like you ain't bust a nut in years," Kevin said and then laughed as he turned to leave. "Come on, nigga," he barked at Flip, who was now holding his own dick. "Fucking pervert!"

"Shoooo! That bitch got skills," Flip barked.

"What the fuck?" Sharon giggled as she filmed. The look on Mr. Thortonson's face told her all she needed to know.

"What's going on, Sharon? What's going on in his car? Is he in danger? Does he need help?" David asked in quick, steady motions as he combed his hair in the vanity mirror.

"Nope!" Sharon kept giggling as Bob Thortonson's face broke out in pure ecstasy. "He's cumming."

"What?" David stopped combing to spy out the Toyota's window a block away. It was impossible for him to see, but he still tried. "What are you saying?"

"She just gave the boss some head, David."

"Keep filming!" David whispered. "Get it all."

David had other thoughts now, thoughts of extortion and blackmail. Maybe a permanent job as an anchorman.

The living room was small, but neat and clean.

"She had very nice taste," Veronica Rawls said, checking out the glass figurines. The table had a hand carved mahogany base fashioned into a large hand to hold the glass top. The hardwood floors were buffed to a high gloss with a centerpiece throw rug under the coffee table. "That's Africa," she said and pointed to Joanna, who gave her a 'no shit' look.

Stepping into the dining room, Joanna lifted the dozen pink roses from the small wood dining room table. They laid beside the glass vase, which held only water.

"She never got the chance to arrange them," Joanna whispered, and felt a strange sense of regret for the woman upstairs. It'd been almost an hour and Timothy Rankins' team of forensics still kept her out.

"Jimmy Choo's," Detective Rawls said and smiled, holding up the four-inch heels. "Expensive taste." She sat on the royal blue leather sectional beside an end table that matched the center coffee table perfectly. "Oops!" she said and then smiled, lifting the glass dish lid. "We got marijuana." She pinched a bud and sniffed. "Damn! Best grade, too," she whispered, looking around. Joanna had left the room. Since no one was watching, she pinched five more nuggets from the dish and wrapped them into one of the latex gloves she carried. "For medical reasons," she smiled, then slid it into her carryall bag.

"That's bad for brain cells," the deep baritone voice said from the doorway, startling Veronica Rawls, who thought no one saw her. "Hi, I'm Detective Madison. Allen Madison." He held out his hand to shake. "Don't worry, I won't snitch you out." He smiled.

"Allen Madison?" Veronica searched her mind's record and knew that name from somewhere. "What district are you out of?" she asked.

"Sorry," he produced his wallet which held his badge and ID card, which read Colorado State Police. "Didn't your captain inform you I was here?"

"Allen Madison… No shit!" Veronica roared. "The same Allen Madison who took three bullets from that crazy assassin up in-"

"The one and only," he said and smiled, and Veronica Rawls knew then she was willing to share more than a smoke with this big, dark, hunk of a man.

Detective Allen B. Madison stood 6'3 and was well built, with perfect skin the color of burnt wood and a snow white smile that made her knees weak.

Veronica had never been attracted to a black man before now, but he was somewhat hypnotizing.

"Ummmm… shit! I'm no drug abuser. Fuck!" Veronica Rawls said, pulling the glove free from the pocket of the carryall. "It was for relaxation and… dammit!"

"Damn, woman! Relax, will you? I'm just a man who snuck up on you." Slowly, he reached and pushed the glove back into the pocket. "Shit, maybe we can share that?"

"Ronnie, who's this?" Joanna said as she re-entered the room.

"He's mine! I saw him first," Ronnie blushed.

"What?" Joanna giggled.

"I mean… I mean…"

"Stop," Allen laughed. "She's funny. Hello, I'm Detective Allen Madison of the Colorado State Police." He shook Joanna's hand. "I'm here to speak to both lead detectives at the request of my boss and your captain."

"About?" Joanna was suspicious.

"The Giant Slasher," he replied.

Both women knew he spoke of Abaddon. Their eyes met.

Last night, neither detective thought their second day off would be full of so much work and information. They sat at a table inside of the interview room looking at the photos from three different states. Thirty murder scenes in all. Mostly married couples, some single women, all of them African American descent. All except one which could have been mistaken as a black married couple. They were a South African couple who emigrated to Texas three years prior to the murders. Both died horribly.

"You're telling us he'll just stop and move on?" Joanna asked, looking at this African husband and wife. They were tied into the Union with duct tape, their throats slashed deeply.

"No, I'm saying when you get too close, he's gone. The bastard plagued Denver for two years. Only during the month of May..." Allen Madison was saying as the detectives studied the photos on the table.

"Mother's Day," Joanna whispered.

"What?" Detective Madison looked confused.

"It's his mother he's killing," Detective Rawls said. "The month of Mother's Day. The wigs, the lipstick, the earrings. We believe the song-" Allen stopped her.

"Song? What song?" Madison asked, flipping through his notes, searching for references to songs.

"The Isley Brothers. The Bose Airwave System CD players," Detective Rawls continued.

"Wait! Shit!" Allen said, reaching for his phone. "Where did you find this Bose system and song?"

"Beside every bed. Didn't y'all? If it's our boy, they have to be there."

Thirty minutes later, Detective Madison confirmed it.

It was listed, but no one thought it had anything to do with the murders or murderer. Texas and Florida also confirmed the systems were present at the scenes. Florida and Texas still had the plasters in evidence and reaffirmed that the CD was there inside, only one song recorded on repeat. An Isley Brothers tune.

"That's where we'll start," he said.

"Too late, detective. A truck was stolen from a warehouse in a New Mexico factory five years ago. Two thousand units of the Bose Airwave System were stolen," Joanna said. "And the CD is home burned. Basic disc found in every corner record shop in America. Same with the wigs, lipsticks, and earrings."

"Has he ever contacted anyone before?" Joanna asked and the nervousness was heard in her voice.

"Never, why?"

"The freak has an interest in our girl here," Captain Jackson barked from the door. "Dammit, Joanna! Why am I the last to hear that our suspect attacked another detective of mine?"

"Another?" Allen Madison asked, surprised. "You're saying the Giant Slasher has attacked two of our own and you were one of them and survived?"

"He didn't want me dead," Joanna said and felt her stomach tighten and became aware of the soreness inside. So bad she wanted to rush into her uncle's arms, to cry on his chest. To have him comfort her as that little girl he and Aunt Sheila held so many nights while she cried herself to sleep. She wanted to scream out that he had raped her. Had spilled his seed in her most precious gift, had her sprawled naked and delved thoroughly. "Excuse me," she almost cried. Both men noticed the change in atmosphere. She left the room.

"Is she alright?" Madison whispered. "As she seen anyone about the attacks?"

"He only beat her up a little," Veronica lied, protecting her friend. "But I saw a doctor about the blow to my head. Feel this," she said, diverting attention from her friend.

"Ouch!" Madison said, rubbing the large knot on the side of Veronica Rawl's head.

"Yeah, ouch!" she squealed, pulling her hand away.

"Sorry," he smiled. "Who saved y'all?"

"No one! He let us live," Veronica said. "I'll fill you in on everything at dinner tonight." She smiled. "Where are you staying?"

"The Quality Inn. Airport Row," he told her.

Stop being stupid, Sharon. He's just a man, she thought, sitting at her desk, watching the office door from across the room. David's a piece of shit. He has no right and it's blackmail, illegal, and that means jail time. Get up and open your mouth, stupid. Sharon continued to think, convincing herself she had to tell Bob Thortonson what David had planned. How he tricked her into participation.

Slowly she rose from the empty desk and crossed the room full of news collectors and sorters. Sharon froze at the door. A bead of nervous sweat rolled down the small of her back. "Mom always said the truth is the answer," she whispered as Bob Thortonson snatched the door open before she could knock.

"Sharon, right?" he said and smiled fatherly like.

"David's a snake!" she blurted out, more from fright than anything. "And he tricked me into it!"

"Wait... slow down, and come in. Tell me what David is up to," Bob said, unsure of what he was about to find out. "Come in, dear."

"Who's the Giant?" the trainer whispered as he watched the man place plate after plate on the olympic bar. "Wait, he can't be serious."

"Don't know him. But I assure you, he's serious. The fool started with four-thirty - fifteen reps, three sets, and has been climbing ever since. Won't take a spotter either," the other trainer said.

"Shit!" the trainer whistled as the Giant broke the five-twenty easily, with a slight growl.

"Grrrr!" the Giant roared, throwing the weight up.

"Damn! Who is this guy?"

"He signed up as Michael Angel," the desk clerk whispered. The Giant pushed out thirteen reps easily.

"Yeah, who is it?" Captain Jackson barked in his normal, irritated sounding voice. The door opened and the officer entered with a grave look upon his face. "Well?"

The patrolman looked toward the stranger first, then back at Detective Rawls before looking at the captain in the eyes.

"It's alright, officer," the captain said. He understood the officer's reluctance to speak in front of a stranger, especially after the mistake the desk sergeant made speaking about a case in front of the media last year. "This is Detective Madison. He's on loan from Denver."

"Sir, there's been another one..." he said as he looked at Madison once more. "Belmont Plateau Diamond Field."

"Hold up. Our boy has changed his-" Detective Madison started to say when Rawls shook his head no.

"Apollyon, the copycat," she said, gathering the photos.

"Apollo who?" Detective Madison frowned.

Entering the room, looking refreshed, Joanna interrupted. "His name is Apollyon. It's Greek for Abaddon. And the Bible describes him as the king of the abyss... a gate keeper of sorts."

"Just lock the damn room," Captain Jackson barked. "Better yet," he turned to the squad room. "This room is off limits to anyone that's not directly involved with the Abaddon and Apollyon cases. Understood? If you enter, you will be suspended without pay!" he yelled, then turned to the detectives. "Get going; I'll lock up."

"I'll be damned!" Madison whispered, closing the Bible.

"Tell us about it. Just when you think you have God figured out, He goes and drops some shit-balls in your Metzo soup," Veronica Rawls said, then laughed.

"I got to get me one of these," he whispered, looking down at the black, leather bound book. "Nephilim and abyss... Giants and kings of deep, dark holes... wow!"

I was raised as a Methodist and knew nothing of an Apollyon... or angels and human beings having children together," Veronica joked. "And when we say Giant," she turned and winked. "I mean, big as shit!" She held her hands almost a foot apart.

Joanna winced a little, and it didn't go unnoticed by Madison or Rawls as she turned into the park.

"Well, the copycat is average and the one we have to concentrate on now." She jerked her head toward the crowd up ahead. "The circus is here already."

They all noticed the news vans parked up and down the park's sidewalk. The crime scene had been secured and the lot had been closed off so that no one could park closer.

Flashing the lights in the grill of her Dodge Charger, the two police officers moved the wooden road barrier so they could drive the last hundred yards down the Plateau Road.

"Detective Rawls... Detective Staley... hey!" Gloria Velendez yelled from her news van as they climbed out of the car. "Come on, y'all... it's me!"

"Fan of yours?" Allen said, smiling and stretching his long legs.

"She helped us on this earlier," Veronica said.

"I got an idea," Joanna smiled. "Officer, let her in," she pointed to Gloria Velendez. "No cameras."

"Come in, David. Sit down," Bob Thortonson said, smiling. The two large station security guards stood on both sides of the door to his office.

"Bo-Mr. Thortonson, may I ask what this is about?" David frowned, eyeing the two guards.

"Sure, come in," he said, holding the door wide open. "This is about the Abaddon and Apollyon story and some unsuspected investigative reporting."

David looked back as four more security guards headed toward his desk.

"No way!" the personal trainer whispered in amazement. He just watched the Giant dumbbell press the one-fifties for six sets of fifteen.

"Steroids!" the other men whispered in jealousy.

"Hell no! Look at his skin. It's too perfect for 'roids. That's all natural," the trainer said, knowing the business. "I got to meet this guy."

Setting the weights to the floor, Michael sat up and downed a protein shake. His eyes were focused on the television across the room as Gloria Velendez interviewed Joanna Staley, but neither woman was his focus at the moment. It was the tall man standing beside Detective Staley. It was Allen Madison from the Colorado State Police that had his attention.

"Boy, he's here!" Mother whispered in his ear.

Michael looked around suspiciously. He noticed the two men watching him.

"Mother, they may hear us…" he turned away.

"You know they have to die," Mother whispered into his ears.

"Who?" Michael turned back to see if the men were still watching.

"Not them, Boy!" she hissed. "Now finish up playing with your toys…"

"They're not toys!" Michael said out loud as the trainer approached. Snatching the one-fifties from the floor, he laid back, bringing the weight to his chest.

"Uumph, uumph, uumph…"

The trainer watched in amazement.

Chapter Nine

MICHAEL SAT STARING at the television as Mother screamed in his ear.

The re-broadcast of Gloria's interview with the detective had angered Mother to the point of insidiousness.

"All of them, Boy!" Mother screamed. "Tonight!"

"No, Mother… we mustn't…" Michael paused to wipe away a tear. "She's mine. You promised."

"She's a no good bitch!" Mother screamed. "A no good, jealous, underhanded bitch! She wants to be me, Boy!"

"I won't," Michael whispered like a stubborn child.

"Then the white one…" Mother whispered. "You always wanted to know… now is the time, Boy. Let her feel your Glory empty into her stomach. Make Mother feel the pleasure once more. Don't you start that, Boy."

Michael smiled as he pulled himself from his gym shorts. "I can have her, Mother?" He began to stroke.

"Boy! Stop that!" Mother screamed. "My floors, Boy, stop it now!" she demanded as Michael exploded onto the hardwood floors of their home. "Stop this instant! Oh God… mmmm you… you, son of Satan…"

"Abaddon, Mother," he growled and came again.

Allen Madison stepped from the shower and grabbed the large terrycloth towel he traveled with. It was the same one he took to Texas and Florida. He loved that oversized towel. It was the only thing he had left from his marriage. Standing in the mirror he began to dry until the phone rang.

He quickly snatched up the phone. "Hello?" He knew it could only be two people. His boss from Denver or Ronnie, the beautiful white girl who showed interest in him. It was her he was preparing for now. But it was too early to be her calling for dinner.

"Sir," the desk clerk said. "You have a Ms-"

"Detective," he heard Veronica say in the background.

"Sorry… a Detective Rawls is here to see you," the desk clerk continued.

"Ummm… send her up please," Allen Madison said, cursing himself quietly for not showering faster. He studied himself in the mirror as he rushed to dry. He had to admit, other than the bullet wounds to his chest and shoulders, he was a poster child for fitness.

Knock, knock, knock!

"Shit," he mumbled, wrapping the towel around his waist. "Ummm, just a minute…" he froze, shocked as the door opened unexpectedly.

"Thanks," Detective Rawls smiled, handing the housekeeper a ten dollar bill. "My husband is crazy." She closed the door behind herself. "Wow," she blushed, sitting on the king sized bed.

Allen Madison didn't know how to respond, so he smiled as her eyes roamed his body. "What?" he asked, embarrassed.

"Oh, nothing," she smiled, but she never turned away.

"I'll dress in the bathroom," he said and laughed, lifting his clothes from the bed.

"Okay," Veronica said and smiled, standing from the bed following him into the bathroom.

"What are you doing?" Allen said and turned to stare into her eyes.

"I like to watch men dress," Veronica said, smiling and reaching for his towel. He didn't resist as the towel hit the floor. "Oh, damn!" she exclaimed loudly. Her eyes took in the total muscular figure that stood in front of her. Unconsciously, she wet her lips with her tongue.

"So... where do you suggest we eat?" Allen asked, pulling on his boxers slowly, letting her eyes linger down below.

"I have the perfect place. It's quiet and cozy. I'm sure you'll love the food, and dessert will be..." she pulled the waist band of his boxers to have another look. "Wow! That's nice."

Allen now had to blush as he felt his penis start to react to the gorgeous white woman's stare.

"Wow!" she moaned again.

"Shhh, Boy, here she comes. Put that away! Stop it!" Mother whispered as the front door opened.

"Wait... is this your home?" Allen asked as he and Veronica stepped through the front door.

"Not tonight," she replied, taking his hand. "Tonight it's yours."

Kicking her shoes off, Veronica led him on a tour of the home. The foyer where she bragged about the crystal figurines and dishes, the living room and dining room, then the kitchen where she had dinner prepared already. The roasted chicken sat in the oven with the macaroni and cheese. On top of the stove sat string beans and sweet potatoes.

Allen's eyes feasted like a king.

"Damn, woman!" he said.

"What, you thought a white woman couldn't cook?" Veronica asked, then smiled. "Let me show you the best room in the house." She took his hand once again.

"Kill him first, Boy!" Mother whispered.

"No! ...Shit!" Michael said as his eyes darted toward the window, then to the back bedroom closet. He chose the latter. "That's him, Mother!"

"This is my bedroom," Veronica smiled. Allen could see her pride in this room. "I had the middle room walls knocked out to enlarge the bathroom. This deep tub is an antique from the Victorian century. And my six-head shower." She pointed towards the toilet.

"Lift the seat," she said, then laughed, turning to leave. She went straight into her bedroom to change.

"Veronica."

"I'm here, Allen. Please call me Ronnie," she was saying as he entered the bedroom. "You sound like my father... Veronica..." she said, using her best fatherly voice.

Entering the bedroom, Allen's eyes found her standing in front of an armoire, stripped down to a pair of boy shorts.

"Excuse me," he quickly turned away. It was too late. He saw her smooth, toned beauty. The dark hair hanging down her back, the pinkish brown nipples and curvy waist.

"Allen!" she giggled. "Allen..." she said as she waltzed across the floor and took his hand. "Don't be ridiculous. I just studied your prick closely. You can at least admire my breasts." She placed his hand on her left breast. "See? I'm flesh and blood."

"She's a whore, Boy," Mother said into his ears. "Listen to the whore and that bastard."

Michael didn't answer. He still remembered Colorado Springs. Allen Madison came very close to catching him that night. "He called you, 'The Slasher,' Boy," Mother continued.

"Let's eat and talk," they heard the detective say.

"Stupid little bitch! Why would she tell?" he snapped outside the house on the small street. "We could've written our own ticket in this business if she would have kept her mouth shut."

David sat watching the home they followed Bob Thortonson to. "Fired, huh?" He pulled the slip of paper from his pocket. "Darlene Goodjones," he read aloud. "I'm going to sell the information I got to the highest bidder and then Bob can kiss my a-" he stopped talking and slid down into the seat of his Toyota.

The door opened and out came a young black man wearing a blue sweat shirt and jeans. Quickly, the man headed for a blue and beige conversion van parked across the street from the home.

"Okay, who are you?" David said and smiled, clicking off three quick photos before starting his own car to follow.

"Maybe CBS or ABC," he said out loud as the van pulled away. He followed.

"Oh, God, yes!" Veronica whispered, falling onto his chest. Both had sweat dripping onto her expensive silk sheets.

Quickly, Allen rolled her onto her back as he slid from her soft lips. He knew she had ridden him to orgasm twice, but now he wanted to cum again.

"Allen… wait… ohhhh God!" she screamed as he penetrated her moistness deeply once more. Her legs raised into a V instantly as he made her insides dance to his rhythmic pulse.

"Psssss," Veronica sucked in air as another orgasm slammed into her stomach.

"I'mmmmmm… cumming!" Allen growled as he exploded inside her pulsating walls.

"Stop it, Boy! Mmmm shit! Mother needs more," she moaned softly as Michael shot eight ropes of sperm onto the closet wall.

Quietly he opened the closet door and paused to hear them still making love in the master bedroom. He dressed and pulled the ski mask over his face. Unzipping the army duffle bag, he removed the crimson red lipstick. Stepping into the hallway, he froze to listen. They were still grunting like animals.

"Stop that, Boy!" Mother whispered as Michael pulled Glory free to masturbate again. Moments later, he exploded onto the hardwood floors. Then he wrote on the wall.

"Make me cummmm… Allennn!" Veronica squealed as Michael climbed out of the skylight in the highly fashionable bathroom.

He looked over the clock on the DVR under the flat screen. Tonight was great but he knew Tracy's husband would soon be getting off work and it wouldn't end well if Bill caught his baby brother in bed with his wife.

"Trace, it's 3:30…" he said and bent and kissed her bare bottom. She only moaned, fully asleep now after a night of pure lust. "I'm out, sexy."

"Lock the door," she moaned, rolling onto her side.

"I'm gonna wash up first," Butchie said, smiling. He wasn't under any delusion about love or lust, and this was nothing but lust. His brother's wife was a freak and he was always available.

Climbing from the king sized bed, Butchie walked out into the hallway. I gotta piss, he thought as the large hands wrapped around his neck. He heard the whisper in his left ear.

"I am Abaddon!"

The clock on the dashboard read 3:45 a.m. and the small seat was becoming uncomfortable as David watched the supermarket. He had followed the van here last night only to get stuck waiting for the black man who drove it.

This has gotta be him, David thought. Well, one of them. I wonder which, he stopped his thoughts and sat straight up as the passenger door swung open. A nightmare dove upon him without warning. "Wait… ugh… uggghhhh… arrrggh!" he screamed with each knife thrust.

He had one final thought as he died: I'm sorry!

Sliding from underneath her leg, Allen smiled as he eased off the bed. He had planned on cooking some omelettes and whatever else he could find for breakfast and serving them breakfast in bed. She was so beautiful, lying there asleep with her hair spread out in a halo on the pillow.

"Mmmmm," she moaned softly and rolled right back onto her stomach. He felt a familiar stir in his groin and was tempted to climb right back inside her softness, but three hours was much more than either of them needed. Even if his penis wanted more.

The clock read 6:30 a.m. and he wanted to eat, wash, and maybe make it back to his hotel to change. Allen stepped into the hallway as the sunlight played games with his eyes from the skylight in the bathroom.

The Crest toothpaste sat in the sink. As he pissed, he noticed the newly fallen dust on the high gloss floors. Instinct told him to look up, and now that his eyes had adjusted to the brightness of the morning sun, he saw that the glass had been shifted recently. Quickly, he shook and flushed. Without any thought, he used his finger to rub some toothpaste all through his mouth and rinsed. Looking in the vanity mirror, he smiled.

She could be Mrs. Madison, he thought as he turned and saw Veronica standing there, smiling.

"Come back to bed, sexy," Veronica cooed. Slowly, she walked naked to the toilet and sat to pee. Without a second's hesitation, she passed gas loudly. "Excuse me."

Yup! She could be Mrs. Madison, Allen thought again. He turned to leave and froze in the doorway.

"Where's your gun?" he whispered. The urgency in his voice had Veronica up and moving. He followed nervously.

Hello, Allen. Tonight Death was mine to control and I chose to grant you both life. You're a long way from Colorado Springs, boy. I've taken what was yours. I guess we're even now. Ha-ha-ha! She was sweet to the taste. I wonder, how she does it, sugar. But white will tell one day.

Hello, Veronica.

"He was in my house again?" Detective Rawls whispered, pissed. In her hand she still held her Glock .40; so did Allen.

"So!" Joanna Staley said as the Crime Scene tech fingerprinted both detectives to eliminate them from every other fingerprint they found. Her eyes were on Allen's.

"Helen was my sister…" he began and then hesitated to control his emotions. "She and her husband were victim's number five and six in the Springs."

"But how does he know you?" Joanna asked.

"I almost had him. Could have killed him, but he jumped in the river and we lost him." Allen looked at Ronnie. "I didn't have the shot. But I took it anyway."

Veronica held out her hand to him and he took it.

"It's time to come clean, Allen," Joanna said from the other side of the room. The look in her eyes told him she meant business. Besides, it was evident that The Slasher had something planned for the three of them, especially now.

"Can we do it elsewhere?" Allen said and looked around at the crowded house. The women knew his emotions were tied to the case because of Helen, his sister and now Detective Rawls.

Two hours later, they sat inside of the Old Country Buffet, eating breakfast and talking.

"She was my only family, besides my father... the captain," he began.

"Fraternal?" Joanna asked, indicating the police association.

"No, Army! Anyway, when my brother died, Father raised us on the bases. Some here in the States, some overseas. Helen and I were really close, but she was my sister. She fell in love with this Army brat like herself and married young. Father never approved. He wanted us to follow in his footsteps. I did just that for a while when I enlisted at seventeen, quickly gaining rank in the military police. But I wanted more than Uncle Sam wanted to give. So I decided to leave after eight long years and joined the Colorado State Police as a second class detective because of my MP background."

"You can do that?" Veronica asked with a mouthful of ham and grits.

"Of course," he smiled. "I married that year and she was killed in a car accident two years later. After that I buried myself in work. Case after case..." he paused a moment, as if he was thinking about his own past.

"I mean, I solved cold cases from murders to robberies and found I had a knack for the unsolvables," he continued. "That's when it happened. I got a call from the commissioner..." he went on with his story until he finished with the day he tracked The Slasher to a GNC of a mall in Pueblo.

Detective Madison paused as if he needed to recall the story. Slowly, he said to himself, "I wasn't sure, but I found a connection with the first killing of a single mother named Carla Jannins and my sister." He paused again. He seemed to be fighting his own emotional state for control.

Veronica reached across the table to take his hand. "It's okay, Allen... we get it."

"No, I need to hear this, Ronnie. Please continue, Allen," Joanna stated flatly. It wasn't that she had no feelings, she actually felt his pain the most because of her gift. No, that wasn't it at all. She needed to use it to dig deeper into the mindset of Abaddon. "Please... while you're..."

"Sorry, Allen, it's her... thing." Ronnie used her hands to indicate some kind of spooky mystical happening in the air, like most people do when describing Joanna's gift.

"It's alright; I actually need to talk about it," Allen sighed and continued.

"Anyway, there I was. In Pueblo, a connection, the GNC! It seems that both shopped there for supplements and vitamins. It was a stretch, but I followed up on it anyway."

"How?" Joanna asked.

"Receipts. Anyway, before I even got to the store, I spotted this huge monster of a man standing with his back turned to me. Call it a hunch or intuition, but I just felt... something. Here I was, ready to follow this hulk of a man because of a feeling I had. This may sound funny, but at that moment I thought Helen was speaking to me from somewhere..."

Both women saw the tears in his eyes as he paused as he spoke of Helen.

"All I could do was follow. That's when I realized I had to get a look at his face. I watched him climb into a small blue Topaz... Mercury... I couldn't help but think how strange. This Giant man, climbing into such a small car. At that moment I should've pounced on him, guns blazing. But I didn't have enough. I still needed to see him. I tried, but fate kept me at bay. Traffic lights, pedestrians, once a child darted across the two-lane highway as I got close. Then it dawned on me. The plates. I could call them in. So I radioed in the plates. That would come back to victim number seven, Shana Thompson. We found her because of that call. But I still hadn't seen his face. I hit my lights and siren by then, and he bolted. Straight into a summer school zone during dismissal, kids everywhere. I had to break off pursuit. Departmental rules."

"It's law now!" Veronica whispered.

"Law or not, it caused The Slasher's escape! We found Shana Thompson's body along with her boyfriend that same day. I went back to the GNC and the clerk knew just who he was. She referred to him as the preachy boss with muscles. Her description was vague. Tall, very muscular with long dreads. No facial hair, but polite. No book photos or prints."

"But how-" Joanna began to ask.

"Wait," Allen held up his hand. "I receive a call from some old lady claiming to be The Slasher's mother." He paused to let the words sink in. "She directed me to 137432 Travant Plaza, a stucco home. By now, The Slasher was up to thirty six victims on his 28th day straight. I was desperate and needed to find my sister's murderer, so I went alone to the address with the intention of just watching, until he reappeared. That's when it happened."

Allen closed his eyes as if he could see it all happening again. "While I was watching, I heard a loud crash on the roof of my car and it shook violently. I jumped from the car with my gun drawn. There she was... eyes staring blankly. Her neck had been broken and she was naked..." A tear escaped down the dark skin of Allen's cheek. He sat silently for a moment, staring down at his empty plate.

"Allen..." Veronica whispered.

"Let him finish, Ronnie." Joanna knew he needed this. To purge his system of this nightmare. "Go on, Detective."

"She was raped after she had been killed," Allen continued.

"Who?" Ronnie asked.

"The clerk!" Joanna said.

"Yes," Allen confirmed. "The sales clerk from the GNC. It seems he thought she could possibly ID him. But she couldn't... she was just..." His thoughts roamed again for a second. "Then I saw him. He stood no more than fifty yards away on what we call the salt flats. He had planned this and wore a ski mask, but I swear the son of a bitch was smiling. I felt it and my heart leapt out of my fucking chest. He roared my goddamn name, like we were old high school buddies. I froze when I heard it. 'Big Al', he roared down at me. He taunted me with my sister's death... how... how she... screamed for me too... oh God..." He placed his head in his hands and wept softly.

Simultaneously, all three cell phones rang as the two women sat, quietly watching Allen Madison grieve. Both Joanna and Veronica answered their phones.

"Yeah," Joanna whispered. She had an edge to her voice from transforming in her mind to see the eyes of the Giant Abaddon. She instantly saw the alertness on Ronnie's face as they both received the same news.

The car was silent as they pulled into the parking lot of the Pathmark on City Line Avenue. The ride was strange because neither woman wanted to interrupt Allen's thoughts, but now they had to focus on the homicide at hand. It was confirmed that the victim was an ex-intern of the Fox News station and somehow connected to the Abaddon and Apollyon case.

"Allen, are you-" Veronica Rawls whispered as he stepped from the car.

"Sure," he said and then winked with a half-smile.

"Look who's here," Joanna said, heading for Gloria Velendez.

"Program Director Bob Thortonson speaking."

"I am Abaddon," the wicked voice growled through the line.

"Ummm... wait! Call this number. It's safe, 215-555-1122." Bob hung up immediately. Seconds later, his cell phone rang.

"Yes, Abaddon?" he half stated, half questioned.

"This is Mother, you bastard!" she laughed, and it chilled Bob's blood. "Do you know?"

"Yes, Mother. I do," Bob Thortonson smirked and read the address off with guilt in his heart.

"Good, because today is Mother's Day and Mother wants a special treat! We'll call you back…" Mother paused and Bob heard what seemed to be a conflict in the background.

"She's on Coulture Street. Third house from the corner of Pulaski Avenue… she was…" Abaddon hoarsely whispered as Mother cut in.

"Stop that, Boy!"

"What side of the-" Bob Thortonson tried to ask as the phone went dead.

Sitting there, he contemplated whether to call the police or get footage first. Using the office phone, he dialed Gloria Velendez.

"Yeah, Bob, it's him!" she instantly answered, recognizing the number. Since she was in the van talking to Joanna, she used her speaker phone. "I ID'd the kid."

"Fuck him! He was a snake."

"Wait, Bob-" she tried to grab the phone but Bob kept talking, and Joanna's hand pushed her away.

"Listen, Glo," Bob used her nickname. "He just called and there's another one on Coulture Street. Third one from the corner. Get over there while I call the police."

"We're here with Glo… Bob," Joanna smirked.

Chapter Ten

WILLIAM JONES COULDN'T help but smile as he exited the 23 bus on the corner of Germantown and Coulture Street. Usually, he would have been home by now, but when the foreman asked for volunteers to do overtime cleaning of the subway tracks, he quickly jumped at the chance to make time-and-a-half for five more hours. All he knew was that Tracy wanted wall-to-wall carpeting and her Billy Boy was gonna get it for her. Stopping at the corner store for his early morning bag of weed, a pack of smokes and a 24-ounce of Olde English, Billy headed home.

"They both locked," Joanna said as she approached her partner, who just tried the door on the northwest side of Coulture Street. Just as they both looked up at Allen Madison, he pushed open the heavy steel security door of the third house on the west side. All three locked eyes as if they were sure of what was inside.

"Can I help you?" the heavyset man asked.

Instantly, Joanna and Veronica crossed the street holding their badges, to assist Allen.

"I'm Detective Staley and this is Detective Rawls," Joanna said as they approached, causing the heavyset man to quickly turn from Detective Allen Madison who still stood at the top of the home's steps.

"Like I said," he said as he studied their badges. "Can I help y'all? And why is he peeking into my doors? I own this property and I worked my ass off for this home!"

"And you are, sir?" Detective Rawls asked.

"My name is William Jones, but why-"

"Is there a Mrs. Jones, sir?" Rawls asked.

"Yeah! Why?" he asked, now more concerned.

"Do you know if she's home, Mr. Jones?" Joanna asked.

"Of course, she is… wait! Why y'all keep looking at him? Is Tracy…"

At that moment, he realized that something was very wrong. Dropping the bag that contained his purchase from the Ritz corner store, he yelled for his wife. "Tracy!" Without another word, he broke out running, taking the cement steps two at a time. "Tracy! Tracy!"

It took everything Allen Madison had to hold off as their bodies hit the sun porch floor. Seconds later, both Joanna and Veronica held him to the floor along with Allen's help.

"Mr. Jones… please, sir… please," Allen said as the Bose system instantly came to life upstairs.

All three detectives rolled away from Mr. Jones as they reached for their weapons. Before they could warn him, William Jones leapt to his feet and rushed to his wife's side.

"Tracy!" he screamed, taking the stairs two at a time.

"Shit!" Joanna barked in hot pursuit, with weapons drawn.

"Please, Mr.-" she tried to warn him, but it was too late. The scream that filled the home would forever chill Joanna's soul and would always haunt Veronica's nights. That scream now placed them inside of Allen's nightmares forever.

"Poor bastard," Allen whispered as the ambulance slowly drove away.

"He'll never be right again…" Joanna turned away to conceal her own pain. "Shit!" she mumbled as the gray Lincoln town car pulled up.

"Who's that?" Allen whispered to Veronica when he noticed the drastic change in all of the other officers present.

"The fuckin' mayor… damn!" Veronica replied as the second man stepped out of the Lincoln. "And the commissioner."

"You! Come here!" the mayor's assistant yelled, pointing a finger toward Allen. "Did you hear me? Come here!"

Smiling, Allen pointed his finger at his own barrel sized chest. "Who… me?"

"That's right, you," the assistant barked again. "The commissioner needs your assistance."

"So?" Allen walked away, shaking his head.

"What's that officer's name? How dare he-" William, the assistant began as he turned to the mayor.

"William, shut the fuck up! You're a damn drama queen," the mayor whispered so no one but William heard him. "Wait in the car, will you?"

The commissioner heard it though, and winked at the assistant, which infuriated him.

"Fuck you, Frank!" he mumbled.

"No thanks! I only do women… fag!" the commissioner shot back, then flagged the two lead detectives over.

"Sir, this is Detective Joanna Staley and Detective Veronica Rawls. They're both the leads on this holy mess."

Both detectives were surprised that the commissioner even knew their names, much less that he would introduce them to the mayor.

"Detectives," the mayor said, smiling. "Give me some good news… please. Look, I won't bullshit you, because I'm a straight shooter. Ladies, we have the world's attention now.

The feds just informed me that they're sending a task force of profilers along with the FBI agents to take over this case."

"But-" Joanna started to interrupt as the captain stepped beside them.

"Joanna," he whispered sternly.

The mayor smiled. He could appreciate her unwillingness to move over for the big fish.

"No, let her speak her mind. Detective?" he said, and smiled.

"They'll just get in the way, Sir," she complained. She went on to explain the connection they shared to the perps. She explained the news station's connection and how they've spun a closely watched trap and needed just a few more days to snare at least Abaddon if not Apollyon also.

"Well," the mayor said, then laughed at her excitement. "We'll just keep that information to ourselves... right?" He looked toward the commissioner and captain. "But we must hand over that other info pertaining to the case to the profilers of the FBI... understood, detectives?"

"Yes, sir," Detective Rawls smiled.

"Turn over on your stomach, sexy," he whispered into her mouth. "Let me have you from behind." He lifted himself from her body.

"Can I take a hit first?" she cooed. "Then you can make me scream your name from behind. I like to cum while I'm high," she lied. There is no way he could create an orgasm inside of me with that! She thought to herself as he handed her another dime rock. "Put it in while I hit this."

Carmen Beckson rolled to her knees and lit the pipe. She deeply inhaled as she felt him slide inside of her unshaven lips. To her surprise, the mixture of crack and penetration caused her to climax. She quickly exhaled the gray cloud and moaned it out. "What's your name? I'm cumming..."

Her heart froze as he whispered, "Apollyon!"

Swiftly, the rag covered her mouth as she struggled to free herself. Her last thought as her body shook once more was, I'm cumming!

"Get the damn panties, nigga!" he said and smiled as he loaded the trash bag full of her clothes. Lifting the pink, soiled panties, Kenneth rubbed his erection as he sniffed the soiled crotch.

Climbing from the van, he headed into the house as the dark greenish bag slung over his shoulder.

"Kevin... yo, Kevin!" he yelled, expecting to hear his baby brother answer from his bedroom as usual. Quickly, he headed down to the basement. Using the key from around his neck, he unlocked the large cabinet that sat to the far end of the basement.

As he pulled the two doors wide, he smiled at the six stackable plastic luxury bins, each with a colorful top to indicate the contents. Deliberately, he dumped the contents of the container with the red rope onto the cement floor. He knew he needn't worry about Kevin catching him because of the phobia that stuck him early in life.

The basement meant death to his younger sibling. It's where death took their parents years ago. It's the same place there Joseph, their father, made them watch as the neighborhood kingpin fucked Karen, their mother, before the shotgun blasts took both their lives as final revenge.

It's the same basement that Joseph tied the rope around the rafters and his own neck while they begged him not to, and Kevin tried to hold his father up as his feet hung, kicking wildly. No, he needn't worry about Kevin coming downstairs.

Slowly, Kenneth undressed and lay on top of the contents of all the bins to masturbate once again. The bras with their fasteners stabbing into his skin. The panties with the different scents of pussy juices around his head and face. Even the shoes played into his sexual fantasy.

"I am Apollyon… uuumph… I… uuumph… Am…
Sssss… yess, yess, yess, I'mmmm Apollyonnnnnn!" he
moaned as he had the largest explosion of the day.

He smiled to himself as he spotted the plate of rocks on
the kitchen table.

"Sorry, Kev," he whispered, stealing six crack rocks from
the plate and a few plastic bags to place them in for his next
adventure. "Yo, Kev! Dammit, nigga. What I told your dumb
ass about leaving this shit everywhere?" He smiled, knowing
he was putting on a show to mask the fact that he stole what
he needed already.

"Yo, Kev!" Kenneth barked as he approached the stairs.
Looking up, he noticed the bedroom door to the back was still
closed. Which meant Kevin was either still asleep or he was
out tricking again. He put his money on tricking.

"Man!" he yelled, climbing the stairs just as the music
came booming to life from his brother's room. He paused as
he heard the golden oldie roar to life. "This nigga," he shook
his head and went to his own bedroom humming the Isley
Brother's tune as Ronald Isley sang: "Somebody said… I was
living in the life…"

Kenneth slowly closed the door, smiling as he thought,
Fuck that bitch, Kev.

"Kill it, you son of Satan!" Mother giggled as he slid into
the dead woman's body for the third time since they made the
Union.

"Uummph! Uummph! Uummph! Uummph!" he grunted for
the next twenty minutes until his mother screamed loudly,
"I'mmmmmm cummmmmmmmin, Boooooyyyyy!"

"This nigga in there fucking old lady Betty," Kenneth
laughed as he peed, listening to his brother grunt over the
same song for the last ten minutes.

Kenneth knew about those late nights. His brother would sneak Betty's old ass up into his room to fuck. So many nights, he himself tricked with the 58-year-old woman.

The only reason she never made it to forever was her age and the fact that she was too damn skinny.

"Tear that pussy up, nigga!" Kenneth yelled as the song started up again from the beginning.

Kenneth shook off and flushed the toilet. For a moment, he thought about going down to his collection and imagining Big Monk fucking his mom again while he masturbated, but he shook the thought from his head as he listened to Betty whispering behind his brother's door about killing it. He had to smile.

Kenneth froze as he heard someone crying. He knew it wasn't Kevin because the voice was too harsh. Slowly he walked to the bedroom door and listened.

"Kev... Yo, Kev, you alright, man?" he asked as the door suddenly flew open and there stood a Giant. He couldn't believe his ears when the Giant said:

"I AM ABADDON!"

"Wait!" he cried out as the large hands encircled his neck. So badly, he wanted to explain how he idolized him. So badly he needed to let him know he did it all for them. So badly... so bad... so...

"Wait... I... am... just... like..." he tried to say as the darkness took him forever.

Chapter Eleven

"BOB THORTONSON'S OFFICE," Bob said, irritated at the news of the Feds moving in. He received the news from the executive upstairs that he must cooperate fully with them upon their arrival, tomorrow afternoon.

"This is Mother," she giggled into his ear.

"Mother," Bob Thortonson repeated, looking around as if he were being watched.

With a yell, Mother cackled. Bob could tell she loved the effect that she had on him. He had to admit he was afraid of them. So was the whole city, for that matter.

"I already told you, Bob, you'd be the first to know," Mother said and continued to cackle. "You'll tell the authorities for my boy. He's tired."

"But…"

"The proof of who he is, is in the home. The basement. He was filthy," Mother growled and her voice merged with Abaddon's for a split second. "And I left the Union to prove it was I…" the voice suddenly changed for a moment. "Abaddon."

The line went dead in Bob Thortonson's hand. Nervously, he dialed Detective Joanna Staley. Then he had the network break into the morning program for a special report on the death of Apollyon.

"What the hell is going on?" Veronica whispered while pointing out of the window of the Jones's house. Allen and the other two plainclothes officers all watched as the news reporters ran to their vans. Equipment and cameramen loaded their things in a hurry, some even running as if there was some kind of danger of missing the scoop.

"Son of a bitch!" Veronica said. "Where is Gloria?" she asked as she scanned the street for the Fox 29 van.

Stepping outside, followed by Allen, Veronica quickly stopped the fast moving Daily News writer. "What's up, Macky?" she asked.

"Mmmm hmmm, now the shoe has changed feet," Macky said and smirked. Veronica knew he was referring to all the times they had refused to relay information to the press.

Slamming his car door, he started his engine only to pause long enough to lean out of the driver's side window and say, "They say Abaddon just did half of your job for you."

"What?" Detective Veronica Rawls growled.

Sucking his teeth, the reporter responded like the detective was a child. "Abaddon just killed Apollyon in his house. It's all over Fox News."

Quickly, Detective Rawls re-entered the home. "TV," she barked at the officer standing in the living room. She pointed to the wall.

"This is the living room of the alleged Apollyon. As you can see, on the table there is a plate with what appears to be crack cocaine, bags, and a scale. Up these stairs, it is said, lays the body of the rapist and murderer Apollyon, who had been plaguing our city parks for the past few weeks. He is the copycat killer, who idolized the terror, Abaddon.

But it seems that he, Abaddon, didn't appreciate the attention from him," Gloria Velendez continued to speak as she quickly moved through the home.

"Down these stairs is the so-called evidence to prove the identity of Apollyon. How do we know these facts, you ask? We were contacted by the Giant, Abaddon, via telephone only minutes ago, revealing the location of the bodies. We will not go upstairs where the bodies are located because that's the main crime scene, but I will take a moment," she continued as the camera followed her down the stairs into the basement, "to show you the basement where Abaddon said there was evidence of Apollyon's guilt."

The cameras followed her down the stairs.

In the moment before Gloria Velendez screamed, the microphone caught the sound of her feet running. The cameraman Jimmy had mistakenly let the camera capture the scene briefly on the live feed.

On top of a pile of clothing was the body of a black man whose eyes were open. His neck laid at an odd angle, which seemed to be stretched much too long to be human. As the camera bounced, the red lipstick could be seen on the wall in written script, but was unreadable because Jimmy was hot on the heels of Gloria Velendez. Both were terrified.

The Charger pulled onto Peach Street. The small urban neighborhood was located in the lower-class section of Philadelphia where the drug infestation was rampant. The homes were so bunched together that it was almost impossible to breathe or stretch.

Detective Allen Madison just watched in amazement. He never saw such poverty where he came from. Not that there weren't ghettos where he lived, but they didn't seem so depressing, so helpless, so filthy and neglected.

"What?" Joanna asked, seeing the look of despair on his face. "Wait until you see South Philly."

"No shit!" Veronica whispered as they climbed out of the Charger.

"Officer," Joanna barked. "See that reporter?" She pointed as they passed Gloria Velendez and her Fox News van. "Place her under arrest and transport her from the scene to the round house."

"What's the charge?" he asked as he pulled out his cuffs.

"Accessory to murder after the fact," Joanna barked loudly enough for the other reporters to hear. "Also interfering with an official crime scene, disturbing evidence, and aiding and abetting a suspect. Book her under my name and badge."

"If you say so," the officer said and grabbed Gloria by the arm. "Turn around," he demanded.

"You can't do this… Joanna… wait," Gloria demanded as she was placed into cuffs. "Jimmy, you're getting this? Get his badge number and car."

"What is she being arrested for?" A reporter from CBS yelled from the crowd.

"You heard the detective like I did, lady," said the officer. "I'm following orders."

"Hey, detectives, can we get a statement?" another reporter yelled as Joanna and the other two detectives climbed the cement stairs.

Veronica Rawls turned toward the crowd of reporters, but pointed to three uniformed officers. "I want all reporters moved to the end of the block. I don't want anyone within five houses of this crime scene. If they live in any of these houses it's either on their porches or inside. If they resist, book them. Same charges!"

The groans came from reporters and neighbors alike, but no one resisted. Some even found neighbors to rent them space in or on their property.

Entering the small house, all three detectives froze. There were way too many people on the scene.

Joanna approached three officers with her badge raised. "Everybody get the fuck out! And put those phones away.

Ronnie, take their badge numbers." She pointed to the three officers with phones out.

No one moved for a second, until more detectives raised their badges. One yelled out so loudly that an officer from outside came to look inside. "What the fuck did the detective just say? Get the fuck out and secure the perimeter. Front and rear! You… with the smart phone. What's your name?" the big, burly white guy roared. All the others rushed to leave the scene, not wanting their names in a report of misconduct somewhere, especially not on a case of this magnitude.

"Thanks, Mike," Joanna said, then winked at him.

"Anything for you, beautiful," he smiled.

"She's kind of old, ain't she?" Detective Allen Madison said as Veronica made note of all of the items in the room.

"This wasn't a planned victim," Joanna said, pulling open the mouth of the dead woman. "She was just in the wrong dealer's bed."

"So why kill Apollyon and his family? It was - I mean, he took some of the heat off," Detective Mike Boosey asked from the door. He watched the three detectives going through the procedures of canvasing the grid.

"Are you kidding me? Apollyon presented a direct challenge of power and respect that The Slasher… I mean, Abaddon, thought was God-given," Allen said over his shoulder.

Looking up, Joanna nodded her head. "He's right. Abaddon sees himself as one of God's greatest creations. He named himself King of the Abyss. There was no way he could let Apollyon live while he lives."

"Well, he had great taste in music," Officer Mike said.

"Who?" Joanna asked, turning to Mike.

"The kid," he pointed at the dead brother. "Did you see his collection of blues? Muddy Waters, B.B. King, Albert King… Shit, this kid was way too young to understand Big Momma Thornton."

"The blues," Detective Rawls said, then smiled. "Not no more!"

Just as she finished laughing, the phone on the night stand rang. All four detectives stared at the phone as if it was a foreign object.

"Shit, y'all!" Veronica smirked. "Really?" she whispered, picking up the line on the third ring. "Hello?" she answered. She alerted Joanna with her eyes.

Joanna dashed over to the next bedroom's phone.

"Is this the whore?" Mother cackled into her ear. "Yes, yes, girly. I recognize the squeaky innocent voice." Mother laughed and then said, "Was he good inside you, whore?"

"Mother? You jealous bitch!" Veronica came back, ready to match her nemesis word for word. "What is it, Mother? Is it that you really want him inside you? Are you really some kind of-"

"Don't detective!" Abaddon's voice rang out, replacing Mothers. "She'll-"

"Quiet, Boy!" Mother roared, shouting down Abaddon. "So, little whore," Mother said, then giggled. "You want to push my buttons, huh? Well, I'll push yours first."

"I don't have any buttons, bitch! Unless you take your own life and deprive me of the satisfaction of putting two high points in your dyke ass!"

"Oh no?" Mother cackled, and her voice changed once more to Abaddon's.

"What about him?" Abaddon growled. "The tall dark man standing to your right?"

Detective Rawls turned to look at Allen Madison and realized they were being watched. Her eyes instantly went to the bedroom window and locked with Abaddon's.

"He's on 52nd Street," she yelled, dropping the phone. "The house directly behind this one."

Rushing toward the window, Allen spotted Abaddon's back as he left the room's window across the alleyway.

"He's on the move!" Allen yelled as all the detectives in the house made their way to the home on 52nd Street. The first officer to run out the back door to cover the rear fell over two dead cops laying in the alleyway.

"Clear!" Mike Boosey yelled from the kitchen door.

"Clear!" Allen yelled from upstairs in the back bedroom. Just then, he heard a scraping sound coming from the bathroom. "The roof!" he shouted, rushing in.

Jumping onto the sink, Allen reached for the skylight glass. It slid with ease out of the way. Joanna and Veronica both entered the bathroom as Allen's feet disappeared through the skylight.

"Allen… no!" Joanna screamed, climbing onto the sink top. With little effort, she jumped to grip the edge of the skylight. This time, her hands held true. Effortlessly, she pulled her weight through the roof.

Crouching with her firearm ready, Joanna scanned the rooftops. She spotted the Giant leaping from the roof ten houses away, but there was no sign of Allen Madison.

Quickly, Joanna ran toward the Giant only to realize that each house was separated by a three foot drop to the next rooftop, to compensate for the steep angle of the hill. On the third drop-off, there he was, still and lifeless. His gun lay only ten feet to his right, unfired. Slowly, she sat by his head and cried with her head on her knees.

"Joanna! Allen!" she heard Veronica call from further down the block, then again from up the block. "Allen! Joanna!"

Ten minutes later, Joanna heard the voices of the other detectives coming from the rooftops to her left. They finally came for them.

Every night from then on passed with another murder, and another taunt from Mother.

Chapter Twelve

THE CITY OF BROTHERLY Love is the fourth largest city in America and not one television was turned to any other program. Tonight the interview of Abaddon and someone named Mother was being aired at 8:00 p.m. eastern time. Bars were crowded, and department stores had people standing in the audio and visual sections turning televisions to Fox 29 News stations throughout the city. Even police and other city officials found somewhere to watch. Criminals, drug dealers, and other undesirables stopped movement to also watch. It seemed the city froze for Abaddon.

Most other television stations had to make a deal to have a live feed of the interview from Fox 29, who quickly agreed as long as the station flew the Fox 29 station logo on the screen.

Joanna laid in Veronica's arms as the program started.

Gloria Velendez began:

"Tonight, America, I was awakened by my boss, Bob Thortonson. He ordered me to collect my cameraman, Jimmy, and to come to his home in Bryn Mawr, a suburb of Philadelphia. I was given no explanation. Just an order."

Gloria paused as the hideous laughter could be heard in the background.

"America, this may very well be…" she began and then paused as a tear rolled down her face. Quickly, she used the back of her hand to wipe away the tears. "If I die tonight… Mommy, I love you. Daddy…" she sniffed loudly. "Daddy, thank you for being my Daddy Bear. I love you so much."

"Stop it, Bitch!" the voice of an old lady was heard from the background.

Gloria's eyes shot to the right side of the camera. Everyone watching knew he was there.

"Mother, she's frightened," Abaddon's round voice whispered from the same area, and America sat up, collectively afraid.

"Ummmm…" Gloria said and then wiped her eyes quickly, trying to pull herself together, to be the great journalist she dreamt she would be. This was the story of a lifetime and she was determined not to blow this shot at greatness. She knew this night everyone would remember her and Abaddon.

"Tonight I am going to interview Abaddon and Mother in the bedroom of Bob and Marge Thortonson, who sit in what the Giant Abaddon has informed me is the Union," she said, pushing herself to stay in the moment.

"Show the world, Boy!" Mother cut in and Jimmy slowly turned the camera toward the bed where Bob and his wife laid taped together in the Union, naked. Since this was recorded last night, the station blurred out the focus enough so that their nudity was not displayed.

The camera slowly eased back to capture Gloria Velendez. "As the world knows, Abaddon has killed over 48 people. Brutally raping most of the women as they laid dying underneath him," she reported. "The men, mostly husbands, suffered quicker but much more violent deaths. Ladies and gentlemen, it gives me no pleasure to introduce to you… Abaddon…"

"And Mother, bitch! Say it!" Mother screamed as she rushed to stand over a cowering Gloria Velendez, completely naked except for the ski mask.

Gloria quickly covered her face and head with her arms as Jimmy screamed, "Please don't, Mother!"

"See, Jimmy knows," Mother cackled.

Softly, Abaddon's hand reached out to stroke Gloria's rich, dark hair. "You're safe," Abaddon reassured her. "Don't worry, Mother never breaks her promises."

America watched as both voices came from the strange, naked Giant's mouth under the mask.

"I'm so scared, Daddy," Gloria let escape from her mouth, cringing as Abaddon sat beside her. "Please... Aba..." she began. Not being able to form a coherent word, she began to pray in a loud voice.

"I won't let her..." Abaddon said as Mother took over again.

"Let me? Hah! Boy, I let you, not the other way around."

And that is when the Giant's eyes went to the camera.

He spoke to America. "I am Abaddon! The King of the Abyss. My reign is a thousand years. I will soon cleanse the city of all transgressors who escaped from the Abyss. For I am!"

"How?" Gloria whispered trying hard to pull herself together, considering it her professional duty. She kept on being drawn to his lap where his hand constantly rubbed. "How can you do this when you're the most feared killer this city has ever seen?"

"No, he's not," Mother said and then began to laugh. "He's a pussy lover! I killed every bitch he's ever entered."

"But I..." Gloria began and caught herself, not wanting to reveal too much. But not in time to fool Mother.

"What? You think we're crazy? I am Mother and I refuse to let my boy fuck nobody but me. This is a gift and it's called Glory." That's when Mother lifted the penis that was blocked out by the station's edit.

"Mother is very jealous and she loves me," Abaddon let out a strangled whisper.

"That's right, Boy! You tell her. That's my boy."

"Mother will soon sleep for eleven months…" Abaddon began, but Mother cut him off.

"Quiet, Boy!" she yelled.

"But not before…" he continued.

"Don't tell them, Boy!"

The Giant stood to masturbate. The station blocked out the lower half of the screen, but the sperm could still be seen landing on Gloria's face; shock and disgust displayed on her features.

America was shocked. The world had never seen reality TV like this.

"Tonight, I must have her once more!" Abaddon growled, sounding like a wounded animal. "I am Abaddon!"

The screen went black and then Gloria Velendez came back on live. She spoke with concern in her trembling voice. "To my women… no wait… to the black women of Philadelphia between the ages of 25 and 40, between the weight of 145 to 160, give or take ten pounds…" she paused as the camera zoomed in for a close up. "He's still out there, if only for one more night. Be afraid of this very insane, cruel man. If you can leave, leave this city. If not, group together and arm yourselves. Do not stay alone, even with a husband. You are all targets. So be safe out there. This is Gloria Velendez for Fox 29 News."

"See, Boy!" Mother whispered. "Why did you chance telling her?"

The woman watched the Giant stand from the love seat in the corner of her bedroom.

The tears rolled down her face as the voices merged into one.

"It made no difference, Mother. Tonight will be special for you. Then you'll rest," Abaddon said, then smiled down at the dark skinned woman in with the red wig and lipstick, "Tonight, Mother, you will not sleep until I've finished completely."

"Yes, Boy… make… Mother… scream," Mother said, then laughed, stroking Glory to a full erection.

Sharae Rockemore laid taped to the bed post, spread eagle, naked. Her thick thighs struggled to stay closed, and the blood circulation in her hand numbed her arms as she fought to free herself. But she was helpless and slowly becoming hopeless; ready to give up. Because even if she freed herself, he would still have her. He was too big for her to even think about escape. She knew her 158 pounds was no match for the Giant and when he entered her, she knew he would stretch her insides with his huge penis.

Sharae had to admit even though she was terrified, she was wet down there, aroused by the sexuality on display. She had fantasized about having a man as big as he was. Even bringing herself to orgasm as she entertained that fantasy. But not like this, her mind screamed. Never like this.

"Taste her, Boy!" Mother ordered as the music came to life.

Softly Abaddon took one of her large, chocolate nipples into his mouth. His hand went down to her Devil's Flower to massage her Devil's bud. With the sensual movement of a lesbian lover, he rubbed until Sharae's body betrayed her, forcing her to shake and quake in an explosive, squirting orgasm.

Crying and sweaty, her body exploded under his large hand and his thick fingers softly slid into her swollen lips, causing another eruption and another release of her female juices. He had full control of her body.

"She's ready, Boy! Kill it!" Mother cried out. His Glory dripped onto Sharae's chubby stomach, her dark brown body fully exposed. There was no modesty for her that night.

Tonight, Abaddon refused to waste his seed by just masturbating. Tonight she would get her wish. He would kill it.

"Noooo!" Sharae cried out, but she knew she had no way to stop him as his mouth found her round stomach, then her thick waist and finally her throbbing vagina, which he called her Devil's Flower.

Abaddon closed his eyes as he sucked for hours, making her body his until she begged him to stop, to give her some release from his sexual torture.

"Now, Boy…" Mother screamed, looking up at him from Sharae's eyes. "Enter me fully."

Kneeling between her wide spread legs and trembling thighs, Abaddon slammed to the hilt inside of Sharae's Devil's Flower, going in and out of her all night long.

"Mother," Abaddon whispered as he came inside her body again. But there was no answer. "Mother, please," he begged, but still no answer came.

Sunlight was now beginning to creep into the sky and he knew the city would soon be alive and busy checking on friends and loved ones. They would be praying that he and Mother had spared them grief, that the nightmare had passed them by.

"Sleep, Mother… I love you," he said, then closed his eyes and kissed the dead, still body of Sharae Rockemore. She was so beautiful, he thought. Marveling at her soft, smooth dark skin, her large breasts and hips. The hairy thick lips of her Flower. She was thick, just the way he liked his women.

There were no knife wounds, no broken neck or even fingerprint evidence of being choked.

No, Mother didn't deserve that last night. She got her wish.

"I killed it, Mother," he said and then smiled as he pulled from inside of her body and his sperm made a ribbon as it shot from Glory one last time.

The women awoke to the sound of the constant pounding on the door. Joanna realized that last night might come to haunt them in the very near future, but what was done was done.

"I'll start the coffee," Veronica volunteered and smiled, pulling one of Joanna's hockey jerseys on, to cover her total nudity.

"That's probably my boyfriend," Joanna said nonchalantly, gently pushing the covers away from her nude body.

"Who?" Veronica smirked, openly staring at the display of flesh before her.

"Tommy. He's probably wondering why my bedroom curtain is closed," Joanna said, then laughed.

"Pervert! You gonna ruin that boy," Veronica said and couldn't resist the sudden urge to touch Joanna's hot flesh again.

"One day. When he's older," Joanna said as she got out of the bed and walked to the front door, naked. She peeked out the peephole and caught a glimpse of the Giant as he smiled over his shoulder and disappeared around the side of the complex.

Joanna fell back as if she had been hit by a bullet and called out, "Ronnie, it's him!"

The women hurried to get dressed and ran out of the apartment, fully armed.

Pulling on their clothes as they ran, they knew he was already long gone. But the envelope nailed to the door captured their attention, even though they were caught in the high fever of the chase.

The letter was addressed to both detectives. Veronica read it.

My Dearest Detectives,

Today, Mother sleeps and I'm alone once again until… Well, never mind that. But now I'll be the thorn in the side of all wrong. I'll be in touch and you'll never have to worry about that bump in the night being me for now. At least until Mother wakes again. I'll make sure you two are the first to know.

Abaddon.

"Ronnie, he's gone," Joanna whispered, sudden relief and a strange sadness in her voice. She had been primed for the chase. She had wanted to take him down. She had wanted to taste the sweet victory that would be hers when he was brought to justice. This way… everything seemed so incomplete. Gone, she wasn't sure what that meant.

"Until next year at least," Detective Veronica Rawls said, taking the letter and placing it in an evidence bag. "And I'll be waiting on his ass."

Joanna was still not satisfied.

She took her time that afternoon.

It was such a beautiful day and she refused to rush it. Yesterday, her sister agreed to watch Emma while she drove down to Dover Downs for an interview. One thing for sure, there would be much more money taken in if the position she applied for came through.

"Emma, baby, sit back," Beverly said as she made the right onto Tilpohokon Street. "What's the safety rules while Mommy is driving?" she asked as she smiled at her five-year-old daughter.

"Always wear my seatbelt, and never stand up while in the car," Emma answered.

"What else, sugar?" Beverly asked, reaching over to tickle her only child's tummy.

"Never lean out the windows," Emma said as she looked toward the ceiling as if to say, "Gosh."

"Good. Now what's my number and our address?"

"Mom!" Emma said and then frowned. "I'm five, not two. Gosh, I'm not stupid, remember?"

"That's right: you're not. So I expect you to finish that book by the time I get home. And I need you to listen to Aunt Sharee when she tells you to take your nap."

"But how can I finish this book? It…"

"Nap time is non-negotiable."

"Non-negotiable? What's that mean?"

"That means you have no choice, sugar."

"Oh I get it."

"That means what Mommy wants…"

"Mommy gets."

"You are so smart."

"I told you I wasn't stupid."

"No you're not. I'm glad we got that out of the way."

"Me too, Mommy."

"So nap time is not negotiable; understand, young lady?"

"Yes, Boss," Emma said and then laughed as her mom pulled into an empty parking spot outside Sharae's house.

"Boss, huh?" Beverly said and then turned to tickle Emma senseless.

"I'm sorry! I'm sorry! Please," Emma laughed, trying to guard her stomach and neck, her most ticklish areas. "I'm going to pee!"

Beverly smiled and kissed Emma as she undid the seatbelt that held her child in safety. "Now, what's my name?" she asked as she helped her child out of her booster seat.

"Mommy," Emma said and continue to giggle.

"That's right… now let's go," Beverly said and climbed from the car and went to open her daughter's car door so she could get out.

"Mommy, Auntie Sharae's door is wide open."

"She must have seen us coming," Beverly said as Emma ran up the steps and down the path.

Beverly laughed to herself as she opened the trunk to grab the small bike with training wheels. She watched Emma pull the heavy security screen door open and rush inside.

"Girl, this job come through, we moving out of this crazy city," Beverly said, coming close behind her daughter. "I swear, the first thing I'm gonna do is hire you somebody to clean," she continued as she picked up shoes that were parked at the front door.

Suddenly, Beverly realized that the house was too quiet. She knew that because Sharee lived alone, there was always something on... the TV or the radio... something to keep her company. Still, Beverly was smiling as she walked into the kitchen.

"Girl, what..." Beverly began, mildly surprised when she found an empty kitchen. "Emma..." she called out and then waited for a response. Then, "Sharae... is everything alright?"

By this time she was climbing the living room staircase. At the top of the staircase, she smiled, seeing Emma sitting in the doorway of Sharae's bedroom with her knees pulled into her small chest.

Quickly her smile erased as she spotted the tears rolling down her daughter's face. "Emma baby, what's wrong?" she wanted to know as she knelt beside her daughter. Not once did she look into the bedroom; she only had eyes for her grieving daughter. If she had looked into the bedroom, she would have seen the writing on the wall.

Emma just cried and pointed to the wall inside the room.

"What is it, sugar?" Beverly whispered, pulling Emma into her arms. When she stood, she saw what Emma was pointing to. The lipstick stood out in blood red in the sunlit room, and instantly Beverly focused on one word: Abaddon.

Gently lifting her daughter up, Beverly moved them both out of the site of the murder scene. "Baby, close your eyes!" Beverly cried out, and closed the bedroom door without looking toward the bed, where she knew her poor little sister slept eternally.

If only she hadn't been alone, Beverly thought as she let her daughter back downstairs. Perhaps this wouldn't have happened. The reporter told all women to beware. Gone, gone like that.

The tears began to flow from Beverly's eyes, but she was holding on to her daughter too tight to wipe them away.

"She was only twenty-four," Detective Veronica Rawls whispered from the passenger seat.

"She looked much older," Joanna observed. "He probably believed her to at least be in her thirties."

They drove down Ogantz Avenue.

"Why no slash this time? No neck breaks or strangle marks. Nothing."

She's still dead. But how? Joanna asked herself, not wanting to voice the question out loud. Lately, Ronnie had taken this case too personally.

"Jo, she was his last..." Detective Rawls whispered, looking out the window.

She had tried to hide the fact that she had just wiped the tears from her face. Was she crying for his last victim, or was she crying for the loss of Allen, or was it for the innocent girl who seemed to be in deep shock? Who, no doubt, would need mental help from this day forward.

"I'm going to quit," Detective Rawls whispered, still looking out the passenger window.

Joanna drove on without responding.

"Did you hear me? I'm going to just walk away while I'm still sane. Maybe talk to someone about the dreams..."

"What dreams, Ronnie?" Joanna finally responded.

"Nothing!" she snapped, and then cried softly, watching the passing houses, the children playing, totally unaware of the dangers of this God-forsaken city. She envied their innocence. Suddenly, she knew she would never leave her job because she wanted to protect that. Someone in this city deserved not to live a life of worry and pain.

Pulling over by a playground, Joanna shut off the motor and turned toward her partner, determined to get to the bottom of her problem. "Ronnie," she said, reaching out to take her hand. "Look at me, Ronnie," she whispered, as one would to a lover in distress.

"Jo," Veronica began, and it all came down on her at once. The unbearable weight of total helplessness. "That poor child!" she cried out, a sob in her voice. "Look what he's done to…" "Shhhh…" Joanna said, suddenly realizing that this was not the time or the place. Maybe after they made love, when they were naked and warm with each other, lost in each other's bodies. Perhaps that was the time, she thought. But now all she could say was, "She will be alright. Believe me. I want to tell you a little story about this little girl who woke one morning to the screams of her mother and father being murdered for $200 and some jewelry."

It took a good twenty minutes and a lot of tears to tell her story, but Joanna explained as best as she could why she knew that little Emma, the shocked child, would survive the horror like she had survived her horror.

When Joanna finished, she looked at her partner in the eyes and said, "I swear we'll catch him. He'll never see a courtroom. Do you understand me? Never! I swear!"

They both knew it was a promise of murder and that they had appointed themselves judge, jury, and executioner. For these two women, the situation couldn't be handled any other way.

"You promise?" Detective Veronica "Ronnie" Rawls asked, and then smiled sadly.

"On my parents' grave," was detective Joanna Staley's reply and promise. Then she sealed it with a kiss on Ronnie's pillow soft lips.

"Wow," Michael Angel said and smiled as he watched the women kiss. It made him feel warm and hard in his pants. A quick flash of a picture of the two of them naked and making love shot to his brain and enflamed his whole body. He hadn't expected to see that and he considered himself fortunate. He followed at a safe distance until they pulled over in front of that playground. He had no choice but to pull past them and circle back.

He was still aroused as he said to himself, "So you're more than partners now!"

His thought was that the pressures and stress of the manhunt had brought them together in this strange and sexy way. He was all for it; he wanted to see more. There was that all-familiar tingle, but now that Mother was asleep, he had complete control over his urges, or that was what he told himself.

"I love you," he said and smiled. "Both of you," and then he giggled.

"No, you don't," someone whispered in his ear.

"Mother?" he cried out, but it couldn't be Mother.

Two little girls danced by his car window, arguing about some boy.

"No, you don't, Gwen!" the tall kid yelled again, a voice of authority at such a young age. "He wouldn't let you have his number!"

She spoke loudly to a short, heavy-set girl who started to run toward the gate of the playground.

Michael Angel smiled at himself and pulled out of the parking lot to pass the Charger on the driver's side.

As far as he was concerned, it was official; a certainty in his heart. Still, he spoke the words as he headed home. "I love both of you."

Chapter Thirteen

I'm Back, Both of Us!
May 1. Eleven months later…

"**D**AMN!" HE SAID and stopped to stare at the expensively decorated living room "What did you say you do as a living?"

"I'm a court clerk. Why?" Melisa Montrose said and then smiled as she flopped onto the velour sofa, kicking off her pumps.

Sliding onto the sofa beside her, Jimmy lifted her right foot to his lap. He expertly began to massage her foot, bringing a soft moan from her lips.

"That's nice," Melissa whispered, closing her eyes to fully enjoy his attention he gave her foot. She had danced all night with Jimmy and was impressed that he had a good job. They danced, drank, and talked all night long. And when he finally told her he had no kids and was recently divorced, she had no problems with convincing him to come home with her for the night. In her mind, this was what grown folks did. She herself had just ended an abusive marriage and had no kids to worry about. She saw herself as young and single and ready to mingle.

"Can you do that everywhere?" Melissa asked, then smiled, looking Jimmy in the eyes in a boldly seductive manner. She found no reason to be shy with him. They both knew how they wanted the night to end.

"What's that?" he said as he reached for the other leg to pull her left foot onto his lap. Softly, he laid it onto his hardening penis. He saw the lust in her eyes as she used her right foot to trace the impressive length of his penis.

"Make my body feel that good… mmmm," she cooed.

"If you'll let me," he said as he massaged her feet and she pushed down on his hard on with her toes.

"Let's shower," she finally whispered. Slowly, she took him into her small hand, sensually stroking his penis. His thickness felt good in her hand as she led him upstairs with her own version of the sexy massage. She was a woman who gave as good as she got. She was a very selfish lover.

They entered the bedroom with no hesitation and Melissa, ever ready and more than eager, began to undress him in the middle of her bedroom. Then she led him into her fashionably decorated bathroom. She moved ahead of him, bending to turn on the faucet of the tub, giving him the full view of her bare ass.

As he looked down at her, he heard a voice: "This bitch is…"

"Quiet, Mother!" he groaned softly. He heard the shower water hit the tub basin.

The voice in his head was loud: "Are you," Mother whispered. "Boy… stop that… mmm, please. Boy, stop… it," Mother moaned as he exploded inside of the dark closet.

Jimmy loved the way her body moved. Most men would say she was overweight, but to Jimmy, she was juicy, thick. The extra pounds made for a hot night of soft sex. Long ago he realized that chubby women seemed tighter, much moister, and loved to freak. Most of all, he loved to hit it doggy style.

They were made for that, as their ass spread wide at the hips. He wasn't a very large man but he was above average and loved to try to bring that gutteral moan from thick, juicy women, especially when they came and moaned loudly and called his name. He really loved that. It made him feel like he was the man of their dreams, the lover they had been waiting for. When he pleased the women, he pleased himself. That was the kind of man he was; he wasn't a selfish lover.

Melissa let the water hit him in the shoulder as she began to lick down his body only to be stopped as she tried to kneel. She closed her eyes as his mouth found her oversized breast and worked his way down her body until her clitoris rested between his lips, where his tongue went to work; he was determined to rock her world by sucking her fat pussy.

It wasn't long before she was screaming, "I'mmm... cummmmmin, Oh God, Jimmmmmmmyyy!"

It was music to his ears.

Melissa screamed and shook violently.

Her appreciation of his oral skills really turned him on, made him feel that he was The Man.

Then that voice again: "A whore, Boy! Is that what I've become? A whore for anybody," Mother whispered as Melissa screamed again. "Stop him, Boy! I don't want him inside my body!"

"Wait, Mother... mmmmm!" he moaned as he shot more cum to the closet floor.

"Shhhh! They're coming," Mother whispered as she led them into her bedroom. Her throat was raw from her screaming and she felt a little weak in the knees from his exciting lower invasion of her body. She had no fight left in her. She was in total surrender. Her mission was to make him feel as good as he made her feel. She felt totally blessed to be with him. He was a man who took his time with a girl; she totally loved him for that.

"Fuck me hard," she came right out and said, almost begging with passion.

Jimmy turned Melissa toward him, with one hand he pushed her to her knees.

"I want to suck dick," Melissa told him, coming out of herself, being a new woman for this new lover. She greedily took him into her mouth as he closed his eyes. She even gently squeezed his balls. She was not a novice when it came to sex and her head game was on point. She was really going all out that night because Jimmy had inspired her to go beyond her normal routine. She was more than ready to pull out all her tricks for this night.

Only God knew what went through his mind as he heard that voice once again. That same horrifying voice that haunted his dreams. The same voice that made life so frightening. All he could say was, "You promised!" as he heard, "I am Abaddon!"

"This is just in Fox 29 News has the exclusive," Gloria Velendez said into the camera. She had long ago been promoted to anchorwoman after all the national attention she received from the Abaddon and Apollyon case last year.

"This morning a letter was received as I collected my mail from the bin on my desk. It was addressed to…" she began and then paused, thinking of censoring herself before she continued, wanting to be real and not offensive. Still, she felt she owed it to her viewers to give them the raw honest truth, figuring that might save some lives.

She held the envelope up for the camera.

"To the pretty Spanish Bitch," she continued with a look of sad resignation on her face. "I must warn you; this will cause terror amongst the populace of Philadelphia. It starts with the headline: "A Letter from a Serial Killer.""

Then she paused to swallow, her throat tight from so much emotion. It was also plain to see that she was fighting to control over her fears. She knew she had to be a warrior for truth. She had to press on.

"Dear Victims, I read somewhere that a killer is created. Some say it's the circumstances around him that saturates his instincts to murder his victims... I overheard somewhere that a child is born to be a killer; it's just in his blood," and again, she had to pause before she could continue. "Does a man have a choice in the matter when it's kill or be killed? That's up for debate. But self-survival will kick in and nature will prevail..." she paused again to regain her composure. She knew she had to continue. There was no other option. She was all the way live on the air.

"I've seen what so-called society tells the world when one of its created killers snaps and murders his wife and tries to do likewise to his son. The way they'll use the media to influence, to deceive the public's thoughts, to disguise the legality of insanity. They'll take no credit for the monsters of their own creations. None at all! Hah hah, hah! Fuck them, and fuck you, and fuck me. I just don't understand. So maybe you can help me. I have a question to ask this city. Ready??"

Gloria stopped to look up at the camera as it focused on a close up of her frightened face. "Here it is," she continued. "Which killer am I? Hmmm. Good, God damn question. Which killer... am... I?"

After another brief pause, she said, "He's signed it." She laid the letter on the desk for dramatic effect, then continued, "In the mind of a... killer. Ladies, especially my black sisters out there with a little extra weight, between the ages of 25 to 50, please, please take what I say to heart because it could mean your very life. I beg you, please be careful. The monster is back. He goes by the cursed name Abaddon and he's already proven himself very, very deadly, and the police seem to be no match for him or... Mother. God help us all."

The reporter finished with a whisper and the station went to a commercial break.

"Bob Thoronson's office."

"Hello, Bobby," Mother said, then laughed. "How is Mrs. Hairy Pussy?"

"Mother?" Bob said, sitting up straight and feeling nauseous. This was the moment he had dreaded even though he knew it was coming. He expected the insane calls to begin, just not so soon. He wasn't ready. There was no way he could be ready. He gripped the phone tightly.

"Stop whining, Bobby."

No one called him Bobby.

"Be a man, Bobby," Mother taunted, playing with him like a cat would play with a mouse. "I know you got balls, Bobby. I seen them. Ain't talking about with Mrs. Hairy pussy. I mean that crackhead bitch. You filthy old bastard." Mother laughed, a voice like a knife to his heart. "I see she has a nice apartment over there in Manayunk and she's clean. Ten more pounds and she'd be mine."

"Mother, please…" he said, suddenly feeling weak, like there was no way he could move from the pain she was about to unleash on him.

"Shut up, Bobby! Listen… I'm woke now, sooooo?" Mother laughed, sending chills down Bobby's spine. "She's there… waiting. 1592 Plymouth Street. Tell them all." That's when Mother's voice changed instantly. "I am Abaddon… I'm back…" and then there was that laugh.

Quietly, Bob sat with his eyes closed. As if that would send him into a darkness that would shield him from what was about to come. He had no choice, so he prayed for the women of the city. Not confident that his prayers would be answered, but he knew he had to do something. To put up some hedge of protection as feeble or ineffective it might be. Someone had to do something.

Detective Joanna's eyes fell on her partner. She wondered how she would take the news of his return. Sure, they knew from the FBI profilers that this day was coming. They knew of the month of May and that because of his dissociative disorder, Mother would surface, but not once since that day last year had they sat and discussed his return, or what would be done or said.

For months, she and Ronnie had solved sexual assaults, murders, and child attacks, but the Giant was altogether different. Today she watched Ronnie's every move, trying not to be obvious. This morning they watched the broadcast together with the rest of the task force that was formed in April in anticipation of his return. That would be Abaddon!

The Feds wanted the lead and the power struggle began. She lost the war of authority, but she still had the upper hand. Abaddon was in them... she and Ronnie were in his plans. Was he planning with Mother for them or was it like what Mother had said, that he loved them, wanted them and desired to protect them? One thing for sure, he had most definitely been deep inside of her body more than once. Well, once physically, but many times in her dreams had he probed her womb deeply, causing her to wake as her body spasmed in orgasmic release.

For her, the dreams started only a month ago in anticipation of his return. So badly she wanted to tell someone, but who could she tell that the most feared rapist, the most feared murderer had invaded her insides... deeply, and yet, she had survived. No, that information had to remain between the four of them: Ronnie, Abaddon, that old bitch Mother, and herself. All this ran through her mind as she watched Ronnie answer the phone.

Instantly, the look she received from Ronnie served as the signal that it had started, and she remembered her promise to Ronnie, and not just to her friend and lover but to God! She knew she had vowed to uphold the law, but this time, because of this mad man, she would deliberately break a commandment. Because of Abaddon, and the threat he held over the city, he would die.

By her hands, she would commit murder.

The news vans were everywhere. Channels 3, 6, and 10. Channel 17, Channel 29, stations from Jersey, Delaware, and as far as New York were lined up and down the street.

"God damned media circus!" Ronnie commented in wonder and disgust as they pulled up. "Feds already here," she added as she noticed the four black cars blocking the small side street.

Stepping from the Charger, both detectives spotted their captain standing at the bottom of the home's steps.

"Captain," Joanna yelled as they crossed the street.

"Detectives," he nodded in greeting, "Alphabet boys… they asked for the two of you, pronto. It's been a mess in there." He shook his head. "Feds all in the evidence. Dumb sons of bitches! Fucking sons of anarchy! We don't need this shit! Too many cooks in the kitchen! Fuck!"

"Did they disturb the room?" Joanna wanted to know as she interrupted the captain's rant, moving up the cement steps to the home.

"I don't think he'd let them," the captain smiled, speaking of the only Fed profiler he liked, the one that gave respect, so it wasn't hard to give respect back to him. Some called that professional courtesy.

Joanna noticed the smile on Ronnie's face as they observed one of the other Fed profilers.

Ronnie turned to Joanna. "What?" she asked, still smiling.

"I saw that…" Ronnie whispered. "He's gay."

"No, he's not…" Joanna stated with much conviction. "He's just conscious of his appearance. I think they call that being metro-sexual. Don't you see how he studied all this?" she added as she ran her hands down her slender hips, then giggled. Sex was always the way she took her mind off the horror they would eventually see.

"Please, Ms. Model-thin Ass," Ronnie said, then laughed as they entered the open living room. "For God's sake, close that blind," she said as she pointed when she noticed the neighbor across the street with his Nokia camera and Zoom 5000 lens. "Where's Eric?"

"Bedroom," one of the FBI techs said from the kitchen.

Climbing the stairs was like stepping into another world through a narrow portal. Upstairs were only four profilers and one agent, Eric Wilson Jr., who was the lead agent and the only one with a sense of investigative prowess.

"Detectives," he called out and smiled his million-dollar smile.

"Agent," they both responded, Neither asked if it was their boy. The Bose Airwave System, the Union, and the sperm was his signature; these told his story.

"Everybody out!" Agent Wilson said as Joanna stepped toward the bed. He himself went to a corner to observe her do her thing. He saw no reason to get in her way. She was a professional at work.

Joanna opened the closet and scanned the floor, the walls, and the clothes. She stepped inside and her hand moved in a motion that mimicked masturbation. She closed her eyes and Agent Eric could have sworn her body trembled as if she had an orgasm. He looked away and found himself looking at Ronnie who nodded as if to confirm his observation. He really didn't know what to make of either woman.

"No, Mother…" Joanna moaned softly as she came from the closet.

Agent Eric knew what was happening now.

Joanna was on the Laz-E-Boy that sat in front of a full-length mirror with an ornate oak frame. Her hand continued to imitate masturbation as she growled softly.

"What…" Eric half-whispered, somewhat startled by the detective's strange behavior. Ronnie touched his arm and shook her head no. Her finger was to her lips and he understood that he was to be quiet while this unbelievable police woman did her thing.

Slowly, Joanna stood from the Laz-E-Boy in the room and crossed the room toward the bed. She reached for the floor only to stand empty handed, but seeming to hold something in her grasp.

Agent Eric watched in fascination as she pulled the invisible wig onto the deceased head. Then she looked to be applying lipstick to the dead victim's mouth, then the large hoop earrings were invisibly put on and arranged. She straddled the body and continued to simulate masturbation, only to pause and reach for the Bose Airwave System and pressed Play.

"Somebody said... I was living the life..." the Isley Brothers sang out as Joanna opened her mouth to speak.

The words horrified Eric, coming out in a raspy voiced growl.

"I am Abaddon," Joanna said, then slammed her lower body into the dead woman's pelvic area, simulating penetration, then making a motion that had her slicing the aorta with an invisible knife.

"Don't!" Joanna whispered as she came to, wiping the tears from her face.

Never before had it been so real. Never before had she been able to climax in character. But that day she had had multiple orgasms. Her lower body was rocking and jerking out of control. There was no embarrassment because she had no control over her actions or emotions at that time. She felt herself entering Melissa and she heard the snap of Jimmy's neck. She became a spirit for that moment... no... more like twenty minutes as he violated Melissa's body. The sadness, pain, and sorrow of Abaddon had surged through her body as she spoke his name. She felt the childhood suffering. The repulsive touch of Mother. She really went there, and it wasn't a pleasant experience.

Joanna moved away from Ronnie as she came near her. The touch of Ronnie or anyone for that matter, felt repulsive. She had come out of trance with the echo of the screams of the victim's pleas, only to realize she had mounted Melissa for sick sexual gratification. She had felt Glory slide inside of Melissa.

Joanna fell to her knees and screamed, rolling along the floor beside the victim's bed. "Ronnie, don't! Oh, God, I was him!" she cried out.

"Wow..." the profiler whispered, holding the camcorder at the bedroom door. Behind him were two others. "Did you see that?"

"Did you get that?" Agent Eric whispered, only to receive a nod from the profilers who stood in awe. "Oh God, Eric... she's a transfer..." he whispered.

"Ronnie, get me out of here!" Joanna cried, standing up from the floor on shaky legs. And although it was obvious that she needed it, she wouldn't let anyone touch her.

"Wait..." Eric said, trying to stop any movement as Ronnie pushed past everyone to take her partner away from the scene of horror.

"A what?" Joanna whispered as she balled up under the down filled quilt. She was unusually cold.

"Scientists call it Transpose Criminal Phenomenon Reaction. But we call it Trans for short," Agent Eric said calmly. "It's very... very rare. Actually, you're only the second or third to exist, to my knowledge."

"How? Why me? Why now?" Joanna asked, filled with questions. Then she shook uncontrollably under the quilt.

Ronnie looked on in concern.

"Only thing we know is now that it's started, it'll get stronger..." Agent Eric informed them. "More real. Soon, you'll be there with him and then..."

"Then what?" Ronnie had to ask, noticing his reluctance to continue. "There's more, right?" she asked, her frustration coming out in anger.

"Then..." Agent Eric began again and stopped, not wanting to say it.

"Then what, dammit!" Ronnie almost screamed out of control. "What, you…"

"Ronnie, don't…" Joanna whispered. The truth was hard for her to hear, but she needed to know. "He's not at fault here. It's…"

Then Joanna's voice instantly changed, no longer her voice, but the voice of Mother, rushing from her mouth, proclaiming, "Abaddon!"

Noticing them both staring at her, Joanna said, "What?"

Neither one said a word.

"Dammit, Ronnie… why are you looking at me like that?" Joanna demanded to know.

"She'll become… insane," Agent Eric finally got out.

"How long?" Joanna demanded. "How long before I… this happens?"

"No one knows." He hated to be the bearer of bad news. He hated hurting this beautiful, vulnerable woman.

"Trans what?" the captain roared. "Fuck that, she's out!" he barked. "That's it, Joanna! You hear me? It's over. No more Abaddon. No more cases. No more force. You're done!" he went on, screaming now. He was no longer Captain Jackson. He was now Uncle Dad protecting his niece. His final word: "Done!"

"It won't make a difference now," Agent Eric said from the hard, wooden stool in the corner of the captain's office. "Trans can't shut it down or control it. And there is no record of one being able to stop the insanity as it approaches. Even when Jon Paul LaVue stopped his investigation of the Strangler of New Hampshire, he still became the strangler and murderer. Twelve more victims after he captured the real strangler."

"So you're saying my daugh… my niece… will become some kind of… manic?"

Then he began to cry as Mother's voice came from Joanna's mouth. He wept openly saying, "Oh no, Jo Jo."

"Something ain't right, Boy," Mother said and looked around as the car pulled into the dark driveway. "I feel like we have company... a watcher," she whispered.

"That's impossible, Mother. I was careful as always. We were not followed. I checked and double-checked," Abaddon growled.

"But I can..." Mother protested, only to be interrupted.

"Plus, we're ten blocks from..." he began and stopped and smiled, his hand going down to his penis. "From her. Mmmmm."

Clapping her hands, Mother yelled her disapproval. "Stop that, Boy! Oh no... mmmmm. I said, stop that! You no good son of Satan! Stop it!"

"Do you really," Abaddon said as he pulled his penis out of his pants so he could masturbate freely. "Want me to stop this?"

"Well..." Mother stared at Abaddon in the mirror. "Maybe just one. Boy... mmmm... or two." She moaned loudly as he worked up an explosion.

Opening the basement door of her mother's house, Stephanie had no idea he was out there. Sitting in his car, masturbating until she stepped from the enclosure of the two houses.

"Hey, you," Stephanie said and smiled, letting him know that she was down for whatever type of chick, never underestimating the freaky nature of most men. Seeing a man masturbating in public was no big deal to her. She eagerly walked up to the side of his Capris Classic and peeked in. "Damn," she exclaimed as she watched his large dick explode, cum coming from the top onto his hand. "I can do that for you, for ten dollars," she let him know, although she was not a whore or a prostitute, she was just that fun loving girl many men found extremely attractive. But she knew her limits. "I can't take that much dick," she let him know, then giggled, cracking up at the absurdity of the situation she found herself in.

"She saw us, Boy! She has to die!" the voice of Mother whispered in Abaddon's ears. "She'll tell. We can't have that!"

"She's skinny, Mother…" he began before Mother cut him off.

"I said kill, not fuck, Boy!" Mother barked in his ears. "Use them muscles, Boy!" Then Mother began to laugh. "Because you can't think."

Slowly, he let down the car window. "Get in," he growled and hit the electric locks so she could climb in to her death. She was a young and dumb crackhead and he felt no sympathy for her. As far as he was concerned, he was just the agent of her fate.

As he saw it, she was meant to die that day.

"I can suck that big muthafucka," young Stephanie said and then smiled, trying to sound sexy and sophisticated, but to Abaddon, all she came across as was a ghetto THOT. A greedy nasty ghetto whore. She reached across the seat to wrap her small hand around him, gripping his massive Glory. "God damn, Mon," she said, letting a little Jamaican accent slip out as she leaned over to give him a blow job, much sloppy top with plenty of saliva and deep sucks and tugs and moans.

"I'm-a blow this muthafucka's mind with my head game," Stephanie told herself. But he ain't getting none of this tight pussy. Muthafucka too big with that horse dick.

"Don't let her, Boy," Mother argued in his ear as he closed his eyes to enjoy the head. "Don't… mmmm, shit, Boy," Mother moaned as the crackhead whore sucked for dear life, trying hard to earn her ten dollars.

"This is big," Stephanie observed, then paused for a moment to give her jaw a break. "Cum in my mouth, Big Dick Muthafucka." Then she took him to the back of her throat. Deep throat this muthafucka, she thought.

After a few more deep pulls, Stephanie found herself laying across his lap. Suddenly she sat up and wiped her mouth. What she had done wasn't pretty, but she got the job done, handled her business, earned her ten dollars. "What's your name, then?" she asked, making small talk as she continued to masturbate his still hard penis. "Damn, it' still hard."

He smiled as he exploded again in her stroking hand. He growled with malice. He let her know, "I am Abaddon!"

So badly, Stephanie wanted to scream, but his large hands snapped her neck instantly. He had no more use for her.

Ronnie sat up in horror as she heard him speaking from somewhere inside the apartment. She didn't know how the .40 Glock ended up in her hand as she rolled to the floor from the bed.

Much to Ronnie's shock and amazement, Joanna laid on the bed, groaning in ecstasy. Her hand seemed to be on an invisible string moving up and down between her thighs. Suddenly, she moaned and bucked as if she were nearing her climax.

"I am Abaddon," Joanna roared and grabbed the same pillow Ronnie had just vacated with such force, the pillow burst as she twisted on the bed.

"Don't... call... mmmmm, shit..." the girl said and groaned. "Don't call me that."

Then she came in the girl's wide mouth.

"What's your name then?" she asked and then smiled as she wiped her mouth. Her hand felt so good on her large penis as she came again.

"I am Abaddon," she growled, snapping the girl's unsuspecting neck. Her hands felt so strong as they wrapped around the girl's neck. The feel of bone snapping, the sound of the sudden gasp made her explode again, a hard and violent rush that took her breath away.

"Put her in the trunk, Boy," Mother said, then giggled. "Let's go!"

Turning out of the dark driveway, Abaddon looked up at the street again. "Ten blocks, Mother," he whispered.

"1826 Pittville Street," Detective Rawls said to the agent on the other line. "It was him… coming from her mouth." She paused as Joanna came out of the bedroom, obviously still in a trance, her hand moving in masturbation motions.

"She's now in the living room," Ronnie told the caller. "Should I wake her?"

"No! Just watch her! And, Detective, stay away from her. For your own safety. She'll possess his strength," Agent Eric whispered. "I'll get the ball rolling on that address, but it's probably over by now. We're always too late."

"But… I thought you said she'll see what he's doing?" Ronnie whispered as Joanna laid on the floor, humping and grunting like an out of control sex monster.

"I am Abaddon!" Joanna roared as she made a slashing motion with her right hand. "Ummmph, ummmmmph, ummmmph…" she continued as Ronnie watched her and Agent Eric listened.

Suddenly, Ronnie froze and aimed her .40 Glock at a humping Joanna who looked at her and whispered in Mother's voice. "I know, whore!" Then she giggled in a maddening cackle. "I see you, too!"

Chapter Fourteen

"I CAN'T, RONNIE," Joanna whispered, defeat in her voice as she sat on the passenger side of the Impala.

"I've seen what's in there. I did it," she said and began to cry.

"Oh no, baby," Ronnie whispered. She softly turned Joanna toward her by grabbing her chin. "Look at me… make no mistake about it. He, that monster that did this shit is not you. That bastard with his sick ass sadistic mind did it. Not you; not us. You're one of the good guys. We have to shut him down. Sit here and I'll be back when I finish my walk through. We will end this."

Stepping from the car, Ronnie spotted the first of many news vans pulling into the small street. "Officer," she called out to a uniformed policeman. "No one is to get near that car or the detective inside. Am I understood?"

"Yes, Ma'am," he said and then nodded, noticing the urgency in her voice.

"And have a few officers keep the press at least a hundred yards from the scene." Ronnie continued, making sure the officer understood that she was serious about keeping her friend safe. Satisfied, she then turned to enter the home of Katherine Shuman, the deceased.

"Detective Rawls," Agent Eric called out as she entered, standing and then making his way over to her. "How's…"

"Bad," Ronnie let him know. "She can't even come inside."

Suddenly Joanna appeared in the doorway.

"Move that news crew away from that driveway and dammit, Mike, put that cigar out," she barked, giving orders and shaking up everything in the room, moving like the boss everyone knew she could be. She even smiled as she continued. "It's bad for your health." Surveying the scene, she said, "He came in from the bathroom skylight."

"Jo?" Ronnie said and frowned, but secretly glad that her partner was on the scene, taking charge.

"It's a job, right?" she quickly turned to Eric. "He dumped the girl behind Abbots Fords Project. The green dumpsters."

Then she walked away, giving orders to police men in uniforms, gathered around the crime scene. "Get outside and keep the neighbors across the street."

"Yes, Ma'am, they'll be there by noon," the clerk said. "We're just confirming there will be someone there to expect delivery." After a slight pause, the clerk read back the address and phone number. "Very well, Miss Vincent, twelve noon."

After she hung up, he pressed the white button on the intercom system.

"Michael… Jesus. You're truck is loaded. Let's go, fellas."

"Yo, Michael…" Jesus said, making sure he was a good distance away from his friend as he pulled his shirt off. "Can you tell?"

"Oh God," Michael said and then laughed. "It's only been two months. Put that shirt back on."

"Yeah, I know… but can you tell? Marie said she noticed I was bigger when we made love last night." Then Jesus flexed his torso.

"I think she meant your head, skinny."

As usual, Jesus charged the hulk of a man and dove at this back with little effect. And as always, Michael just pulled him over his shoulder and carried him down the stairs of the truck, struggling.

"116 Sharpneck Street," Jesus pointed as Michael pulled the truck in front of the address. Pulling the invoice clipboard from the dash, he said, "Freaks."

"What?" Michael asked as he turned toward his friend.

"Floor to ceiling, bedroom," he said and then laughed. "Better put on a shirt, big guy. She might want some and I at least want a chance."

"What, jealous, Jee-sus?" Michael flexed his biceps

"Damn!" Jesus whispered as the muscles in Michael's arms seemed to stack onto more muscles.

It was Jesus who rang the doorbell as Michael opened the back of the delivery truck. As she opened the door, Michael was already heading up the walkway. He noticed the woman staring at his best friend carrying the boxes of mirrors with his tool belt securely around his thick waist.

Donna was not shy about showing her appreciation. "Damn," she whispered, licking her lips.

Instantly, Jesus flexed his chest and sucked in his stomach. "Miss Vincent?"

"Mmmmm hmmmm!" Donna moaned and then smiled, eyeing Michael's back as he sat the boxes down and returned for another load.

"Can you sign here… please, Ma'am?" Jesus said, smiling. "He's gay. Now you can sign here and stop looking at my husband," he lied and and laughed inside.

"Shit!" Donna said and rolled her eyes in disgust. Ain't that the way, she thought. All the good looking guys are taken or gay. Damn, what's a girl to do? Then there's the unemployment thing. Damn, either jobless or gay. What ever happened to straight, horny men?

Michael fit the last fastener to the wall when Donna Vincent entered the bedroom with two sandwiches and iced tea.

"Sorry, I don't use sugar in my tea," Donna said, and then smiled, setting the tray on the dresser. "I hope you and your husband don't mind turk…"

"What?" Michael stood up, totally confused. "My who?"

"Your husband," Donna repeated what she had been told. "He's your mate, right?"

Michael turned to Jesus with fire in his eyes. He couldn't have this fine woman thinking that he was less than the man that he was. Ain't down with no gay shit, he thought, looking menacingly at Jesus.

"Hold up, big guy!" Jesus said, and then laughed, taking two steps toward the steps, ready to make a quick exit. "I was just joking…" he began just before he took off running down the stairs. It was not until they reached the corner before Michael tracked him down. Carrying him back to the front lawn of Ms. Vincent's home, Michael dropped him and sat on his chest.

"Tell her!" Michael said and slapped Jesus twice in the head. "Truth!"

"But I still love you…" Jesus said, still being the funny guy.

Donna looked upon their antics and allowed herself to be amused, especially now that she knew the truth. The way they carried on was strange, but funny. They were manly, yet playful with each other. Secretly, she wished they were playing with her, especially that hunky looking Michael.

"Tell her!" Michael said, looking up at her. "I'm not gay!" That was when he let go of Jesus and slapped him hard on the shoulder with a half-closed fist. "Especially with this."

"Ouch, big guy! Spousal abuse! Somebody call the cops!" Jesus screamed.

Donna found herself laughing even harder.

"Tell her, Jesus!" Michael was insistent, wanting to clear his name.

"All right, all right! Get up please, I'll confess," Jesus said between giggles.

Michael stood and waited, speaking to Jesus, but looking at Donna. "Tell her, skinny."

"All right…" Jesus said as his eyes darted left and right. "Ms. Vincent, he doesn't love me anymo…" he said and then took off running, followed closely by the Giant.

Two hours later, they pulled off with twenty dollars in tip money. But Michael left with more, much, much more.

"She's the one," Mother whispered in his ears.

The blue Impala sat idle as their eyes remained locked.

"What is it, Ronnie?" Joanna asked, then looked away.

"You know what, Jo. Why the sudden…"

"Look, what am I supposed to do? Sulk and die? Fuck that! And no, I will not be a test study somewhere. If I die, it'll be after I kill this bastard," Joanna said, trying hard to mask her pain and worry, but the tears escaped anyway and Ronnie couldn't help but notice.

"Jo…" Ronnie said, reaching for her hand.

"Nope! Stop!" Joanna said and pulled away. "I don't want you feeling sorry for me. I need to be alone tonight, Ronnie."

That was the last thing Ronnie wanted to hear, but she respected her friend enough to let her have her way.

Joanna climbed from the car and walked toward her apartment. Not once did she look back, but she knew Ronnie watched her all the way, until she disappeared inside, feeling all alone. Standing, she looked to her window and there he was, wiping away tears as he watched her from his window. Holding her hand out to him, Joanna had to smile. There was no doubt that there was someone there for her. Moments later, she stood in the open doorway as Tommy walked into her arms.

He looked happy and hurt as he asked, "Why, Joanna?"

"I had too much on my plate, Tommy," Joanna confessed, slightly bowing her head. "But now I got to make sure I'm…" she stopped mid-sentence.

Although Tommy was concerned about her, he still felt the need to push her. He wanted to know where he stood with her. He had known her too long to feel any comfort in this limbo. "What? Make sure of what?" He questioned as she stepped into his apartment.

"Do not ask questions, Boy!" she chastised him. "Just follow Mother…" she said and smiled strangely. "I need you to learn how…"

"How to what?" Tommy asked, innocently. Still confused, but more than eager to please.

"How to pleasure my Devil's Flower, Boy. I want you to learn to use all that Glory."

With that, Joanna reached down and took him in her hand, cupping his balls and stroking his penis, feeling it swell. That made her smile. "I want you to kill it, Boy!" she whispered.

Her voice was strange, Tommy thought, as she led him into the bedroom. But he had no thought to move away from her, to not follow her wherever she led him. This was the reunion he had hoped for. He had had his doubts, especially with Veronica in the picture. But now he was determined to ignore the strange voice.

"When you come to me, Boy…" Joanna said as she began to disrobe. "Remove all your clothes!" Then she began to giggle and the sound did frighten him a little bit but his teenage hormones controlled his mind and actions.

Ronnie punched the keys with a steady rhythm. She punched in the subject she needed. The screen flickered and a picture of a man with a handle bar mustache and goatee filled the screen. His name sat under the picture. From the name she expected the face to be a French white man.

So, Mr. Jon Paul La'vue, you're black," she thought and for some reason she found it ironic. For the next thirty minutes, she read about the case study carried out by the black detective after he was himself captured for the murders of twelve victims committed in the same fashion of the Strangler of New Hampshire. "A flower was placed on their chests..." she read out loud. But the question was, "What happened to you, La'vue?" With even more curiosity, she continued to read on.

"I'm gonna..." Tommy groaned as he did what she instructed. He stood at the bottom of the king sized bed. His hand moved up and down the length of his penis.

Joanna laid with her legs wide open and her two fingers rubbed in a circular motion on the wet bud of her clitoris.

"Boy, wait for Mother... I'm... almost..." she wailed as her back arched. "Come with Mother, Boy!"

Tommy couldn't hold back any longer as she screamed. He exploded with such force it shot onto her smooth pussy lips and fingers as she bucked wildly beneath him.

Jon Paul La'vue one day entered the squad room smiling at his partner of eight years. He whispered something to the effect of... "A flower for penitent or penitence." It wasn't until later that his partner understood his words. They were words of Albert Fish, the Strangler, to his victims as he strangled them to death.

"A flower for penitence," he would whisper as he took their lives with a strip of cord.

"John Babin stood only 5'5"..." Ronnie continued to read.

"How?" Tommy whispered as he held his mouth inches from her moist flower, her Devil's Flower, as she kept calling it, which was so much unlike Joanna. Still he chose to ignore that.

Spreading her hairless lips with the fingers of her left hand, she grabbed the top of Tommy's head. "Suck it, Boy!" she said as she pressed his mouth to her vagina. As he licked and sucked, she grinded into his face. Guiding his movements with the thrust of her pelvis and the movement of his head with her hands.

"Use your tongue more. Boy… mmmmmm, yessss," she went on. "Find my bud you son of a…. Ahhhh, mmmm, yesssss. I'mmmm cummmming, Boy!"

"It's believed that Jon Paul La'vue's first victim was his lover and friend, a Ms. Fancine Del Larue of South Berkshire Place. That's where they shared a flat. She was the last to be discovered, but the coroner placed her death around two weeks before the capture of John Babin…" Ronnie read on, speaking softly to herself.

"No! No! Boy!" Joanna screamed. "Take it out!" she said as she pushed on his chest. "Take it out, Boy!"

"But…"

"Boy, I said, kill it!" she barked up into his confused face. He was so willing to please that her tone of voice upset him. "I can't do nothing with that lovey dovey shit!" She gripped his long, thick penis.

"Look at this, Boy!" she growled. When he looked down at his penis in her left hand, she slapped the dog shit out of him. "This is named… Glory, Boy!"

The shock on his face showed the surprise and pain that she had caused him. But she rubbed gently onto his penis, appeasing him, and calming him down. Making him think this was like all their other times together.

"Jo…" he tried to say as she slapped him again with such force his head turned and he almost fell off the bed.

"Fuck me like that, Boy!" Without another word, she slapped him again, causing spit to fly from his mouth. "Now use Glory to pleasure my Devil's Flower, Boy!" Once again she slapped Tommy senseless and giggled.

Feeling she wanted it rough, Tommy grabbed her throat but not to hurt Joanna, not for payback, just to get into her new game. She giggled and slapped him again.

"Bitch!" he screamed with his thickness at her moist opening.

"Mother, Boy!" she said just before slapping him again. "Mother!"

The transformation came on slowly. It took somewhere between eighteen months and three years. This is only an estimation because no one knows just how early the actual Transferable Criminal Phenomenon began.

Jon Paul La'vue was clever to begin with, so it's believed he hid the first signs from everyone. But it's known that he took over the strangler's case twelve months prior to their first break in the case.

"Ummmmph! Ummmmph! Bitch!"

"Argghhhh.... Ohhhh shit!" she screamed. "Ohhhh, yesss," she screamed and slapped him again. "Call.... Ohhhh, God.... Mother.... Boy!"

Tommy found that she had him so excited that he really was trying to hurt her. Many times he had high school girls begging him not to go so deep. One even measured him with a plastic ruler. Seven and a half inches, he remembered her telling him. Now he slammed all that into Joanna's body and she wanted even more.

"Call... me... Mother, Boy!"

"Take it, you Mother.... I'm..."

"No! Stop that, Boy! Don't you dare..." her legs flew out in a vee as she cried out in pain and pleasure. The muscles in her vagina tightened around her young lover.

"I'mmmmm cummmmming!" Tommy screamed as Joanna's body convulsed beneath him. She, too, had an orgasm.

When they finally captured Jon Paul La'vue, he was declared clinically insane. In a federal inquisition, his diary was put into the record. The following is an entry dated three days before the capture of John Babin:

13 February 1963

Today she whispers all her transgressions of unfaithfulness. The breath of life no longer travels through her pores. The blood travels on emptiness, void of love or compassion. My flowers are sorrows until they're places on the souls. A flower for penitence.

Jon Paul La'Vue
The Strangler

"Oh no, Joanna," Ronnie cried out, slowly standing from the desk. She looked around the squad room. Who could she tell, was her thought.

Their eyes locked as he entered the detective's squad room.

Ronnie rushed into his arms. "We gotta help her!" Ronnie cried out, holding nothing back.

"We can't," Agent Eric whispered.

Chapter Fifteen

Stop Me If You Can

THE DARKENED ROOM was silent and misery settled in the air. Martha sat trembling with Ronald taped behind her. She could feel the warmth of his blood pressed into her skin. She could smell the coppery scent flowing from his heart onto their bed, which was now their death bed.

This was him.

She knew it the moment the basement door flew open and the pot of mashed potatoes fell from her grasp. "Scream!" her mind demanded. "Run, bitch!" it demanded, but she knew she would not. Not with Ronald, Jr and his father upstairs unaware of the monster down here with her. No, she had no choice, even when he smiled and whispered his name.

"I am Abaddon," he had softly growled, standing there nude in the doorway leading into the basement.

All Martha could do was tremble as sure death approached with the speed of a charging cat. The power of his hand clamped above her elbow, then over her mouth. He had them and she knew it and prayed what she read was true. The Giant Abaddon never took a child's life… ever! It wasn't until he had Ronald in his strong grasp that she remembered something else. Her man, her husband, Ronald, would surely die a horrible, painful death.

"I understand you, Abaddon…" Martha whispered, trying desperately to reach his humanity, if there was any left in him. "I can feel why you must do this." Her voice shook. She knew she was on shaky ground but also knew she had to try to save as much of her family as she could. She was even ready to sacrifice herself for her husband and her son. Her life meant nothing to her if she would lose them without a fight.

"Mmmmmm," he moaned, sitting on the bedside ottoman at the foot of her bed. His eyes momentarily met hers in the large vanity mirror with the custom cherry wood frame. His hand moved frantically up and down his bare, brown penis.

"I do," Martha whispered again and then paused. "It's her… your mother," she continued. "She made you hate women…. She's the cause of your suffering."

"I love you, Mother… mmm," he said, just before he spilled his seed on the floor.

"But, she must have hated you… Abaddon," Martha continued, moving like she was navigating through a lethal land mined field. She knew just one misstep would mean death for her and her family. "She must have wanted you dead so bad. Why else would she have made you into this monster?"

"Don't listen to that bitch, Boy!" Mother suddenly barked.

Martha watched him caress his cheek as Mother's voice came out of his mouth.

"She doesn't understand our love, Boy."

"I love you, Mother," Abaddon moaned, obviously in that languorous peaceful place where men went after orgasm. In this good feeling place, he continued to masturbate, his hand moving like it had a mind of its own. He handled himself like he was totally alone, oblivious of Martha closely watching him, making her the voyeur that she never wanted to be. She was sickened by his public display of such a private and personal sexual act.

"Love?" Martha whispered. "That bitch don't…"

"Shut up, whore!" Mother yelled as the Giant leapt to his feet.

Even though she was terrified, Martha stood her ground. Too much was at stake for her to break down now. "Look at me, Abaddon. Is that your real name? Abaddon," she whispered. "My name is Martha. I know if you were my son, I would never…"

"I said…" the Giant charged at Martha with his hand raised, but it was Mother's voice that spoke. "Shut up, whore!" she started to slap Martha as the other hand grabbed his left.

"No, Mother!" she screamed loudly. Suddenly the two voices became one.

"What, you love her, Boy?" Mother mumbled softly.

"I only love you, Mother. Please… you know I do."

"But does she love herself, Abaddon?" Martha whispered, drawing him into a debate that would distract him long enough for her to do something to save her family.

"Michael," he growled, staring at Martha, the peacemaker.

"Don't, dummy!" Mother shouted and Martha could see the struggle the two were having. One wanted to attack her and one wanted to protect her. "She knows your Goddamned name now."

"She's gonna…" he mumbled as he began to rub Glory once more.

"Not this whore, Boy! Her!" he began as he turned in the mirror and their eyes met.

"Michael," Martha said as she licked her dry lips. "Mother doesn't love you. She hates you. Listen to what she calls you…"

"Don't listen to her, Boy!" I'm warning you! She means you no good! She's just running her mouth to save herself and her family. This dumb bitch doesn't know it's too late!"

"Boy!" Martha smiled and returned the sarcasm, fighting with every tool she had. "Is that love… Michael?"

Slowly he took two steps back as he frantically masturbated. The growl that escaped his throat sent a deadly chill though her blood as he shot jets of sperm in the air and ran toward the bed screaming loudly like some mortally wounded animal.

"I am Abaddon!"

"I am Michael," Joanna screamed as she ran from her bed into the living room, slamming into the wall.

"No, don't!" Agent Eric whispered quickly as his team moved in to help the fallen Joanna. "Reset the camera, Jill," he ordered the agent by the kitchen door. It was the camera that faced the bathroom and Joanna had knocked it down as she ran out of the bedroom.

"Kill it, Boy! Oh yessss! Kill it!" Mother's voice rang out in the apartment and it felt to Martha that the walls were shaking with Mother's hideous cackle.

Suddenly she was active, moving like an evil spirit in the room.

"Ummmph, ummmph, ummmph, ummmmph," Joanna grunted loudly as she humped the floor with such force she developed a rug burn. "Ummph, ummmmph, ummmph… mmm!" she finally shuttered and her body stiffened. "I love you, Mother."

"Shut up, Boy! How stupid are you!"

The team of profilers watched and listened as Joanna transed the struggle between Mother and Abaddon.

"She knows your name, Boy!" Mother said as she rubbed his face with Joanna's right hand.

"No one knows us, Mother. I'm careful," Abaddon said while masturbating with Joanna's left hand.

"She can see us now, Boy! I told you that!"

"She knows I love her. She'll never..." he said and then looked down at Martha's dead body.

"Shut up! Stop it!" Joanna said as her head turned toward the table where nothing sat but a place setting. "It's 3:02 in the morning. Take me home. And shut that baby up, dammit!" Mother screamed.

"No, Mother!" Abaddon whispered.

"I only meant feed it and change its diaper," Mother said and then giggled. "I'll never let you hurt a baby, Boy."

Joanna stood and headed into the bathroom.

"Eric," Ronnie said, holding her watch up for him to see. It read 3:45 a.m.

Delores nervously looked at the white Capris Classic as it parked inside of the restaurant's parking lot.

"Mack, I-"

"Delores, stop that!" her husband said as he shook his head, reluctant to get into another futile argument.

"I'm just saying-"

"Woman, for the last three years we've known that man, and not once has he shown a violent bone, so just stop it."

"Oh yeah? What about Tony and Fat Boy? He destroyed them easily."

"Yup! For you, if I remember correctly. So stop it."

"But his name is-"

"Stop!" Mark barked. "Get his table ready."

"Hello, Delores!" Jesus breathed heavily as he rushed into the restaurant. "Here comes the big guy!" he said and then laughed before he sat down.

"Hey, Mack! Delores!" Michael smiled as he gave his usual greeting. Then he looked toward the table and sucked his teeth.

Jesus smiled and waved.

"Hey, Michael!" Mack yelled from the grill. But Delores rushed into the back and Michael felt her avoidance. For some reason, her feelings toward him had changed. He had no clue as to why.

"What'd I do?" Michael whispered to Mack, obviously offended and concerned. He always considered Delores a friend.

"It's not you, it's me," Mack lied, not wanting to feed into any dissension.

"Hey, Jeeeee-sus!" Michael yelled out, still feeling uneasy by Delores' reaction to him. But Mack had assured him that everything was all right, so he decided to go with that.

"Come on, Big Guy, how many times must I say it? It's pronounced like this… 'Hey-Zeus,'" Jesus said and then smiled, showing no impatience with his friend. "Besides, did you see the paper this morning?"

"Nope! Why?" Michael asked as he sat and dunked the tea bags one at a time.

"Oh nothing, Big Guy," Jesus said and then giggled, sliding the daily newspaper across the table with the headlines facing him. "Read that."

"I told you, Boy," Mother whispered in his ears. "Now everybody's gonna know."

Delores came from out of the back of the restaurant with herself back in character. "Hey, Big Guy," she said, and smiled as she walked up to the table.

"She knows, Boy. So does he! Look at them!" Mother whispered. "You can't let them live, or…"

Before anybody knew what happened, there was the blood-curling sound of Jesus's neck snapping.

Delores screamed and turned to run as the hands closed around her throat.

"Oh God, no! No, Michael!" Mack yelled and pulled out his .38 Smith and Wesson from his back pocket. He heard his wife's head as it slammed into the cement floor and burst like a melon.

"Oh, God, no!" Mack cried out, flipping open the gun, trying to load at least one bullet. Damn, Delores, he thought as the first shell fell to the floor. If she hadn't complained so hard about this gun it would have been ready.

"I will not have a loaded gun in this restaurant," Delores once told him.

Mack went up in the air, gripped by large hands and came down with his back broken on the granite counter top, signaling his demise.

"Kill him, Boy!"

Michael froze for a second as a tear rolled down his face. "Sorry, Mack," he whispered as the butcher's knife slammed into Mack's head and stuck in the counter.

"What happened here, Jack?" Detective Williams asked, thinking this was all deja vu.

"Three murders," he answered.

"Please say it's not the Jeffersons."

"Why? You knew them?" the officer said as he pointed to one of the covered bodies on the counter-top. He shook his head. "It's bad, Williams… messy."

"Worked an assault here last year around this time. Some Giant motherfucker named Michael Angel stopped two fellas from screwing with an old man and his wife."

"Well, he should have been here today. May have been a different outcome. This is bad. Shit." The officer shook his head again.

"That bad?" Detective Williams asked, lifting the cover from Jesus. His head had been nearly turned backwards. "Holy shit!"

"Wait until you see her."

The officer turned away as the detective lifted the sheet. He quickly recovered the exploded head of Delores. "Gun shot?" he whispered.

"Nope. Head slammed."

"And that one?" Detective Williams said as he pointed to the counter.

"Broken back, butcher through the head," Tim, the coroner said, shaking his head. "This city."

"Brotherly love, my ass," Detective Williams said as he picked up the Daily News from the floor. The headline froze him as he read.

MICHAEL, THE ANGEL OF THE ABYSS, STRIKES AGAIN

"Son of a bitch!" the detective screamed and rushed to his car.

"Goddammit!" Franklin Testervana yelled at the three-man crew loading the delivery truck. Today was bad for everybody. First he came in that morning alone because his wife's freaking stomach cramps sidelined the bitch. That left him with no clerk to confirm deliveries or make calls. Second, that little spic and his freaky big friend hadn't shown up. "Who's gonna deliver and install in the Northwest District?" he barked loudly, for the hundredth time that morning.

"Billy, call your sister. See if she needs a few extra hours this morning."

"She has classes in the morning."

"So what! Call her!" Franklin barked, not caring about what anybody else had to do. He needed his work done here.

Suddenly, the lot filled with police cars. No sirens, no lights, just fast moving police vehicles. Instantly, they all heard orders being shouted, guns, and moving feet.

"Down! Down! Down!" someone shouted as the whoosh of a helicopter was heard overhead.

The tall mailman climbed the porch divider that say in between both houses. His eyes studied the living room through the open curtain as he slowly pulled two envelopes from his bag. "Clear," he mumbled as if he was reading the names on the letters. "They're set."

"Alpha to field. Move in," Agent Eric ordered his team of extractors. The street seemed to quietly come alive as a team of ten assault agents dressed in tactical black moved up the steps, weapons ready. If you weren't aware of what the mailman really delivered, the sound of the two explosions would have terrified you.

"On three…. Two… one."

Two loud bangs came from both the front and back as both doors simultaneously flew off their hinges and crashed to the floor in a cloud of broken wood and dust.

The clatter was loud: "Move, move, move… FBI… FBI."

The shouting alerted the entire block, scaring the neighbors shitless.

"Clear!" one shouted.

"Clear," another echoed.

"Clear," the team shouted, one by one until the house was cleared room by room.

"I told you he wouldn't come back here," Joanna said as she entered the house. It all seemed so familiar and that depressed her more than anything. He's not going to make this easy, she told herself.

"Take the bedroom," Agent Eric told her.

"No, Eric… I need to see the basement." Then she looked down and her eyes focused. Suddenly, she was no longer Joanna.

In another room, Ronnie said, "Hi Mother," and lifted a picture from the mantel over the false fireplace. They all studied the picture of the dark skinned woman sitting in a hammock beside an army sergeant. Her hair was long, curly, and red. She wore bright red lipstick and large hoop earrings.

160

She wasn't that heavy in the picture, and Michael couldn't have been more than eight, but still her hands seemed to lay on his chest in a sexually suggestive manner as he stood in front of them.

"I wonder if it started that early?" Ronnie whispered. "The sexual molestation."

"No, she never touched me… him, until he turned old enough to…" Joanna began whispering. "Anyway," Suddenly she turned and headed for the kitchen like she already knew the layout, like nothing was a mystery to her.

Agent Eric and Detective Ronnie watched as Joanna pulled on a pair of workout gloves from the kitchen shelf. She pulled them on tightly and grabbed a power drink from the fridge.

"It's getting worse," Ronnie whispered as they followed Joanna down the stairs into a makeshift gym.

"Dammit, Eric," one of the extractors said as they entered the basement. "That's four-ninety!"

Without hesitation, Joanna slid under the weight, on her back. The agents all watched in doubt as she grunted under the strain.

"She can't possibly think-" the first agent began to say as Joanna pushed the weight into the air with ease. "I'll be damned!"

Eric pointed them toward the stairs, and silently mouthed for them to leave quietly.

Before the team turned to leave, Joanna had finished ten reps and easily placed the weight back on the rack. Standing, Joanna began to strip away her clothing, only to sit back under the weight, comfortably naked. Twelve reps came as easily as the first ten. She stood in the mirror and flexed.

"Boy, all them muscles and no brains," Mother's voice barked from Joanna's mouth. "But Mother still loves you, Boy." That was when Joanna caressed her own face.

"Now hurry and finish. Mother wants another one tonight."

Joanna dropped another plate on both sides.

A profiler stood with a camcorder, filming her every move.

"How?" Mother screamed. "Shit! What now?" she continued as Michael sat in his car a block away, watching the news crews, police, and neighbors crowd the small block where he lived, his hands feverishly working his middle.

"We need another car, Mother," he whispered.

"We need to kill that bitch!" Mother screamed. "She's always watching us, Boy! I know what it is. That bitch wants to be me! And you, too! That bitch is crazy!" Then Mother cackled. "Crazy bitch!"

Mother continued to cackle insanely as Michael pulled away.

It was her favorite ritual after a long night's work.

Bathe, then turn on the television. She would pull the blinds shut, then the curtains, and the cushiony softness of the quilt would feel so good against her skin while she melted into the bed. Not once would she have thought of the fact that she was completely naked. All that Donna knew was that if they didn't find her a man soon, her checking account would be overdrawn with the cost of D batteries and porno DVD's.

"Come here, Long Brown," Donna said and she settled into her nightly routine. She pulled the large vibrator from the nightstand. "It's just me and you, once again." That was when she sucked on the black, hard rubber, taking almost half of it into her wet mouth. Searching with her hand, she found the universal remote and pressed Play. Instantly, the 42-inch flat screen filled with a real porno star driving into the chubby sister on the floor, one she could identify with.

"That's what a bitch needs right there," Donna moaned and spread her thick, round thighs and rubbing the long vibrator on her pussy lips.

"Fuck me, Brian Pumper," Donna cooed along with the actress on the screen, and then the doorbell rang and stopped her sexy thoughts. She sat up straight, cursing somebody's poor timing. Quickly, she pressed MUTE and listened.

The doorbell rang again.

"What the fuck?!" she whispered. This is not the time, she told herself as she rushed to pull on her red silk Louis Vuitton robe, covering her thick, fleshly body.

"Just a moment," Donna said, knowing she would shoo the unwanted intruder away with the quickness. I should have put the Do Not Disturb sign on the door, she told herself and then laughed at her horny silliness.

Still, she took her time to step in front of the wall-to-wall mirrors to straighten her box braids and moisten her lips. Her eyes found the flat-screen just as super porno star Brian Pumper sank into the chubby girl from behind, giving her some serious back shots.

"Be right back, love," Donna said and then giggled, rushing to open the door.

"Who is it?" she asked pleasantly as she looked from the vestibule window.

He looked up and smiled and said, "How about lunch?"

Chapter Sixteen

THE INVOICES FROM Custom Mirrors and Frames littered the entire squad room. At least fifteen uniformed men and women searched the deliveries of Michael Angel and Jesus Garcia.

"1892 Pittsville," one woman officer yelled, holding up the invoice. It was the latest victim. "Who uses handwritten files anymore?" Ronnie whispered, reaching for the third victim's invoice on the list. They had already found every victim of last year's rampage in the files. The object was to separate all possible new victims. They knew his type, so the process of elimination would be fairly easy. It was the manpower that would cost the city. Overtime was welcomed by most. To that end, the mayor and city council had authorized two hundred added bodies for positive elimination work. Most officers would have to use their own vehicles, but the city would pick up the tab for the gas.

"Five in West Oak Lane," Joanna said as she held up the new possibles. The chubby white officer standing in line took the slips from her. "That's my district," he added quickly.

"Wait; two more," Agent Eric said as he handed the officer the invoices. The entire group had been instructed on what to look for in possible victims. The profile: between the ages of 25 and 40; weight no less than 135 pounds; height 5'5 or less; no less than 140 if taller, but no more than 170 at any height; brown skin and clean of drugs. Only problem was that too many women in the city fit the profile.

"Got four in Mount Airy," the captain said.

"That's my call," the young, black woman officer said, snatching up the invoices. "14th on the move," she said and smiled.

Joanna stood from her desk, but not unnoticed by Agent Eric and his team of profilers who kept their cameras and eyes on her at every moment. They needed every bit of documentation on the Trans that they could record. To them, she was a case study. It wasn't just the fact that she stood that alerted them, it was the way she flexed and cracked her neck every few seconds. Too bad the police woman who just stepped away from the captain's desk hadn't noticed.

Officer Phyllis Compton stood 5'6 tall and was about 135 pounds, solid. Just his type.

With a strength like she never experienced before, Joanna grabbed hold of Phyllis's neck and around her waist. Officer Compton screamed as she was raised into the air and slammed to the desk.

"I… am… Abaddon!"

"Shit!" the captain yelled as he knocked Joanna to the floor of the squad room with his shoulder. It took five detectives to hold Joanna down.

But it was too late for Officer Phyllis Compton.

Ding dong! The doorbell rang once again that afternoon, but this time Donna would not answer it. She was busy this time; she had her company.

She was his for the taking.

"Damn…" Donna smiled down as Michael rubbed himself up and down.

"That's…" she began and then swallowed and licked her lips. She always wanted a big one like that. "I mean… seeing one and taking it is two different things," she told him as she glanced over at her flat screen TV.

Michael just held out his right hand.

"Maybe I better get that…" Donna nervously whispered as the doorbell rang for the third time. She stepped toward the bedroom door.

Michael's speed was unbelievable. "No, don't," he said as he placed a kiss on her neck. "It's just Jesus, hating."

"The little Spanish guy?" Donna asked, recalling his partner, then giggling.

"Yup! He wasn't supposed to pick me up until four."

"Oh, so you were that sure of yourself?" Donna said as her hand caressed Glory, knowing she wanted him in her bed the first time she saw him. She was never shy around a man she liked.

"Weren't you?" he said, making her feel good about herself. Flattered that he saw her as a woman that got what she wanted. He boosted her confidence in herself and that made her want him even more. She felt herself getting wet for him.

Michael was listening to Mother as Donna continued to stroke him. Slowly his eyes looked down on her small moving hand.

"Well are you… ready?"

"I… damn… it's bigger than I've ever had."

"Maybe it's time to try something new."

"You can't just ram it in."

He couldn't help but notice her nervousness. Still, he could feel her body heat and knew she was ready.

The doorbell rang again.

"I'll go nice and slow," he promised her.

Her body shivered.

166

"I swear."

Donna moaned deeply as Michael covered her body with his, crushing her beneath his man weight.

"Thirteen in all," Agent Eric said.

"How many unnotified?" Detective Veronica Rawls said.

"Two or three. But we've set cars in front of those until we can locate and eliminate or identify them as possibles."

With a quick glance toward her partner Ronnie whispered, "We gotta-"

"She'll be under surveillance at all times," Agent Eric said, "But…" he took Ronnie's arm and led her outside where he could speak frankly.

"What is it?" Ronnie sad and then looked back at Joanna.

Agent Eric also looked back. "It's becoming real for her. She's becoming-"

"I know," Ronnie said, deeply saddened as she looked back at her lover and partner. "Maybe we should-"

"No, not yet. Let's see if she can lead us to Abaddon first."

"And that shit earlier?"

"Probably just a reaction to last night's murder," Agent Eric said, but he didn't seem confident at all.

Detective Rawls picked up on that and it made her feel even worse. Her partner had killed a woman, a fellow officer, and was not in jail. And had no remembrance of what she had just done. She was in her trance state, but a life had been lost and when Joanna found out it was she who had taken it, Ronnie had no idea how she would react. Would the guilt put Joanna in a funk she couldn't snap out of? Or could Joanna never recall what she had done and never have to absolve herself? But still, an officer was dead and that would have to be dealt with officially.

"I'm almost..." Donna cried out as she rode up and down on him.

She had chosen to be on top, out of fear. His overwhelming masculinity frightened and excited her.

"She's ours, Boy," Mother moaned into his ear. "Mmmmmmm... she's good, really knows how to ride a dick!"

Michael said nothing as her breasts swung over his face and he exploded for the second time inside of her.

"Please... I'm gonna..." Donna said as she sped up her rocking motions with her heavy hips, out of her mind with lust. He was drowned in her juices. She was stretched wide and loving it. I can take it! She thought. "God! Yes! Just..."

"She's gonna cum, Boy!" Mother cackled, highly amused at the salacious antics of the chubby girl going for her nut. "And when she does..."

"No!" Michael growled, being pulled between Mother and the girl that was giving him her all of her hot, wet, fleshy self.

"I gotta... I... gotta..." Donna moaned, misunderstanding his no. All she knew was that this was the best she ever had. She even thought she might squirt all over his dick and balls. Just like she had seen in her pornos. She was becoming that nasty porn star and she felt no shame. She was enjoying herself too much.

Donna moved her hips up and down as she fell forward, smashing her heavy soft breasts onto his rock hard chest. Her mouth found his and her vaginal muscles vibrated on his shaft. She moaned into his mouth as he held her hips down, her mouth parting slightly and almost on top of his. She had to let him know, "I'm cummmmiiiiinnng, Michael!"

"No," Michael whispered, once again trying to defy Mother's command.

"I think... I love you... Mich... Oh God... Michael!" Donna whispered, her voice raspy, all the strength rushing out of her body in the wake of her explosive orgasm, which was unlike any other orgasm she ever had. What's going on here?! She asked herself. Shit, this dick is too good!

Donna rested on his hard, wet chest. Greedily, she thought about round two as she felt his hips pump into her... even deeper this time. This man is gonna kill me, she thought.

"Ahhhhh, shit!" Donna cried out in pain. Her nails dug into his chest as she rose up to escape him. She tried to roll away from him, but he had a firm grip on her wide hips.

"Let me get myself together."

What she wanted to tell him was that her spirit was willing but her flesh was weak, but if he let her rest for a moment she might go at it again. But the reality was that she needed a nap before she took him on again. Unfortunately, he was ready to take her again, whether she was ready or not. Her dream lover suddenly became an evil, unfeeling sex monster.

Talk about too much of a good thing, she thought. Shit.

"You said you love me..." Michael whispered as he delved deep into her, going balls deep into her like the pornos she loved to watch.

"Please... Oh no... God..." Donna screamed loudly as Glory plundered her pink insides, pounding her like she was a piece of meat.

"I am.... Mmmmmm."

"Say it, Boy!" Mother cackled, enjoying herself although it was obvious that Donna wasn't enjoying herself. Boy was killing it and Mother couldn't have been happier. "Kill it and make her call your name!"

"I... I... I'm cumming!" he screamed as Mother cried in his ears. He wanted her love. He needed her love. He always wanted that. And this night he was so close! He just wanted to please her.

"Stupid son of Satan... yo dumb boy..." Mother continuously scolded as he split open Donna's body with his Glory.

Donna pushed up on him, determined to take it, no matter the pain.

"What the fuck?" Officer Zanidaski said as the woman's screams drifted from the home. Rushing to the driver's door, he pulled it open. "3514 to dispatch," he screamed frantically. The panic in his voice got an immediate response.

"Dispatch... go 3514."

"8116 Sharpneck... he's here! Inside!"

"Who's there 3514?"

Breaking protocol, Officer Zanidaski screamed, "Bitch, who else?! That goddamn Giant... Abaddon..."

"3514, this is 3519 in response.... 3514, this is 3522. 3514... 3514... 3514..." the response calls came in instantly, also breaking the protocols of his dispatch.

Officer Zanidaski ran toward the home's door. He tried the door and found that it was unlocked. He stepped into the home. "Shit!" he said to himself when he heard the scream coming from the bedroom.

"Oh Lord Jesus... Oh God... please," Donna cried out.

Officer Zanidaski slowly climbed the stairs with his gun out. His gun hand trembled as he reached for the bedroom door. When he opened the door and looked into the darkness, he said, "Freeze, goddammit!"

Instantly, Joanna rolled across her desk and raised her arms as if lifting someone. "I am Abaddon!" she screamed and brought the invisible person down across her knee. Then, just as quickly, twisted what seemed to be a neck breaking action.

"Oh no!" Agent Eric whispered as Ronnie closed her eyes, knowing another officer was dead.

"Kill that bitch, Boy!" Mother yelled as Joanna stood and rushed across the squad room.

Ronnie barely managed to move as Joanna broke another phantom neck and ran from the squad room.

"He's dead!" the duty officer growled, standing by his cruiser as the captain pulled up with the Feds on his tail.

"Who? The Giant?" he asked, jumping out of his car.

"No… Bobby Zanidaski… the bastard broke his neck and back." The duty officer turned away, crying.

"He didn't want to kill this one," Joanna whispered from the bed. "Zanidaski caused…"

"What, bitch!" an officer shouted from across the room. "Say it again…" he took a few steps her way. "Say it-" he began, but never saw the right hook that put him down, lights out.

"Get this piece of shit off my crime scene!" Captain Jackson roared, rubbing his knuckles. "Anybody else?" No one accepted the challenge.

"He didn't. Mother tried to convince him to and he fought her. It wasn't until…" she began, then looked down at the dead officer. "He has her car now. The white Capris Classic is two blocks north on Mt. Pleasant Street."

"Steven, Mary," Agent Eric ordered two members of his team to go find the car.

"I know where he's going," Joanna whispered. The entry room grew quiet. But she spoke no more as she sank to her knees to cradle the dead officer's head in her lap and began to cry. "I'm sorry, Bobby. So very sorry."

"She's sleeping," Ronnie whispered as she held a bottle of pills. "Demoral."

Agent Eric patted the sofa next to him, and Ronnie sat down and leaned her head against his shoulder. "Get some sleep," he suggested, but it was more like an order.

Ronnie didn't fight him as her eyes darted toward the bedroom where she just left Joanna. He likes me, she thought as she smirked and drifted off to sleep. It was a moment of peace she really needed.

"Goddammit! She's gone!" Agent Eric screamed.
Ronnie rolled to her side and then onto her feet,

"What?" she said as she looked at the clock on the DVD player: 5:42 a.m.

"Shit! Why ain't nobody wake me?!" she barked, suddenly realizing she had been asleep for almost six hours.

Then panic set in. "We gotta find her, Eric!" one of his team members said. It was plain to everyone there why.

It was Ronnie who told the tale: "She's going after him."

Or not, was the unspoken other reason.

"Maybe..." the profiler named Steven said.

No one wanted to face the fact that Joanna had become a monster herself and was on the prowl, seeking her own victims.

That thought made Ronnie sick to her stomach. "We got to find her," she whispered again to Eric.

Chapter Seventeen

Here I Come, Bastard

"**B**OY, I THINK YOU'RE crazy," Mother said and then cackled. "Oops! I know you're crying, Boy," she teased. She saw his empathy as a weakness, another reason to criticize him, to bring him down so he would remain under her thumb, under her power.

"Stop that, Mother," Michael said, taking it all in stride, even giggling at Mother's joke. He knew he had to be strong in front of her. Even though he was feeling things he would never share with her.

"They know who we are now, Boy…" Mother said, stating the obvious. "They know about Texas and that father of yours," Mother paused as Michael pulled the wood from the condemned motel door in the far corner.

"So?" he said and pushed the half-rotted door open only to put the wood back up in front of the door so it looked undisturbed.

"So? So?" Mother said and then slammed him on the side of his head. "That means the world knows... stupid! They'll find out what I've..."

"Say it, Mother," Michael said as he sat the two bags on the musky old bed. "What will they know, Mother?"

"You want me to say it, Boy? Alright, I'll say it." Their eyes met in the dusty mirror. "I made you a man, There, I said it, Boy." Then she let out a hideous cackle.

Michael bent to pull the cans of tuna from the bag. "You did more than-"

"Shut up you no good bastard!" That's when the can of tuna flew into the mirror. "I taught you about life, Boy! Not like your father..." Their eyes met in the shattered mirror.

"Mother, don't!" he yelled and shook his head, dismayed and irritated by her random acts of violence.

"Don't what, Boy. It wasn't me who tried to murder you and me! And why?" she teased, staring into his eyes. "Because he heard, Boy. He heard you and Glory doing what he could never do..."

"Stop! Stop! Stop!" Michael said, not wanting to hear this story, not wanting to be reminded of what he had done, what they had done. He wanted to put that behind him, but she would never let him forget. He slammed into the wall, covering his ears. "Please, don't!" he begged, but he knew she would never let him.

"He saw it, Boy!" Mother now whispered and smiled as she tormented him. "He saw how big and long! How deep you went inside me! How you shot your sperm into my belly while I screamed in ecstasy and agony all at once, Boy. And you know what? His dick was little!" Then Mother began to cackle loudly.

He didn't want to hear any of it. "Stop it, Mother," he shouted. He did everything in his power to forget that fateful day.

Father had come home unexpectedly while Mother was enjoying his Glory. When Father saw the truth, he tried to kill Michael first.

"Father, No!" Michael had shouted, but it was to no avail.

Mother got in the middle of the altercation, and Father snapped her neck before Michael could stop him.

"You killed her!" Michael had shouted, in a daze.

"That's something you will have to live with, Boy." Father's voice was scary, unlike anything Michael had ever heard before that day. "Let me go call an ambulance," Father said in disgust as Michael knelt over his dead mother, weeping.

Father disappeared into the kitchen to make the call.

A few moments later, Michael heard the gunshot that forever changed his life.

He ran into the kitchen, but it was already too late. Father was gone.

"Why, Boy! The truth hurts, don't it?" Mother taunted, knowing from his facial expression that he was reliving that day. "Besides, look where you got me," she said as she looked around, taking in her seedy surroundings.

"Ain't this the same place where…"

"Yes, Mother. I worked here last year with Jesus and his son."

"I kind of liked that runt," Mother said, then cackled. "He was funny."

"Stop, Mother," he said, tired of sparring with her, tired of her taking him on one guilt trip after another. And she never stopped, going on and on until someone died.

If someone would have been outside their door, they would have sworn there were two people behind the door, talking, a man and a woman. And if they listened closely they would've sworn it was a mother and her son. But no matter how hard they listened, they would have been wrong.

"Bitch!" he said and slapped her so hard her eye instantly swelled shut.

"No, Chris… don't… please," she begged, looking up at him from the floor.

"I said watch your damn mouth!" he said and reached down and lifted her from the floor by her hair. "What do you mean?" he asked and slapped her again, this time in her mouth. "I ain't doing it right?"

"I didn't mean it, Chris. You…" she began and then stopped to wipe her bloody mouth. "Baby you got the best-"

She never saw the kick coming until it cracked her ribs. "Aaargh," she cried out in pain.

"I know what you need! You been asking for this!" Chris said before he stormed out of the room.

When he left, she crawled toward the door.

Chris returned with a jar of Vaseline.

"No, Chris… please…" she begged, on her knees. "You know I don't like that. That hurts."

"Bitch… so I'm not fucking you right, huh?" he ranted as he pulled out his stubby penis and greased with the Vaseline.

Boom! Boom! Boom!

The pounding on the door halted the assault.

"Bitch, don't move!" he told her as he pulled his robe closed and threw the jar of Vaseline at her. He cleaned his hands on his robe.

"Who is it?" he barked and snatched the door wide open. The horror of what he saw and heard caused him to defecate.

"I am Abaddon!" Debra heard and climbed out the bedroom, screaming as Chris died alone.

"Help me, please!" Debra continued to scream as she banged on her neighbor's bedroom window. She was naked and battered. "He's here!"

"This doesn't fit," Agent Eric whispered as they studied the crime scene. On the floor was Christopher Tyler. His back and neck were broken and he was very much dead, but how did Debra Clark manage to escape the Giant, Abaddon? No, he thought. Something was off.

"Do you think it was…?" Ronnie whispered.

"No one saw the perp. And Debra swears she heard a manly voice."

"So have we!"

Then they knew who killed Christopher Tyler.

"Wake up, Boy. The sun is up!" Mother yelled. "It's time to think of how she's gonna die."

"She's not going to die," he whispered, sitting on the edge of the bed.

"What!?"

"I said she's not gonna die. There's no need."

"Boy?"

"Stop calling me Boy, Mother. I am Abaddon."

"Shut up, stupid! You're what I tell you you are! Now feed me and get your hand off your cock, Boy!"

"Abaddon," Michael whispered trying to have the last word, like an insolent child.

The slap came quick.

As he held his face, Mother said, "Shut up!"

All eyes were on her as she walked into the station house. She felt them watching her every move. When she approached her desk, she heard the whispers. Some called her insane, crazy murderer, killer. But the worst were those who pitied her. Ten years ago, she set out to prove to the world that Joanna Staley needed no help. She could take care of herself in any situation. But now they doubted her.

"Jo Jo," her uncle whispered as he came from his office. "Come inside my office. We need to talk."

It wasn't what he said that infuriated her so much, but how he said it. With so much pity, so much love.

"Damn right!" she barked, staring into the eyes of the closest detectives. "Get the hell away from me, Mike!" she snapped.

"Sure doll, sure. I still love you."

"Sorry, Mike," she said and then kissed his cheek. He of all the cops still had her back.

"Sit down," the captain ordered. Without looking up, he tossed his manila file across his desk. "Remember Debra Clark?"

Picking up the file, Joanna opened the manila folder. A photo of a woman was attached by a paper clip to the left side of the front cover. Her face was so battered her eyes were just a mask of black, her lips split and bloody. Under the picture was the name Debra Clark, age 31, black female. VICTIM was printed in bold type.

"Yeah, I remember her," Joanna said and then closed the file. She had been beaten so bad her jaw needed reconstruction and she suffered a detached retina. Her so-called lover had also sodomized her repeatedly until a neighbor heard her screams of anguish and called for help. When the officers arrived and found her semi-conscious, the bastard was still inside of her anal cavity.

"Remember the perp?"

Joanna nodded, still reading through Debra's file.

"Well, last night Abaddon broke his spine in two different places, then twisted his head around one hundred and eighty degrees."

"So!" she said, smirking. "He was a no good bastard."

"That's not it…" the captain said as he sat up and fixed his gaze on her face, looking into her eyes. "He didn't touch Debra Clark."

"Maybe she's not his type," Joanna said and then giggled nervously.

"That's the other thing. She's thin and light-skinned. That's not his usual M.O."

Suddenly standing, Joanna stared down into her uncle's eyes. She was now catching the drift and didn't like it.

"Just say it, Captain!" Joanna yelled. The shadows of a large man hovering outside came through the window, making her aware of the department's fear of her. His assumption was unmistakable. "You think I did this, right?"

"Where did you disappear to last night?"

"Fuck you!" she roared as she moved toward the door.

Suddenly it opened and a police officer stepped into the office.

"Captain, he's been spotted in the northeast," the officer said.

"Move!" Joanna said as she pushed him aside. He hit the floor, unable to stand under her unexpected strength.

"Joanna Staley, get back here!" the captain shouted. "Dammit, detective. Get off my floor!"

"Yes Ma'am, all forty thousand," he said and then smiled at the white girl in the credit union. "I am moving back to Alabama."

"Sorry to hear that, Mr. Wilford. I really enjoyed your visits," she said and then smiled. "How would you like your money?"

"Fifties and twenties, Joyce, and please call me Abe."

"Well, Abe," Joyce said and then looked around to see if anyone was listening. "We could have had some fun if we met somewhere other than my job," she whispered, placing the bills on the counter as he loaded them into his gym bag.

"Is there a problem, Joyce?" one of the two security guards asked with his hand on his sidearm.

"Oh no, Jason," Joyce giggled. "Mr. Wilford is just closing out his account." She smiled again as she placed the last stack of fifties on the counter.

"Yeah, whatever!" the guard said, becoming super aggressive. "We know who he really is. Place your hands on the counter, motherfucker!"

Michael placed the last stack of money into his pocket and winked at Joyce. "Sorry, beautiful. What you are about to see will not be pretty."

"Jason, Bradley, what are you two-" she froze as the Giant turned with such speed she barely heard him move until she heard the snap of Bradley's arms and his scream as Abaddon used him to ram Jason down onto the ceramic tile floor, instantly breaking his neck.

Lifting Bradley once more, but this time over his head, Abaddon grinned as he brought the helpless man's head down on the edge of the countertop.

Screaming, Joyce passed out as the brain matter covered her face and chest, just before darkness took her to another place. From afar she heard that growl as it said loudly, "I AM ABADDON!"

"No way!" Ronnie whispered as they watched the security footage from the credit union surveillance cameras.

"That's fast, Eric," Steven said, watching the Giant totally destroy the two beefy security guards.

"Was it him?" Joanna asked, stepping into the monitor room of the credit union. All eyes turned toward her. "Don't!" she warned, taking a seat as Ronnie looked at her, puzzled.

"Fuck that!" Ronnie barked. "I'm not trying to hear that. I am not gonna have you waltzing in here like everything is okay. Where the fuck have you been? And why did you take off out the window? This madness has got to stop!"

The room grew silent as their eyes met. No one else spoke as the two partners filled the room with their tension.

"Well?" Ronnie demanded, obviously not willing to let this go.

"I don't..." Joanna tried to whisper but tears overtook her, making her mute. "Shit, Ronnie... I'm losing my mind," she said when she found her voice.

Ronnie reached out and pulled her into her arms and held her tight.

Joanna's sobs were raw and heartbreaking, reminding everyone in the room of a lost child.

"Please… don't let me hurt anyone…" Joanna cried softly into her partner's shoulder. "Promise me you'll do it, Ronnie. I'll get him. I have to get him. He can't be allowed to go on."

Ronnie began to cry with her.

"Don't let me turn into a monster," Joanna said, still holding onto her partner, her friend.

"I… I… promise, Jo," Ronnie said and cried even harder and louder. Then she led Joanna out of the monitor room.

"That car ain't no more good use to us, Boy!" Mother yelled as they crossed Torresdale Avenue. "You can bet they have the plates and color…" she began and then paused and smiled. "There!" she pointed out, raising his arms as her own voice came from his mouth.

Michael looked down the long row of used car dealerships on car lot row.

"Quickly, Boy… that one there!" Mother pointed to the third car lot up the street. "See that sign?"

"No questions asked," Michael read aloud, rushing toward the car lot.

"Howdy young fella," the old white man said and smiled, offering his hand to Michael. "Let me guess… truck?" he said as they shook hands. "I'm Bob of Bob's No Hassle Used Cars. My motto is No Hassles or Heckles. Just Sales." Then he laughed.

Looking around, Michael spotted the black on black Tahoe. "Good, Bob, because I need that!" and he pointed and walked toward the shiny five year old SUV.

"And at ten-five it's a steal. All aluminum, alloyed wheels, fully loaded. Only forty-five thousand miles. I'll tell you what… tags and a full tank of gas on Bob's."

"I'll take it," Michael said as two police cars shot by with lights flashing, but no sirens.

"Good, good. Now there is a bank-" Bob tried to ask as Michael started to pull cash from his bag. "Alright, cash then. Come this way, son."

"Name's Thomas. Troy Thomas," Michael told him.

Forty-five minutes later the shiny black Tahoe pulled past the red Toyota Corolla surrounded by police.

"See, Boy…" Mother cackled. "Listen to Mother and we'll be fine. Now let's find us someone for tonight."

She opened the door after seeing Tommy standing there looking so helpless and lonely. Ronnie's first thought was to close the door when she stepped outside, but to her surprise, he as faster than she thought.

"Joanna!" he yelled, moving toward her room.

"No, Tommy! Stop… wait," Ronnie whispered as Agent Eric stood from the couch.

"Sorry, son, but-" Agent Eric said as he reached for Tommy's arm. Without warning, Agent Eric was tossed to his back with the Jiu Jitsu move of a second degree black belt.

"Joanna… it's me…" Tommy said as he continued to move toward the room.

"Damn!" Agent Eric moaned. "That kid's fast." He sat up, rubbing his lower back.

"Dammit, Tommy. Stop this instant!" Ronny yelled as Joanna stepped from her bedroom in a trance. Just as Tommy reached for her, she ran into the kitchen. He froze as he heard the voice.

"I AM ABADDON!"

"God no!" was all that Phyllis Clark could scream as the Giant came from the bedroom closet. It all happened so fast that her scream seemed to fade into empty space. His large hands covered her mouth as her feet left the floor.

"Mmmmmm," he moaned as he pressed into her back.

"No! No! No! Boy!" she screamed loudly. "She's fat, Boy! Not like me… Mother was never-"

"She's just right, Mother," Abaddon said and then smiled into the mirror at Mother as he ran his hand ran over her large nipple. The water felt so good on his fingertips.

"And she's too black, Boy," Mother yelled back.

"She's perfect, Mother," he replied as Phyllis's eyes took in the scene of both voices coming from the naked Giant that held her from behind. So loudly she tried to scream, but his hand blocked the sound from escaping her mouth. She tried to bite him but his hand was held tightly over her mouth.

"Where did you find this one, Boy?" Mother wanted to know and cackled as he grinded into her soft, wide butt.

"I don't know, Mother," Abaddon whispered as his hand traveled from Phyllis's thick chocolate colored nipple to her throat. "She was just there."

Phyllis knew who he was and prayed for a quick death. She so badly needed air as his hands squeezed her throat. Her last thought before she passed out was of her .35 Glock M&P, sitting on the nightstand.

Looking up at the red numbers of her alarm clock, Gloria Velendez cursed Bob Thortonson. Who else could it be? She thought, looking to her right as Joshua slept with his beautiful cock ready once again. Slowly she reached for the cell phone and answered, turning her back to her new black lover. "Yeah, Bob?"

"Hah, hah, bitch!" The cackle startled her. "So you're waiting on that old nincompoop to call? You're a whore, girl."

"Oh God... Mother?" Gloria almost screamed, causing Joshua to wake. She felt him roll toward her but her mind was paralyzed. She felt the probing of his member as it slipped easily inside her walls.

"You whore, who do you think it is?" Mother cackled again. "Listen to him enter this whore. And tell the world..."

Gloria pressed RECORD on her Bluetooth as Joshua pinched her peach colored nipple from behind. She didn't want this but despite of that her body began to react.

"Listen, you whore, while my boy has his way with her!" Mother almost yelled as Abaddon's voice filled the phone with a growl.

"I am Abaddon!"

In the background, the woman was heard screaming as he grunted over and over again.

Gloria knew he was violating her body as she died. Her body was continuing to be manipulated by Joshua who moved from her nipple down to the vee between her legs, rubbing down and then pushing his finger into her shaved vagina, making her squirm but not because she was uneasy. She was actually pushing into his hand, allowing his fingers to dig deep into her. Then she shook in ecstasy as she cried out and climaxed along with Abaddon.

"Ummmmph! Ummmmph! Ummmmph!"

As she gave into the animalistic sounds of Abaddon's invasion upon the innocent, her lover turned her onto her back and mounted her, entering her body with his manhood and pounding her into submission.

God forgive me, she prayed silently and shook again.

"7681 Briar Road… hurry!" Captain Jackson ordered as he jumped from his bed.

"Honey?" his wife questioned, worried it was Joanna, his niece.

"It's that monster," he told her, rushing from his room in pajamas with only his gun and car keys.

Joanna had given him the address.

"That's eight blocks from here!" Ronnie screamed, rushing toward the car. She and Agent Eric would rush to the officer's aid while his team remained behind to watch and listen to Joanna for more information.

"It's the cops, Boy!" Mother whispered as they looked out the window of Phyllis Clark's home.

"How?" Abaddon said and then frowned, lifting the .35 Glock out of the window. He unloaded five shots and then dropped the gun.

"It's that bitch, Boy" Mother yelled as they headed toward the bathroom "She's gotta die!"

"Open the skylight!" Mother said, then cackled, caught up in all the excitement.

"The roof, Eric! He's using the skylight!" Steven said as he and the rest of the team watched Joanna moving around the apartment.

"The rooftops!" the radio roared as Captain Jackson turned onto Briar Road.

"Get him!" he barked into the microphone as he skidded to a halt. "He's coming down the drain pipes on the corner of 74th and Briar!" Without waiting, the captain jumped from his car, like he was jumping out of an airplane, with that intensity. He was a man entering a war zone because of this evil Giant, Abaddon.

"Freeze, you son of a bitch!"

Hitting the ground, Abaddon smiled as he darted to his right, into the darkened driveway. The shot sailed wide.

"Shit!" Captain Jackson cried out. "He's on foot! I'm in pursuit, down the driveway of Briar Ro-" the transmission cut out.

"Tell them..." Abaddon said, laughing as the captain screamed. "I cannot be stopped... I am Abaddon... King of the Abyss!"

The captain's eyes lost focus. The pain was too great and he could not breathe. The last thing he saw was the smiling face of Abaddon just before everything went black.

Chapter Eighteen

Face Your Maker, Woman

THE SIXTH FLOOR was too crowded. The staff of the Albert Einstein Trauma Center were upset but knew better than to complain. An officer had been injured by the Giant, another raped and killed. There was no regard for regulations or rules and to voice any objection would only cause more grief to the staff.

"What's she doing here?" the tall black uniform said with disgust as Joanna stepped from the elevator.

"Say it again and I'll break your face!" Detective Mike Bosey yelled. Two more detectives stood beside him, showing solidarity, and brotherhood. "As a matter of fact, get the fuck ghost." And when the officer didn't move, he yelled, "Now!"

The uniformed officer left, highly embarrassed.

"Hey, Jo," Mike whispered, letting her know that he still wanted her around and that he was defending her right to be in the squad room.

The panic was in Joanna's eyes as she rushed toward the hospital's waiting room to be with her aunt. The first thing she asked was, "Is he…"

"We don't know just yet," Mike said as he helped clear a path for her.

"Jo Jo!" her aunt cried out to Joanna as she entered the waiting room. "They won't tell me…" she began and almost fell to the floor before Joanna caught her easily and carried her to a seat.

"Abaddon spared him for me," Joanna whispered in resignation, knowing she was still under the spell of the Giant.

"Who?" her aunt asked in shock, but got no answer. Only a blank stare.

Ten minutes later the doctors emerged, flanked by the commissioner and mayor, both of whom had just arrived and sat with the family.

"Mrs. Jackson, he's asking for you," the doctor said with a smile.

"Is… is my husband…"

"Besides a broken collar bone and bruised eye, he's fine, Mrs. Jackson."

Suddenly Dorothy Jackson swooned and fell to the floor.

"She's gotta die, Boy! That bitch!" Mother said forcefully and tossed a can of Red Bull across the room. "I wasn't finished, Boy!"

"Neither was I, Mother," Michael said as he continued to masturbate with his left hand.

"Shut up! And stop that, Boy! We need to leave this city… now!"

"No!" he shouted, defiantly, his mounting frustration turning to anger.

"No what?" Mother growled at the mirror. "She's too close!"

"I'm not leaving the city, Mother. Not yet at least."

"Then kill that bitch! Fuck her if you want, but kill the bitch... and stop that... mmm, Boy... we need to finish!" she moaned and exploded on the floor of Abaddon's motel room. Instantly, their eyes met with the pretty, young prostitute tied to the bed.

Abaddon smiled and charged toward the bed as if he was running a 40-yard dash. Stopping only short of entering her body to whisper into her face the terrifying words of an insane monster. "I am Abaddon!"

The blade cut into the carotid artery and down to her spine.

The room filled with animalistic grunts as he searched for relief.

The team all sat and watched as Joanna finished off the second pizza alone. She belched and stretched and reached for what was left of the salad. She and Ronnie stayed away from everybody in a corner of the room. They didn't want to be there, but they couldn't take their eyes off of Joanna. And they were on full alert if she decided to strike out again.

"Damn, Jo," Ronnie said and then smiled, struck by how her partner devoured her food.

"I'm hungry. Besides, she would never let him eat nothing like that," she said and then giggled. "Always... vegetables this... and salad that... peanut butter, protein, vitamins this... I like pizza!" she exclaimed and belched again.

"So?" Ronnie said and then smiled innocently.

"So what?" Joanna said as she scratched her private area.

"Where is he?"

The room was totally silent while Agent Eric and his team listened.

"You asked me where I went the other night, remember?" Joanna offered and looked Ronnie in her eyes. "Well, I went to see if he was there."

"Was he?" Ronnie wanted to know.

"I think he was. I waited for him to show himself, but woke up at the station, not knowing how I got there."

"So, you gonna tell us?"

"Why? So they can lock him up and conduct some kind of case study? Fuck that…" she said and looked into Ronnie's eyes. "You made me a promise," she whispered as if they were engaged in some kind of conspiracy.

"Joanna, I…" Ronnie began and then it was her time to stare.

"No godammit!" she yelled. "You can't let me become…" Joanna said and then jerked her head toward the profilers.

"I swear, Jo, I won't…" Ronnie said as her tears told the truth. She wouldn't betray Joanna's trust. She would not let Joanna become a monster even if she had to kill her.

"Then I'll keep my own promise tonight," Joanna said and then smiled deviously, letting her lover know tonight was the night they would lose themselves in the warmness of their flesh. "Just you and I alone, girl."

"It'll never happen again!" Agent Eric roared. "No way in hell! Forget about it," he added as he paced back and forth.

"Wait, I don't work for you, or the FBI!"

"That's where you're wrong, beautiful. I can lock you and Detective Staley away until… let's say you haven't seen what I can do yet."

"Just hear me out, Eric… please," she whispered. "If you let her lead us to him and then move in-"

"Hell no! What part of 'too damn dangerous' can't you understand? I don't want anything to happen… no!"

"Is there something you're not saying here, because I'm confused. We got a chance to catch this bas-"

Without warning, Agent Eric pulled Ronnie into his arms and kissed her. Their tongues met as she pressed her body against him tightly. Slowly, he pulled away.

"There, I said it!" he barked. "No! Not gonna happen!"

"Listen to me, Eric," Ronnie said, breathing heavily, caught up in the moment of passion. "We can use this to… shit!" she exclaimed as she slammed her body back against his. Their mouths met again and they began to pull at each other's clothes until they both were naked.

"Let's see what you think of me after this," Ronnie moaned as she melted under the heat of passion.

"I can take it," Agent Eric let her know. "I'm a big boy!" He smiled as she pushed him on his back, moving him aggressively, being that take charge woman.

"Oh… this is going to be so good," Ronnie groaned as he entered her and stretched her, finding welcome in her hot wetness.

"Hey, you!" the watchman yelled as he came around the side of the motel. "You ain't-" he began and stopped as he noticed the body of the dead hooker cradled in the Giant's arms. He mumbled, "Oh shit… oh shit…" as he tried to escape back around the side of the building. The way he saw it, she was beyond hope and he needed to save himself. But at age 59, his speed was no match for Michael's.

The Giant ran him down in the daylight.

"Please… don't…" he begged as he felt the hands close around his neck from behind.

"Boy, he shit his pants," Mother cackled. "Open that window."

"No, Mother," Michael said as he looked around at the traffic.

"You've been saying that a lot lately," she said as he spied her in the side-view mirror.

"What's that, Mother," he said and smirked into the mirror. He knew where she was coming from, where she was headed. And he knew that Mother hated to be defied; Mother needed to be in control at all times.

"No!" Mother shouted. "Boy, you starting to disrespect Mother's wishes a lot!"

"So?" he laughed.

The slap sailed by his face, barely missing him, another reason for Mother to be displeased with him.

"How dare you!" Mother yelled. "Alright," she said and suddenly smiled. "Goodbye, Boy. You're on your own." And just like that, he felt her leave.

The Tahoe was silent for ten minutes. Michael's eyes darted to the rear-view mirror every few seconds until he couldn't take it anymore. "Mother..." he whispered nervously. Still, no one answered. "Mother... I'm sorry." But still no answer. He tried not to panic, but he realized he needed Mother. "Mother!" he said louder.

Michael looked to his left door armrest. Quickly he rolled down the window in hopes that because he was doing as she requested Mother would answer and he would get back in her good graces.

Still there was no answer.

"Mother... please..." he whispered again. Still, no answer. He didn't even feel her presence anymore. It was like she was asleep somewhere far away from him. He had never felt that way before. It felt like there was something final in Mother's departure. He felt like... she would never return. And that thought made him break out in a cold sweat.

What have I done? He asked himself.

Five minutes later, he pulled into Fairmount Park, off of City Line Avenue. There was something still guiding him.

"Over there, stupid," she said quietly. "By the concession stand, Boy."

He was elated.

Mother smiled, knowingly. She knew he still needed her. It was just an example of youthful rebellion, a spark of defiance, but they were now back on track. They understood each other and that was their strength, their hedge against anything that would come at them. They knew that two was better than one, always.

"I love you, Mother," he rushed to say which was his way of apologizing and he felt that Mother knew that. He never wanted to lose Mother.

"And you better remember that, Boy," Mother let him know.

"Do you still want me to leave the city, Mother?"

Looking into the mirror, Mother whispered as her hand massaged his chest. "Not until after she dies. Somehow she's found a way to watch us. I can feel her watching me, Boy. Us."

"But…" Michael began and then stopped, not wanting to upset Mother.

"Are you listening, Boy?!" Mother screamed. "They're using her to find us. She can't be allowed to live!"

"I…know," Michael had to admit. Mother was right. Mother was always right. "I know…" he had to agree.

"The original Timex Road, 8:30pm," Ronnie spoke plainly. The agent in the corner of the white van gave a thumbs up.

"Listen Ronnie. Every few blocks, relay the intersection and all turns with a right or left," Agent Eric reminded her.

"She's good, Eric," the wiring tech said. "She'll never spot us. We won't be within two blocks of her car. The GPS will guide us with your help."

"I'm ready," Ronnie said as she checked her watch.

"Remember-"

"Stop it, Eric!" she cautioned and then laughed. The afterglow of the way he had made her feel was still with her. She felt invincible, in total control. She was that badass bitch, channeling her inner Foxy Brown.

Detective Veronica Rawls climbed from the van and into her car. Unconsciously, she reached for the Glock at her hip and then the two-shot Derringer on her ankle. She felt secure that the evolution explorers she loaded into her weapons could stop a horse, or a giant like Abaddon. Her firepower could even stop Joanna, but she didn't want to dwell on that. Still, she had to admit that her partner posed as a threat to her fellow officers and herself. Slowly, Joanna was becoming that monster that they all feared.

Detective Rawls frowned as she pulled into the parking lot of Joanna's complex. Her eyes adjusted to the crowd of news vans and reporters surrounding the apartment. She couldn't help thinking how parasitic they looked.

"A bunch of freakin' pariahs," Ronnie barked loudly as one of them approached her Impala. "Move!" she shouted as she opened her door.

"Why the special treatment of Gloria Velendez? Does it have anything to do with her wrongful arrest last year?" a reporter yelled.

Then more rushed her way for answers.

"I said, move out of my way, or…" Ronnie said, squinting evilly at those gathered around her.

As she spoke, an ABC camera accidentally hit her in the face as the cameraman pushed and shoved for shots of one of the lead detectives. She was just collateral damage; nothing personal.

"Damn shit!" Ronnie hissed under her breath, holding her head where a small knot had formed. She climbed back into her car and called for backup. Moments later, five patrol cars arrived and she got out of her vehicle.

"That one there!" Ronnie yelled, pointing at the cameraman who an officer slammed into the hood of his car. As the cameraman was bent over with his face pressed into the car's hood, she said, "You're under arrest for assaulting an officer. I warned y'all! Now back up, because I am not playing. This shit is too serious!"

"It was an accident, Detective. We all saw it," someone from The Enquirer said.

"Good, then you'll be called as a witness," the uniformed officer said, taking his name down in a small notebook.

The other reporters tried to get away, but were caught up in the dragnet by the four other officers.

"Fuckin parasites!" Ronnie shouted as she and Joanna drove off. Looking over at her partner who hadn't said more than two words since leaving the house. "Where to?"

"South… take the Lincoln Drive, east side," Joanna told her.

"So he's in South Philly?" Ronnie asked.

"Nope. Just wanted to ride for a while before…" Joanna began but didn't need to finish the statement. They both knew what she planned on doing.

Thirty minutes and miles away from any reporters, Ronnie looked over once again as they traveled in silence. "Jo…" she began.

"Ronnie, please. Just drive!"

"Where? I've been driving for a while now."

"Jump on the expressway. Go north," Joanna said, again staring out of the passenger side window. It was then that Ronnie understood. She was watching.

"So we're there now, huh?" Ronnie said, sounding hurt like her partner was leaving her out of something, not telling her the whole story. Making her feel like she didn't deserve full disclosure.

"Not you and me…" Joanna said, watching. "I'm hungry. Let's eat." Suddenly, her attitude changed.

"If I turn onto Broad Street, we can eat at Mama Rosa's." Ronnie told her

"Naw, let's stay on the expressway. Let's hit Benny the Bum's on Red Lion Road." Joanna smiled out the passenger side window. It went unnoticed by her partner who also didn't notice the white van that stayed three cars behind them.

I see you, she said to herself.

The steaming bucket of crab legs set down by the waitress smelled delicious and Ronnie watched as Joanna dug in with both hands and feasted. As usual, the white mussels accompanied them, and both women gorged themselves.

"So how much longer we gonna play Driving Ms. Daisy?" Ronnie said and then laughed at her own quip. She looked up and saw that the clock on the wall read 11:20 p.m.

"Why... do I scare you now?"

"Come on, bitch," Ronnie said and then giggled, but Joanna could only hear it in her tone. "I'm just..."

"No, you're not," Joanna said and laughed along with her, sounding more sure of herself than her partner did. "You're afraid that I'm gonna go all Abaddon on you and shit."

"Fuck him! It's that giant ass cock I'm afraid of, goddamn, if truth be known!" Ronnie said, then held her hands two feet apart as if measuring the Giant's penis.

"Tell me about it!" Joanna said as she rubbed her stomach. "I'm still afraid of that dick."

Ronnie wished she hadn't brought it up as Joanna stood. But the light was back in Joanna's eyes and that had to be a good thing.

"See what you caused?" Joanna said and then giggled like she was blushing and grabbed a breadstick and held it up to symbolize the Giant's intimate member. "Now I gotta pee." She slid from the large semi-circular booth. Be right back, you freak."

While Joanna went toward the restroom marked Gals, Ronnie spoke softly. "She's stalling for some reason, Eric. I think she may have spotted you."

"He says there's no way," the young redhead said, placing the receipt on the table. "He said to just keep your eyes peeled for her changes. And Steven said save him some of those mussels."

Ronnie placed her credit card on the tray and smiled, then said, "Can you place an order for him on me?"

The young agent smiled and disappeared without another word. The credit card was returned by a short, chubby girl.

"Kiss me, Boy," Joanna said and smiled and pulled Tommy into her arms. Her lips parted and she softly pushed her tongue into his mouth. Her hand slowly slid up his thigh until it was there, rubbing him erect. They pulled apart.

"So where are we going?" he asked from the passenger seat.

"We ain't going nowhere. You're going home and I'm going to work."

"Wait! You made me drive your crazy super-charged car completely across the city, for what? A ride home on the bus? I thought…"

"You thought right, just not right now," she said, then kissed him again. "Now that you're eighteen, we can play openly; do us. So when I get off of work, be ready."

Her eyes went for his erection and so did her hand, stroking his length and squeezing the thickness. "What's my name, Boy?" she said and then cackled.

"Mother," Tommy answered.

She handed Tommy a fifty dollar bill. "Take a cab, Boy."

The change came on unnoticed by him because he was blinded by his hormones.

"I love you, Mother," he smiled and kissed her again.

She smiled and said, "I know, Boy."

"Black female wearing blue jeans; blue, red, and white cross trainer Nikes; a red and white polo, three button; her hair may be in a ponytail under a Phillies ball cap. Remember, she is an officer of the law… but not… I repeat… do not take any chances," Agent Eric Wilson, Jr. said over the radio. "She should be on foot. Approach only with backup and use extreme caution."

Slowly, Agent Eric turned to Ronnie. "She can't be very far."

"She's gone, Eric," Ronnie said, feeling deep guilt, like she had blown another opportunity to help her partner. "She'll try to kill him alone." She turned away to hide her fear.

"We'll find her, Ronnie," he promised, sounding far from confident. But he gave her the hope she needed and the space to contemplate her next move. She didn't want this to end in tragedy.

The darkness was almost complete, except for the bluish glow of the flat screen TV that sat up on the bedroom wall. There was no sound coming from the CNN broadcast.

"Harold..." Vivian whispered as tears rolled down her cheeks. "Oh Harold, answer me."

"Shhhh!" the Giant growled from the high-back chair. His eyes studied hers in the darkness. "You are forever joined in the Union," he stared as he masturbated.

"Please... please don't hurt him anymore."

"He'll never feel again, whore!" Mother cackled. "Now shush that noise. Stop that, Boy," she suddenly yelled at Abaddon. "Mmmmmmmmm... what a waste of your... mmmm... and... seed."

Suddenly he exploded.

"Oh God help Your servant in her time of..." Vivian began to pray although she knew she would die. She knew all about Abaddon, this Giant.

"He ain't listening, girly," Mother cackled.

"God is always listening, Mother," he whispered as his eyes met Vivian's. "Do you believe in God?"

Without answering, Vivian continued to pay, "Our Father, who art in heaven..."

Mother smiled, then said, "I don't like my hair like that."

The suburban rails were dark as she crossed them, but she knew this was the only way. It was hard to focus as the scene of Vivian's mutilation and rape flashed into her mind. Twice she had hit the ground with orgasmic spasms.

"Somebody said... I was living in life," she hummed, not exactly getting it right as she climbed down the embankment.

To anyone else the wood that covered the door would have seemed impossible to break through, but she tugged at it twice and it came loose.

She continued to sing as she pulled the board back into place.

"All this bullshit..." she sang along and laid in the bed.

"Ummmph! Ummmph! Ummmph!" she cried out as she humped the bed, looking into the broken mirror at Mother.

"Stop! Stop! Stop!" Ronnie yelled as they drove up Knights Road slowly. "Son of a bitch!"

"What is it?" Agent Eric said as he pulled two cars in front of Joanna's Dodge Charger.

"It's her goddamn car!" Ronnie shouted and then leapt from the van. She and every tech in the van walked to the car. Inside was a bag on the floor of the back seat, and on the front seat was an empty can of energy drink.

"It's open!" Steven said as he opened the door. They found a bag inside holding the clothes she had on, down to her sneakers.

"She's changed," Ronnie whispered as she looked around at the surroundings. Her eyes focused on a can of Red Bull by the bushes.

"Didn't it say that Michael lived or worked somewhere..." Agent Eric said as he rushed back to the van and his laptop.

The Tahoe pulled onto Neshaminy Terrace and parked.

"Hurry, Boy! The sun's about to come up!" Mother said. "There's no need to be seen by those nosey, rich, sons of bitches."

Michael knew she was right as he climbed from the SUV. Looking around, he quickly decided it was clear and no one would notice him pushing into the bushes. On the other side, the suburban train passed at speeds of 55 miles an hour. He knew there was no need to be worried about anyone recognizing him from onboard.

"Stop lollygagging, Boy," Mother whispered as he made the half-mile walk down the tracks. Finally, he came to the green circuit box which marked the path down the embankment into the empty lot of the old Lincoln Inn motel.

"Stop," Mother whispered. "Did we leave it like that, Boy?" she asked nervously as she scanned the empty lot.

"Yes, Mother! Besides, no one knows about this place but us. Besides, this is a different room."

"She may have been watching us again, Boy… that bitch! If you wasn't so dick happy, you would have killed her that day!" Mother continued to complain as Michael pulled the board loose to enter his abandoned room. He knew it was time to let Mother take control, so he could rest.

Joanna's eyes opened instantly as the bump startled her from her nap. Her eyes found the can still leaning where she had left it, against the rotting door. She heard the thump again as she held onto the .40 caliber Glock M&P.

Then there was a clink.

Slowly, Joanna's eyes turned toward the wall and she smiled. "Good morning, Mother," she whispered.

"This room is much better," Mother whispered, standing in the full mirror, doing her hair. The red wig fell to Michael's shoulders as he brushed the curls.

"You sleep, Boy? Mother has to make sure she's presentable. You never know if your father will decide to come back," she said and then smiled, turning toward the bed. "He loved this shade on me, especially when I gave him head." She giggled at that nasty thought.

"He would just lie there staring up at me in these mirrors until… blam!" she shouted, using her hands to express orgasmic release. "He wasn't as long as you though… as fat either. But he had you beat on eating pussy, Boy!" she continued and then giggled hideously from Michael's lips and began to hum.

Turning back toward the mirror, Mother asked, "What was that?"

"Did you love him?" Michael mumbled.

"Well…" Mother said, then paused. "I did in a way… but I was more in love when we brought you home." She smiled at the memory of the day they adopted Michael. "You were so cute in that cowboy getup. And tall to be only eight years old. You know I was fifteen when he took me from that… well, never mind that. But I was still a pure virgin. Pure… never even been kissed. He used to tell me how beautiful I was. Brought me all these beautiful things. And God… when he took me down to Mexico and married me," Mother said as her hand went to her chest like she was swooning.

"I was fit to die. Imagine those doctors told my folks that I'd never be sane, and there I was getting married to a soldier boy."

Mother's eyes closed as she became lost in thought, the memories as real as yesterday. "Well, the first thing we did- nope- it was the second thing," she said and then giggled. "First thing was he put my legs on his shoulders and made me beg. Fucked me plumb crazy for hours. But next morning we drove up to New Mexico and put the shotgun to my folks for… well, never mind that. Do you think my titties are sagging?"

"Do you think my titties are sagging?" she heard Mother talking through the wooden plank. "I… Boy… stop that! You're gonna shoot that… ooooh yessssss!"

"Do you love me, Mother?"

"Oh yes, Boy… do it again for me, Michael."

Joanna's hand touched her invisible penis as she struggled to regain control.

"No!" she screamed in her head.

Her hand pulled at the wooden board. It came loose easily.

Ronnie watched as Eric jumped from the van.

"The Lincoln Inn Motel. He worked there before he started working at Custom Mirrors and Frames," Agent Eric said as he headed their way. He stopped as he saw the tower with the faded letters that read: The Lincoln Inn Motel.

He pointed as his team turned toward the sign, sitting up high on either side of the tracks.

Ronnie's eyes went back to the can by the bushes.

"Wait!" Agent Eric yelled as she sprinted through the thick opening and up onto the tracks. "Get there!" he ordered his team, then rushed into the bushes himself.

"Shhhhhh!" Michael whispered as he spun around from the mirror toward the door across the room.

"It's that bitch, Boy!" Mother whispered. She's found us," she said as her hand gripped the handle of the knife.

Michael stood still, wearing the red wig and lipstick. He stood quietly and naked as the door stood open and there she was.

"Hey, Michael," Joanna smirked, holding the .40 Glock M&P, pointed at his broad, bare chest. "Or is it Mother? Hey, bitch!"

"Don't just stand there, Boy!" Mother yelled, on the edge of hysteria.

"Yeah... Boy!" Mother's voice came from Joanna's mouth. "Do something, Boy!" Mother cackled, still pointing the weapon.

"Stop that bitch!" Mother barked, gaining some control. "She's not me, Boy!"

"Mother?" Michael mumbled, staring as Mother's voice came from Joanna.

"Mommy…" Joanna said and then laughed as her voice instantly changed into Abaddon's harsh growl. "What should I do now, bitch?!"

"Stop that, whore!" Mother yelled, raising the large army knife.

"Stop that, whore," Joanna mocked in Mother's voice as the Giant made his first step.

"That's right…" all three voices said as one.

"Stop her, Boy," Joanna shouted out, advancing with her gun.

That's when Abaddon charged.

Boom! Boom! Boom! Boom! Boom! Boom!

The first six shots that rang out froze Detective Rawls and Agent Wilson by the embankment as they found the opening. It wasn't until the next two that their bodies slid back into motion.

"There!" Ronnie screamed as she saw Joanna back into the lot.

"This way, Boy!" Joanna said in Mother's voice.

Slowly, Michael came into view from the motel room door, staggering with a knife held in front of his large, wide form.

"Shit!" Agent Eric and Ronnie exclaimed. They automatically trained their weapons on the deadly target. He continued to stagger into the parking lot as blood ran down his chest and dyed the asphalt a deep crimson.

Boom!

The Giant's left leg gave out as Joanna cackled madly.

"Get up, Boy!" Mother coughed as blood escaped from Michael's mouth. "You are…" she began and then laughed as the Giant pushed himself up.

"Yes, Boy… who are you now?" Joanna said in her own voice. She readied herself, standing in her best firing range stance, but the target before her was not made of paper. This target could feel pain, bleed out and die. At that moment she felt like jury, judge, and executioner and she felt that this was the way it should be. She had to end this bloody trail of rape and death. She was destined to make the boogie man in this nightmare go away.

For good. Forever.

"I… am…" he coughed and stood to his full length for the last time. His reign of terror had come to its end. He charged at Joanna screaming, "Abaddon!"

All three officers opened fire. The ensuing fusillade cut him down before he was halfway to her.

Agent Eric's eyes searched Joanna's face as he approached the fallen Giant. From the corner of his eye, he saw Ronnie approaching with caution.

A van came around the building, stealing their attention.

"No!" Mother cried out, trying to rise.

Boom! Boom!

Joanna lowered her still smoking weapon. Her last shot tore away the back of Michael's head, raining bits of red and pink gore down onto the pavement beneath his bare feet. And with a deep sigh of relief, she lowered her weapon. She had slain the Giant. Abaddon was finally dead.

"Jo…" Ronnie whispered as Joanna took two steps back. "Wait!"

"You promised!" Joanna screamed and then turned to run.

"No, wait!" Ronnie whispered more urgently, but it was too late.

Joanna was in full sprint up the embankment. At the top she stopped and turned. "Goddammit… You promised… you promised… you promised… you… promised," she screamed as she turned to run onto the tracks. "You promised!" she roared one last time before she disappeared into the all-consuming darkness.

Ronnie stood but felt like falling. The only thing that kept her upright was the hand of Agent Eric around her waist. And the fear of how deep the abyss was.

"She believes I let her down," Ronnie said to Agent Eric as tears rolled down her face. "I don't know what I should do? What can I do?"

Chapter Nineteen

A New Beginning
Two years later: July 3…

"THIS IS THE EIGHTH one in two weeks," the deputy said as the sheriff knelt over the dead bodybuilder.

"What do you suppose this means?" the sheriff asked as he lifted the flower from the dead man's chest. The muscular dead man had been laid out on the banks of the Mississippi River with his eyes and mouth stitched closed. He had been stabbed once in the heart, and like the others, his penis was missing.

"A flower for penance," she whispered as she walked up to the crime scene. "Hello Sheriff," she said and extended her hand. "Veronica Rawls."

"What?" the sheriff asked as he took her hand.

"Detective Rawls… Philadel-"

"No, I was expecting you," he smiled as he shook her hand. "No, I meant the flower business and…" he pointed at the body. "Why take their penis?"

"It's a message," Ronnie whispered.

"To who? Why?" He wanted to know... needed to know, really. He had never encountered anything like this before and he had been in law enforcement for a very long time.

"The message is to me. She wants to die. The penis is about why. And the flower identifies the problem."

"Hold on, Ms... I mean detective. Am I supposed to believe a woman did this? Killed eight strong, large men in so many days, by herself? Just to deliver a message to you?" the sheriff said in disbelief as the tall black man came toward them.

"Is it her?" the tall black man asked, kneeling over the body.

"Yeah!" Ronnie said as he stood from examining the body. "Sheriff, my partner... Detective Tommy Glenside."

"Sheriff," Tommy said as he took the sheriff's hand.

"Kind of young, ain't you?" the sheriff shot back.

"Yup!" Ronnie said, speaking for Tommy and smiling at the sheriff. "Youngest ever."

"Okay, Ronnie," Tommy said to cut the joke off before she ran with it. "Let's find out for sure." Together, they rolled the body onto its stomach.

The sheriff and his deputy watched in horror as Tommy used his gloved fingers to pull something from the corpse's anal cavity.

"Lord Jesus... what the tarnation kind of freak..." the deputy sheriff whispered as Tommy bagged the rosary beads.

"Sheriff, you got thirty days of hell coming your way," Detective Veronica Rawls said. "This is just the beginning."

The sun glistened off of the high powered field glasses.

"She's here, Mother," Joanna cackled as she sat on the side of the stolen Ford Bronco truck.

"Is he with her, gal?" Mother asked and smirked.

"Ummm hmmm..." she said as she jumped to the red clay mud and began to sing. Then she pulled the door open and climbed in, still singing: "Somebody said... I was living in the life..."

They rode to Jackson, Mississippi in silence. Neither wanted to speak her name. The pain was still fresh even though it had been two years ago. As instructed by the commissioner and captain, Detective Rawls headed to the State Police barracks.

"What?" Tommy whispered as he looked out the windows as they crossed the bridge. He felt Ronnie's eyes on him for miles.

"Just wondering..."

"What?! If I can do it? Don't worry; if the time comes, I'll take the shot. Ain't no way she can live like this! I care too much for her, we have too much history for me to let her live like this. I expect you to understand all that. I can take her out."

"I thought I could too... until our eyes met." Ronnie had spoken about last year when she tracked Joanna to Orlando, Florida. Well, it was really more like it was Joanna who had tracked her down. She was with Agent Eric Wilson, Jr. that time. But she had decided to bathe while Agent Eric ordered food from room service, only to be surprised by Joanna when he opened the door. She was stronger, Abaddon strong and faster too. He never had a chance as she took him in the doorway, dressed like a room service waitress.

When Ronnie came from out of the bathroom, there she saw Agent Eric tied to the bed and gagged.

Joanna was still there, smiling and flexing her neck muscles.

"Ronnie," she had said and smiled, tossing Agent Eric's ACP semi-automatic .40 caliber on the floor at her feet. "Bitch... you promised... now they're taking me, Ronnie. You promised you wouldn't let me become like them."

"Let us help..." Ronnie tried to say as her eyes remained on the gun.

It was him at first, laughing before he spoke. "She, Jo Jo," he said and then chuckled again. "It's us against them."

"The whore is weak, Boy!" Mother had cut in.

Ronnie had looked at the gun as it seemed to suddenly appear in his hand. That's when their eyes met.

"Do it please," Joanna whispered.

"I can't do it!"

Joanna stood from the bed. "Remember a flower for penance," she had whispered as she turned to leave.

Then Mother spoke out again. "Next time it's do or die," then she cackled.

But Agent Eric wasn't the one to die that night. They found the waitress dead in the stairway.

"Well, I'll do it!" Tommy said with a confidence in his voice that Ronnie wanted to believe in.

Bringing her thoughts away from the past, she followed Tommy as they checked in, gave ballistics and prints, and went to their hotel.

"I'll take the steak medium rare with the fries and house salad... yes... and two sodas, root beer, yes... how long?" Tommy listened intently as he ordered room service. "Good, thank you," he said just before he hung up.

Tommy crossed the room and looked out into the night and the lights of the darkened city. He had twenty minutes to shower before his food got to the room. The first thing he did was check the room door. It was locked, then he quickly undressed and headed for the shower. Of course, he took his .44 Desert Eagle with him.

He never left home without it.

"Room service," she said from the hall.

"Just a minute." He smirked and walked toward the door with the towel around his slim hips. In his hand he held his gun. He had heard too many stories about how Joanna had taken Eric and Ronnie by surprise. He was determined not to be like them. He opened the door and then stepped back.

"Come in, please," he said pleasantly. He slipped the gun behind the pillow he had taken from the bed. The door opened wide and her head peeped around the corner.

"I see you've been listening!"

"I better, or…" he began but he didn't care to finish. He didn't want to voice any more negativity.

"Look who finally got here!" Ronnie smiled with her hands up as they entered together.

"Kid!" Agent Eric said and then smiled.

"Agent," Tommy acknowledged with a smile and extended his hand.

"Get dressed. Let's go eat," Agent Eric said.

"But… I…" Tommy said as he pointed to the hotel menu.

"So! It's on the government," Ronnie giggled. "Get dressed, big boy."

"Man!" Tommy said as he rubbed his full belly. "This southern style food is… whoa!"

"Yeah, Agent Eric agreed. "You know I grew up right across the river in Alabama. My family owns a small plantation farm not far from here."

"Plantation? Tommy said and then frowned, not liking the idea of anyone owning a plantation. Especially in the south.

"Trees, not cotton," Agent Eric let him know. "Besides, my mother is black."

"No wonder it's… never mind," Ronnie said and laughed as Agent Eric blushed.

The next two hours they discussed strategy over beers for them and soda for Tommy. And they agreed on one fact: Joanna must die!

After dinner, Agent Eric and Ronnie went to their room and Tommy went to his. Kicking off his shoes, he laid back and closed his eyes. Instantly, he sat up. What was it?

Something was out of place. He just couldn't put his finger on it, but he felt an unease that was almost physical. His eyes searched the room quickly and then focused on the food cart. It held his steak order and sodas. But he was too stuffed from the barbecue from Famous Charlie's Pit and Grill to think about any more food.

Slowly, he laid back and closed his eyes again.

"I wonder if they always just leave your food in your room? I didn't even have to..." and suddenly he sat up in a panic. But it was too late. She was there and he had no chance. At least that was what he thought he would say.

"Please don't, Tommy," Joanna whispered.

She stood naked at the foot of the bed. Those eyes, that face, that body and he knew it all. That same soft voice he fell in love with at 15 years old.

It was then that he knew he couldn't do it.

He had the skills. It was a fact for the last thirteen years he had practiced Jiu Jitsu and even Abaddon would have had no chance against him in a hand to hand match. His gun was now in Joanna's hand. Joanna, his first and only love. No, he couldn't do it; he couldn't take her out.

"I won't," he mumbled.

"Tommy, do you still love me?"

He didn't answer, but they both knew he couldn't deny it.

"I need you to love me again, Tommy. I've been so alone. I'm... I'm," she began but couldn't continue to speak because of her crying.

"Jo," Tommy said as he held his hand out to her, beckoning for her to come to him, to join him in his bed.

She did.

Tommy made love to Joanna for the first time ever. Not to Mother, not in a window of fantasy, but to Joanna Staley, the woman. She had never felt so needed. He had never felt so wanted. They filled the emptiness of each other, until he slept in her arms.

"Kill him, Girl," Mother whispered as she cuffed him to the bedpost.

"No!" Joanna roared.

"Wait!" Tommy yelled as the cuff tightened around his wrist.

"I love you, Tommy," Joanna cried as she headed out the door.

"Jo, take me with you," he yelled as the door closed behind her.

She came in as a whisper and left the same way.

"Damn!" he whispered as she stripped right there in the middle of the gym.

The mirrors she used to inspect the shape of her muscles presented an image she was very proud of, exposing all of her hard work and discipline. "She looks incredible," he continued as she stood there in the skin-toned bikini, checking out her abs.

Their eyes locked and she turned to him.

"Hey, you!"

"Me?" he said and then smiled, going along with her game.

"Yeah, you," she said, then asked, "Is my stomach unbalanced?" As if to answer her own question, she flexed her stomach muscles, her prominent six pack.

"It's perfect… Miss…?"

"Joanna…" she said and then smiled. "How about my lats and back?"

"Let's see…" he said, using his hands to turn her both ways, taking in all over her well-toned body. "Perfect!"

"How about you help me stretch?" Joanna said with more sex in her voice than he could ever imagine.

"My pleasure."

"Dammit, I see your pleasure, big guy," Joanna laughed, brushing her hand across his bulge.

"I wish," he said and smiled. "Carl Monrone." He extended his hand.

"Joanna Staley," said, accepting his hand. "And if you're not married, your wish is my command. After I stretch, it can do the rest." She looked down. "I'm sure."

"So?" Ronnie sat on the bed, frowning.

"She's fast!" he lied with a straight face.

"So why not scream? I ain't buying that bullshit, Tommy. I've seen what you can do, remember?"

The room was quiet for a moment as Tommy looked away. He had to say it. "I couldn't... I... love..."

"Dammit, Tommy! She's not who we used to know. She's now a cold blooded monster. She must die!" Ronnie screamed in anger and frustration. "She'll strike again, tonight. Dammit," she said just before she jumped up and stormed out of his room.

Agent Eric stayed behind. "I couldn't either, kid," he whispered. "She didn't take me at the door. It's those eyes... right? Well, next time... I won't look. I will kill her dead."

"Eric, I've always loved her," Tommy confessed in a whisper. "I don't know if..."

"You can, kid. You will or one of us may die." Agent Eric started to leave. "And don't worry about Ronnie. It's all about her guilt. She had the same chance. She's just sorry she didn't take it. She knows next time, it's her or Joanna."

Tommy sat for hours, thinking, in deep thought. Not of his mistakes, but of the night he just spent with the only woman he ever loved: Joanna.

The screams filled the small warehouse as she stood over him with the surgical stitching needle. This was the start of the ritualistic killing.

"Oh God, nooo, nooo please! Stop this, please, no!" he continued to scream.

"Quiet!" she whispered. "Mother doesn't like noise." Climbing onto his lap, Joanna straddled him. "This is gonna hurt." Instantly, she cackled and the sudden chance to her voice sent chills into his spine.

"No more words from the filthy gal," Mother smirked.

"Please no! Don't! Don't! … ahhhhhh!"

The first stab of the stitching needle went through his lower lip and out of the top. Then she pulled it tight at the corner.

"Hold him, Boy!" Mother screamed as his head turned away wildly, trying to avoid the next stab of pain.

"Yes, Mother," Abaddon's voice whispered. She grabbed his head with such strength he couldn't budge.

The needle stabbed into his lower lip again…

Ronnie looked at Agent Eric as he slept through the third ringing of the hotel phone. She smiled with a satisfying smirk. Last night she proved that women ruled in every bedroom across America. She picked up the phone. "Hello," she answered.

"Good morning, partner."

There was no mistaking who was calling. Ronnie rolled to her feet, still watching Agent Eric. She sat in the armchair before she spoke again. "Jo Jo," she whispered.

"Yeah, it's me, Ronnie." Joanna paused. "I see you got my message."

"Joanna, this has got to stop. Baby… we still love you. Let us help…"

"You know there is no help for the Trans. Well, there is death," she said and then cackled, turning instantly into Mother as she continued. "You made promises to this bitch, girlie. Why didn't you keep your part of the deal, whore? She did! Now me and my boy live with this bitch in the way."

"Mother, you old bitch!" Ronnie shouted, waking Agent Eric. "I swear if it's your voice coming from my Jo…"

"She's ours now… whore!" Mother cackled. "Besides, you might die soon. My boy still…"

"No, Mother, don't," Abaddon yelled.

"So the undercover faggot is there too," Ronnie said and then laughed out loud, taunting Mother and Abaddon and Agent Eric sat up. "Did he ever get… you know… that cock?"

"Wow!" Mother said and then laughed. "So the whore wants to play. Well, whore, last night she took it for him. Yup! Up the ass, and also in the mouth. She loves the taste of cock. Why didn't you tell me she loves cock so much?"

"Oh God, Ronnie…" Joanna screamed.

"Shut this bitch up, Boy," Mother cackled. "She's getting good at it now, gal. It's easy for her now…" Mother paused and then said. "There's another one on the river waiting for you, whore. Under the bridge. Better hurry; I seen a few gators down there." Mother cackled again.

"Yazoo, Ronnie. Yazoo. Bamlets," Joanna cried out.

"Boy shut that…" Mother screamed again.

"I'm trying, Mother. She's strong!" Abaddon yelled and a loud slap could be heard over the phone.

Ronnie closed her eyes and cried, but not just for Joanna. She cried because of the helplessness she felt and the promise she was not able to fulfill.

"They found him, detectives," the sheriff said as he came out of his office. "Let's go."

Ronnie and Tommy followed him.

Twenty minutes later, they examined the dead body of the body builder.

"It's her, Sheriff," Tommy confirmed as he pulled the rosary beads from the rectum of the deceased.

"Lord, please have mercy on the soul so foul she could do this," the sheriff prayed as he watched Tommy continue his examination of the body.

"Her name is Joanna, Sheriff. She has a given name now also. Like the perp we chased down in Philadelphia. I told you before we killed him, he took on the name of the King of the Abyss. Abaddon."

"Yeah, I remember that case."

"Well, Joanna just informed me that she wants to be called Yazoo Bamlets."

"Are you sure?" the Sheriff said and frowned. "Yazoo? Bamlets?"

"That's what she screamed as she struggled with the other personalities. Yazoo, Ronnie. Yazoo… Bamlets. That's exactly how and what she screamed before disconnecting," Ronnie whispered, trying hard to control her emotions.

"God, I wish it was that easy," the Deputy said.

"What?" Tommy asked as he stood.

"Well, Yazoo is the township across the bay. You ever hear of a federal prison complex called Yazoo? Well, it's only thirty minutes west of here and Bamlets was an old department store that went under during the Bush administration's wars. But…"

"Shit!" Ronnie yelled as she and Tommy took off on a dead run toward their car. "Sheriff, please," Ronnie yelled over the hood of her rental car. "She's there!"

Chapter Twenty

"IT COMES BACK TO Victor Broden of New Orleans. Victim number two," the Sheriff said as they sat behind the small storage warehouse down the road from the Bamlets warehouse.

"She's in there," Ronnie whispered. "Can you have it surrounded and give orders to shoot to kill? Sheriff…" she looked deeply into his eyes, making sure he understood how serious this all was. They wouldn't have many other opportunities to stop the monster that Joanna had become. If she escaped this time, they might never be able to capture her, and the killing would never stop. She found that unacceptable. "Don't mistake her beauty as a weakness. She'll kill with no second thought. Her strength and speed are unmatched. You must tell your men, shoot to kill. We have to end this now!"

Tommy and Ronnie's eyes met.

"Ready?" she whispered.

"Nope," he said as he chambered a shell into the 20 gauge Mossberg he held in his hands.

"I can send in twenty…" the Sheriff began.

"No," Ronnie said quickly, knowing that the less lives put at stake, the better. She knew they had to go in hard and fast, lean and mean. As she stood there, she realized she was crying. She wiped a tear away and then said, "Shoot to kill, Sheriff. Do not try to take… this… thing alive!"

"Shoot to kill, Sheriff," Tommy echoed, but even more sternly. He knew what they were up against; they could not take this threat lightly. Too many lives were at stake, including his and Ronnie's.

They headed down the road as car after car surrounded the Bamlets warehouse.

"It's them, Mother… they'll stop us now!" Joanna whispered.

"Boy!" Mother yelled as Joanna turned from the loft window. Then she turned away from the window and ran to the rear of the warehouse where the Bronco sat parked.

"Shit!"

"Why run, Mother?" Joanna said, and then laughed. "You afraid…?"

"Shut your whore up, Boy!" Mother screamed and dashed for the bed. She flipped the mattress, just as the warehouse door flew open.

"Joanna… Joanna… help us… Jo Jo," Ronnie yelled from the cover of the outside wall. "I'm coming in, Joanna. To keep my promise I made to you two years ago."

"She's changed her mind, whore," Mother cackled. "Too late, you white tramp!"

"Shhhhh, Mother!" Abaddon growled.

"Up here, Ronnie…" Joanna struggled to say and then a solid slap was heard.

"Shut up, bitch!" Mother barked. "Well, you know where we at! Come on!"

Tommy's eyes darted to the metal filing cabinets in the middle of the floor. He held up three fingers, to indicate that he planned to make a move on the count of three.

One… two… three… he counted to himself and then dashed as a shot rang out from somewhere in the loft. Slamming to the floor, he returned fire, but because he couldn't see anyone, he fired blindly.

"Ouch!" she said and then giggled. "I thought you loved me, Boy!"

"I love Joanna, you old fag hag!" Tommy shouted as Ronnie dashed behind the overturned desk to his right.

She pointed to her eyes as if asking if he could see Joanna.

He shook his head no. Then he quickly looked toward the stairs leading up and mouthed, "Cover me." That was when he made his dash and slammed against the far wall, seeking cover, his gun aimed up the stairs, but there was no sound, no shots rang out.

"Watch that fourth step, Tommy Boy," Mother cackled.

Tommy looked and saw that it was missing. He stepped over it and his leg went through the fifth step, up to his hip. He suddenly realized it was a trap.

"Oops! I forgot to tell you about the next two, or was it three?" Mother cackled. "Oh well…"

"Joanna's voice took over. "Stay against the wall, Tomm…"

"Shut… this… bitch… up, Boy!"

"Joanna…" Ronnie yelled. "Show yourself so I can keep my promise," she said, then paused. "Baby girl, we love you so much."

Then Ronnie dashed behind a steel triple wide beam that ran from the floor to the ceiling. It faced the loft.

"He won't let me…"

"Sit still," Abaddon's voice filled the small area.

"Don't let her…" Mother yelled as the gun came flying from the loft. "Dumb Boy, can't you hold a little girl?"

Tommy reached the top of the stairs just as Joanna tossed the gun away.

There she knelt behind an overturned table. Her back was to him. He had the shot.

Take it! He thought as he took aim at her small body frame. His hand wouldn't obey his mind, throwing his plan of action into turmoil. He knew what had to be done, but he just couldn't bring himself to do it. Not to her.

"Joanna," he whispered, praying for another way to end this standoff. He could see her muscles tense as she rose with her back toward him.

"Can I look at you once more, lover?" Joanna whispered. "Just once before you…" she began and then her voice changed.

"You do know I've always loved you, Boy!"

A tear escaped Tommy's eye as she continued.

"The other night, Tommy, we made music, didn't we?" It was Joanna's voice but Tommy knew who was speaking. Who had control.

"Turn around, Mother," he mumbled, holding his aim, in his policeman's stance.

"Haaa! See, Boy, that's brains," Mother cackled. "I guess it's up to you now, Michael." Then she laughed.

"Joanna… can you fight it? Please…" Tommy begged. And out of the corner of his eye he saw Ronnie creep up the steps.

"Listen to you! Whiny little piss dick!" Mother cackled and continued to torment him with a mocking voice.

"Fight it, Joanna. Can you hear me, Joanna! I love you, Joanna!"

"Shut the hell up, Boy!"

"Move, bitch, so I can end this shit!" Ronnie yelled. "Or is that faggot son of a bitch… afraid to die? You know we killed his punk ass once!" she pushed, wanting to end this now.

"I'm here, Veronica," Abaddon roared.

"Not for long. Move… just a little, fag boy."

"Stop all this talking, Boy. Get me out of here!" Mother said.

"Do it, Ronnie," Joanna struggled to say. "Don't wait!"

"Hold that bitch, Boy! She's trying to..." Before Mother could finish, Joanna took two steps. She raised her hand which held a knife.

"Sorry, Joanna." Tommy whispered, his heart heavy. He tapped the trigger of his Desert Eagle twice.

Ronnie also fired and Joanna went down.

"Ron..." she coughed, "Tommy!"

Both detectives approached with caution, keeping their guns trained on her.

Slowly, Joanna raised her hand to Tommy and Ronnie.

Before he could approach, Ronnie touched Tommy's arm. "No... don't," she said, recalling the incident at the motel with Abaddon.

"But..."

"She's still dangerous! Trust me!" Ronnie said with tears running down her face. "Back away, Tommy! Now!"

"But..." Tommy cried, overcome with emotion. This was Joanna, his lover in another life, a better time for him and her. This stuck in his mind as he moved forward. This was all that he could see.

"No! She can still be..." Ronnie cautioned in a panic, taking her eyes away from Joanna for just a second.

"Bitch!' Joanna sat up so quick that Tommy had no choice.

Boom!

The power of the Desert Eagle ripped through Joanna's brain, ending her torment.

The promise has been kept, Ronnie thought as she watched Joanna's body slump to the floor.

www.ingramcontent.com/pod-product-compliance
Lightning Source LLC
Chambersburg PA
CBHW070819180626
46818CB00001B/326